AN ELUSIVE QUARRY

We locked gazes, our hearts beating as one, our breaths gasped hot, in unison. I felt desire vibrating through me, unwanted but no less powerful. I lusted for him. I hated myself for my longing, for wanting to consummate my desire the way we always had: passionate, explosive, no real-world effects. Simple, physical release. I knew those days were gone forever.

The Avenger smiled into my soul, and I knew this time in the Netherwood was different. His smile sent warmth shooting into my veins like a drug. Before I could break our connection, he rematerialized, stroked my lips with the tips of his fingers. He cupped my face in his hands, and the gentle touch of his lips on mine pierced me through the heart. I closed my eyes against it, but felt the connection between us grow even stronger.

"Hunt me." He spoke directly into my mind, even as the currents of the kiss washed away my anger. I sighed, opened my mouth to his...and he shivered away into nothingness.

MICHELE LANG

NETHERWOOD

LOVE SPELL NEW YORK CITY

For my family, and as always for Steven.

LOVE SPELL®

March 2008

Published by

Dorchester Publishing Co., Inc.
200 Madison Avenue
New York, NY 10016

ISBN 10: 0-505-52759-6
ISBN 13: 978-0-505-52759-2

The name "Love Spell" and its logo are trademarks of Dorchester Publishing Co., Inc.

Printed in the United States of America.

10 9 8 7 6 5 4 3 2 1

Visit us on the web at www.dorchesterpub.com.

ACKNOWLEDGMENTS

My deepest gratitude goes to my brilliant, meticulous editor, Chris Keeslar, and to my agent, the insightful and savvy Lucienne Diver. And thanks beyond words to my husband, Steven, for everything—you are my North Star.

NETHERWOOD

ONE

The audience in the Amphitheatre screamed for my blood. I loved it.

I hid a smile as I strode forward, feeling the glint of the hot cyber-sunlight on my bare scalp, along my long, muscle-packed thighs. The last time I came here, I was in search of connection; this time I hunted an outlaw. I'm a sheriff, and tracking down and deactivating lawbreakers is my job. The quarry I hunted today could make my career, wreathe me in glory. But I couldn't make the collar here. Not now. Not in the Netherwood.

The Amphitheatre was a locale, an entrance to a virtual sub-plane of existence that people called different names, a reality whose very ambiguity was one of its charms: the Netherwood, Netherworld, the Inferno—a shadowy place with varying levels of descent. Most people—and by "people" I mean natural-born, biologically derived; not droids, medical clones or alien intelligences—avoided slummy places like it, and instead contented themselves with ordinary lives on the grid. But now I clutched my ionic mace, and I knew the grid's illusion of safety was a lie.

The grid, to make things simple, was the main virtual

world. It grew from humble origins, the PC revolution and the development of the Internet in the twentieth century by DARPA: Defense Advanced Research Projects Agency, the research and development arm of the old American military. But the grid grew beyond the ordinary surface world, overtook it in size and importance. Now the grid—this virtual world that also housed the real one—was where all of us lived most of our lives. This was where I hid from death. We could assume cyber identities, avatar personalities like my own Amazonia. It was where we could live our fantasies. Believe me, life on the surface, in the so-called real world, bored most of us out of our minds. Taxes, pollution, cancer, world wars—if all of that didn't scare you to death, it mired you in ennui like a dinosaur sinking in a tar pit. I preferred the grid's illusions.

The grid cancelled all of that mind-sucking, grownup stuff out. You could get food and directions and . . . well, everything. And the Netherwood, part of the grid, this bad neighborhood in that computer-generated world, titillated me with its virtual and yet very real dangers. It always had.

The Netherwood started out as an ordinary virtual landscape, funded by a gaming guru, Geoff Provocateur, about twenty years before I entered the Amphitheatre as the warrior queen Amazonia. But the Netherwood unraveled pretty quickly, with gambling, cybersex, synth-trading, hacking and computer sabotage becoming the entertainments of choice. Under the cover of the "games"—the virtual arena matches—in the Amphitheatre, illegal and dastardly acts were committed on a regular basis. And crime was my drug. I was sworn to smell it out and obliterate it. No matter how much it sometimes appealed.

Now I was back in the Netherwood, hunting. I was seeking out the people here illegally sating their dissatisfaction with their carbon-based lives on the surfaces of the worlds owned by Earth in the waning days of the twenty-second century. Hackers. Criminals. They were clever, yes, but they were dangerous, because their games led to real-life consequences. As I knew from my schooling, they hacked into sensitive material not part of the general grid and released it to public view—and war or revolution could result. Nobody could predict the unintended consequences of truths set free. Holocaust. It had happened in the past, but would *not* happen again. If the government traced an illicit avatar back to an actual identity, that person would be "disappeared," or even worse, replaced by a government agent cloaked in a familiar face.

The criminal denizens of the Netherwood had to be good—better than the government workers, better than WorldCorps security, better than anybody—to survive. And that expertise carried its own set of dangers. It was so easy to get lost in an avatar, to never leave the Netherwood. Like most of us almost never left the grid.

The roar of the crowd refocused my intention. I risked a glance at the stands and saw something I had missed last time; my blood turned to ice in my veins. A senator sitting under the awning—my eyes met hers and I saw through the avatar. It was nothing admissible in a court of law, the things that helped one see through an avatar—a nervous tic, an idiosyncratic speech pattern, a posture—but my intuition told me I was staring into the consciousness of my grandmother, Violet.

Violet. My life depended on her ignorance. I'd gone

too deep without official sanction, and my presence here—my avatar, my whole existence—was illegal. Whether or not I was a sheriff, whether or not my intentions were good, there was no way for me to prove it, and there was no one I could depend upon to listen. So I bowed and smiled wickedly in the senator's direction, as if daring her to enjoy the spectacle of combat she was about to witness, all legal, harmless. She nodded back, evidently pleased by my attentions. And I saw that I was safe: she hadn't recognized me. My cover had held.

In the mundanity of the Real, I went by my given name and lived in the skinny little alabaster body of Talia Fortune. I had the usual bio-mods for people of my rank, but that was it. Here at the gateway to the Netherwood, I was over six feet tall, my skin of darkest ebony, my strength and power unmatched. The denizens of this place knew me only as Amazonia. My secrecy meant my life.

My adversary entered the arena, and I relaxed as I turned toward him, ionic mace in hand. I knew it would be the Avenger. I had come back here to find him.

His long black hair whipped in the breeze, and he bowed to me, his lips curling in a smile. We had fought many battles here together, the Avenger and I. I won or he won; in many ways it didn't matter. Because we would descend lower after our superficial encounters in the arena, and heal each other's wounds.

I nodded in response, shifted my mace into my left hand and reached for my sonic knife with my right. Kept my center of gravity low. The Avenger had a talent for catching me off guard and throwing me off balance. I studied his face as he drew closer, but avoided a direct gaze into his eyes. I didn't want him to see too much revealed there. Didn't want him to see anything.

"I need to talk to you." His voice, barely a whisper, carried through the stale air and touched my ear in a caress.

"First, fight."

He bowed again, a laugh rumbling deep in his barrel chest. "Yes, you fight more eloquently than you speak, my dear Amazonia."

His accent—cultured, the proper tones of twenty-second-century England—coaxed a smile onto my lips. I winked at him, and simultaneously slashed at his chest with my knife. He jumped away, and my blade only grazed his skin, leaving a tracer of red. The crowd screamed at the early sight of blood. I pressed my advantage, but he lunged backward, keeping lower than I could get without exposing my own flank to his attack.

His mouth moved again, but the bellowing of the crowd drowned out his words. I reached to my belt, pushed pause—

The entire scene froze in place. This was a holo-recording, a six-months-ago visit to the Netherwood. I considered the tableau in which I stood, looked for clues I had missed in the initial thrill of battle.

I looked up at the stands to check out the senator first. Why had she stopped by to view this particular match? We were no superstars of the Netherwood fighting circuit; both the Avenger and I fought only to gain access to the deeper levels of the place, so that we could descend. So that we could uncover secrets. So that we could take pleasure together in the shadows. Or that was ostensibly why we came.

The senator I thought was my grandmother leaned

forward, her purple robes looking almost wet in the deep shade of the awning. My body hummed with tension, and I tasted acid in my mouth, like something had crawled in there to die on my tongue. My grandmother had found a miraculous reprieve five years ago upon her death, when her consciousness had been downloaded onto a psy-chip—the first human mind to "reduce down." Now wealthy people reduced down as a matter of course, but it had been Violet, the founder of megaconglomerate FortuneCorp, who had famously led the way. My magnificent grandmother had cheated death, and people with enough money and power followed her lead and shifted to life only on the grid when their bodies died.

Of course, Violet wasn't just my grandmother; she was my employer. And she had the right to do more than fire me if I bungled a job or disgraced the family name.

I had to content myself with the knowledge that my cover had held. If she knew I was Amazonia, Violet had the right and the power to break up the fight and arrest me immediately. The government of the United States still nominally held jurisdiction over the World-Corps, but as a practical matter CEOs like my grandmother used the government's authority to suit their corporate purposes. If she'd thought I was a threat to FortuneCorp, I wouldn't have made it to the end of the match without govbots marching out onto the field and taking me into custody—as cops on the surface hauled my carbon-based body to jail. Yeah, my grandmother was that much of a hard-ass.

But the govbots weren't on their way. It hadn't happened. For the moment, at least, I was safe from my grandmother's intervention.

I shifted my attention to the Avenger, who crouched in the sandy dirt at my feet. I left my recorded body and walked forward, played with his thick rough hair, stroked his big shoulders, rippling biceps. Because he couldn't see me, I dared a look deep into his eyes. Usually such an intimate gaze revealed the artificiality of the avatar construct: you could see the deadness there and kill all illusion of reality. A direct, lingering stare was considered the height of rudeness down here, even among lovers.

But I really wasn't staring into him, because he couldn't stare back and complete the connection. I studied him like a beautiful piece of sculpture, and a sudden realization hit me. His eyes, electronic as they were, glinted with unshed tears.

I reached down to the handheld remote strapped to my belt, tracked the session five seconds back. Leaned in to hear what he'd whispered to me under the roar of the crowd:

"*. . . all of us are going to die . . .*"

My fingers shook as I fast-forwarded through the battle. That one whispered sentence put our encounter into an entirely different light. I already knew how I'd won this particular fight in this surface-level arena, but I had avoided the Avenger's message out of fear, and had lost a greater war in the darkness below.

I recombined with my avatar, reactivated the holo where I found the Avenger after the battle—in his chamber, nestled in the caves of a cyber grove that mimicked the sacred forests of the Druids and the ancient Greeks. He lay on a fur-covered pallet, his body covered with bruises, slashes, and thin tributaries of blood. As I remembered it happening, I strode into the room, knelt beside him.

7

"Poor Avenger." I stroked the scratched, battered expanse of his chest with my fingertips. "Your Amazonia broke you bad today."

He tilted his chin back and half-laughed, half-moaned. "Kiss it and make it better."

I knew his pain sensors must have been turned down during the battle, so the wounds wouldn't feel as bad as they looked. Still, I fought back an absurd flare of regret, and stroked the bruises and cuts with my palms. He trembled under my touch.

Our sparring had improved my fighting skills in the Real as well as in this cyber world we haunted together, but I was grateful to the Avenger for more than this. Much more. I kissed along a weal raised by my sonic knife, traced it with the tip of my tongue. I paused to kiss one nipple, long and lovingly, and then the other.

He made some little sound, and I raised my head. "Feel bad? I can ice you . . ."

His laugh lit up his entire face: he remembered as well as I did our last encounter in a virtual tub of ice water designed to soothe enflamed muscles—which in our case had only heightened the heat.

"My warrior queen, you promised me talk after battle."

"Pleasure first." Again, in retrospect, I had the feeling I'd made the wrong choice. I'd thought that pleasure ruled me, but no. I was afraid—of what the Avenger had to say about death.

His bare stomach rippled as he pulled himself up to a half-sitting position. "Your command is my wish, delicious one."

His lips closed over mine, and I let myself float on currents of electric delight, trying my best to ignore the purple undertone of loneliness pulsing in my veins. Despite my fervent wish to surrender to him, I hadn't let myself go; not here. I never fully had. I couldn't. There were too many illusions too deadly to ignore. Too many hidden dangers camouflaged as simple desire. Our electronic coupling was a falsity. And yet, while this pretense of "lovemaking" made my reality all the more unbearable, I clutched the fantasy to me all the same, was living it again, replaying it. My life in the Real sometimes seemed impossibly banal and gray. It was so much easier to take refuge here, to disappear into my alternate self. To forget why I'd originally come.

I rode the waves of the Avenger's rocking hips and roving hands. As my breath quickened and beads of sweat tickled down my sides, my heart pounded with self-betrayal. My entire life revolved around my job as a law-keeper, around my status as chief shareholder of FortuneCorp. These encounters with the Avenger threatened everything I had achieved in the Real. But I couldn't help coming back to him, time and again. His cyber body felt too good against mine.

His hands slid down the length of my back, cupped my lush, rubber-encased butt. He squeezed me up onto his hips, and my long legs wrapped around him. Grief hunted me close, but I held its gleaming fangs at bay. Barely. Sorrow could swallow me later, leave me an empty shell. For now I kept my eyes closed and traveled deeper and deeper into this personal garden of earthly delights, trying to ignore the fact that the Avenger tempted me like the apple . . . or the snake.

"Can I trust you?" I'd shocked myself with the words escaping my tingling, swollen lips.

"Can you trust yourself?"

It was maddening, how often the Avenger answered my questions with questions of his own. "No," I finally replied. " 'Trust nobody . . . not even yourself.' The first rule of this place."

He sighed. "Our beloved Netherwood, oh yes. But remember, the place is only a means to a larger end."

I nodded. "But there's the puzzle: Who in this sad, mad world shares a common end?"

His hands slid up to my shoulders, massaged the knots and kinks with strong yet gentle fingers. "We are not supposed to speak of such things—why we come here. And yet . . ." His words were hesitant, as if he silently dared me to follow him into the abyss.

I abruptly didn't care about any dangers, didn't mind how close I was to giving my true self away. All of my surface plans and goals seemed suspect in this hidden place, and I found myself speaking truths I'd never before uttered—though not all of them. I said words that were both pretense and dream, lie and hidden truth.

I felt his body shifting under my arms, and I pulled him close, looked over his shoulder into the darkness. "Why do you come here, Avenger?" I asked. "I'm here for pleasure, for knowledge. I want to understand how the World Corporation System hangs together, where its back doors are located, where I can sneak in and do a bit of damage if I so choose. And I want to find out what the corporations and the governments don't want the common people to know." I opened my eyes and drew back, half-gazed into his face. His features had gone completely still, like my words were weapons brandished inches from his face. He knew as well as I did that I'd been careful to avoid keywords that could trigger a security sweep: *virus, hacker, assets, data trees, destroy.*

And I'd meant what I'd said. I was a citizen of FortuneCorp first, the old government second. The secrets and many weaknesses of the old, corrupt governing system held valuable clues to how I could uphold the law in the new. I was bending the rules in service to a larger cause—at least, that was what I told myself. But the Avenger wanted to do more than bend the rules. He wanted to break them.

I smiled again, dared him to join me in danger. "So that's why I come down here, barbarian. Why do you?"

He smiled back, his face suddenly set, like he'd made up his mind. "My dear Amazonia, I come in search of the truth. And I come here for you."

The Avenger refused to say anything more aloud. Instead, he waved his hands in the air and summoned a databox containing a term definition. The clear cube floated in the air above our heads, the letters glowing orange in the muted gray light.

The SINGULARITY: The creation of smarter-than-human computers, with direct brain/computer interfaces. Human consciousness will merge with computers and live primarily in virtual reality. What happens next is an event horizon: a runaway phenomenon beyond our ability to understand.

He tilted his head and looked at me, daring me to say the words, or any words. I studied the box, hunting for understanding. It eluded me. "W-what does that have to do with me? With anything?"

"It's *everything*. Unintended consequences. We're close, so close, my dear Amazonia. To the end. Where will this leave us and our meaningless pleasures when it comes?"

The first time I'd lived this, I'd insisted to myself he was lying—to me, if not to himself. Upon revisitation of the holo-vid, I wasn't so sure.

"Are you messing with me?" I heard myself ask, my voice laser-sharp.

"No. I seek to know you."

"Why? Why make this so complicated?"

"Because we are running out of time. Come to me."

He silenced my questions with a monster kiss, a tidal wave of sensation that pushed all rational thought out of my mind. The databox melted away, incinerated by the intensity of our encounter.

I stopped and paused the holo-vid again. Remembering the rest of our encounter with mingled longing and regret, I detached from my Amazonian body tangled up with his, rotated our entwined virtual forms 360 degrees, felt my body in the Real getting hot and bothered as I saw us gyrating in space, half-naked and sweaty in the dim, veiled shadows. Then I revealed the codes swirling around our cyber bodies, searched for any scrap of identity hidden in the chains of EZ Code woven like fibers into the walls, the floors, our electric flesh.

My body—my own, real, skinny little Talia body—jolted with fear as sharp as an electric shock.

<GO TO FortuneCorp Central Switching>
<GO TO Fresh Havens Planetary Control Center>
<ALL CLEAR>
<ALL CLEAR>
<DATA DELETED>

Fresh Havens. I bolted, logged out from the leafy, electronic shadows of the Netherwood, my human, mortal body bathed in sweat. Based on the dangling code the Avenger had left as a clue, my working theory was correct. The outlaw I hunted in the Real was my Avenger in Netherwood. He was awaiting me at my destination. Somewhere on the planet of Fresh Havens, he looked for my arrival, hopeful. He'd left that last little bit of dangling code behind for me to find. But he didn't know who I was. What I was. Whom I was sworn to destroy.

I took deep, shuddering breaths, feeling strange and uncomfortable within the confines of my natural-born body back on my transport spacecraft, the *Titania*. I swung in my safety harness, still weightless, not yet within Fresh Havens' planetary field. To my left, outside the huge porthole sported by my first-class cabin, the universe lay; cold, black, empty. I stared at stars endless light years away, forever untouchable.

I glanced at a console. The wormhole was two weeks of my time behind us, but in taking that shortcut through the time-space continuum, we'd been out of touch with the Home Office and Earth for two long months. Sixty days: a long time for an outlaw to get away.

My ship was nearly at its destination. I was nearly at Fresh Havens, the terraformed planet where my mysterious outlaw hid. The outlaw I knew: the Avenger. The one I had to betray in order to uphold the law and do my job.

My handheld data device felt warm in my hand, and my fingers shook as I slipped it into its recharger. I stroked the gleaming edges of the black titanium casing as I let the handheld rest. Like most people, I loved my handheld, my navigator, because it was my portal to the multicolored, gorgeous universe of the grid.

Any time I wanted to, my brain waves synced with the electronic signals, made a virtual circuit, and wham, I was in a different world—a better one. I'd spent weeks customizing the basic features of my device when I'd bought it so that I could do what I wanted with it. I felt a physical rush hooking into the grid; by choice, the sensation mimicked a cool slick of water rushing along my body, an electric immersion into a pure cascade of digital consciousness.

But now, back in the Real, I felt a hollowness, a hunger eating my guts out from inside. My fingers traced along the tiny keyboard, and I considered calling up my grandmother, inviting her consciousness up from the virtual landscape she inhabited so I could talk with her about my fears, my hopes as I hurtled toward the planet of Fresh Havens. Then I thought of the senator under the Amphitheatre awning, and felt the tips of my fingers grow cold against the tiny buttons. I decided to let Violet's consciousness remain on the psychip on my handheld, contact her later. She had decided to transfer her consciousness to my handheld so she could join me on this journey offworld. But for the moment, I felt a little wary of her attentions.

Instead, I detached from my safety harness, activated my gravboots and locked on to the *Titania*'s springy, insulated floor. I set off in search of my fellow travelers, the people who had embarked with me on this trek.

Yes, I searched for connection once again; but unlike my adventures in Netherwood, this time I failed. I inched along, tethered by my boots to the spongy black hallway, and as I stopped at the entry portal to each cabin, I could see that every other traveler was sucked into their holo-recordings of grid adventures they'd had, much more diverted by them than by the half darkness of the unadorned ship.

I stood for a long time at the entrance to Riona Sweet's cabin. Alone among the other travelers, she was my age and sex, and I considered going in, touching her shoulder, shaking her back into the Real, even though I knew she was too deeply embedded to return that easily. Riona's blond hair splayed out behind her and her on eyelids fluttered, her mind traveling deeply into electronic dreams. As I watched, a thin gold necklace escaped from under her skinsuit, started floating in the gravfree cabin, still attached around her neck. An old-fashioned charm, half of a heart pendant; I wondered who wore the other half. I watched her dream, tried to imagine who walked in Riona's fantasies, who she ran to encounter in the grid. And if she ran to avoid the Real the way that I did.

I gave up on speaking to an actual human being and clomped all the way around the circular walkway until I returned to my own cabin. Buckled myself back into my harness, released my gravboots, felt myself float free.

My handheld blinked to me in the soft semi-darkness. I had received a message. The *Titania*'s warm, synthesized voice now chirped through the speaker— if a golden retriever could fly me through space and give me a running commentary on how she was doing, the puppy's speech patterns would sound exactly like this:

"*Planet of Fresh Havens within TWO Earth days ETA! Your Uncle Stone will meet you at the entrance gate! He relays the following message: 'Welcome to paradise! Prepare to be blown away! You've never seen anything like it, Talia Fortune!'* "

The transmission ended, and I swung in my harness, alone. Strange: my uncle's earlier emergency transmission had been anything but encouraging. The holo-vid he'd sent revealed a man hanging off the edge of panic, not an enthusiastic tour director gushing through the *Titania*'s forwarded transmission. In his call for help sent to Earth, Uncle Stone had spoken of sabotage, rebel activity, profits slashed. What the planet needed was a sheriff to restore order. My grandmother Violet insisted on sending me.

I wanted to hate the Avenger. It would be a lot easier to blame him for what was about to happen. I didn't want to find, arrest, and execute him. It had been six long months and more since we'd last fought and loved in the Netherwood. If I hated him, it would be so much easier to accept myself as I was, just a sheriff doing her job. But I couldn't hate him. Because he'd made me admit that I was more than just the new sheriff of Fresh Havens or an official of FortuneCorp. I had my own questions and fears and hidden dreams. And I was a woman, with a woman's desires.

TWO

As soon as I saw the planet's surface, I knew Uncle Stone had lied. Fresh Havens was no paradise. The planet was more like a carnivorous plant, eager to devour its latest human sacrifice.

After sending notes through the grid to say good-bye to Riona and the other people who traveled with me, I searched the arrival gate for a familiar face but saw no one I recognized. The gate swarmed with traders getting their cargo onto the transport heading out. The hangar was a cavernous gray shell, cold and a little damp. My sense of adventure germinated into a growing unease. Where was Stone? Was the rebel situation even worse than he'd let on in the official transcripts?

I took a long, ragged breath, rubbed my arms, and scanned the crowd.

My grandmother had debriefed me before we embarked, warned me the outpost was tiny, only about one thousand carbon-based, regular people, the old-fashioned flesh-made kind, and another thousand or so droids and robots, variously designed for pleasure, manufacture, or hard labor. All crammed into a single large bubbledome, built before the engineers had finished retrofitting the native climate for human habitation.

The reality of her words hit me in the face now. Almost no people here. Earth teemed with billions of corporate soldiers, all rushing to compete in a multi-level, complex, and competitive world. Here the landscape dominated the lonely figures hauling loads of raw materials themselves. Not robots, but actual humans at hard physical work. And all citizens of FortuneCorp, all from the English-speaking countries.

Before I'd finished my sheriff's training at Handler Academy, I had rotated through a corporate posting in the Glass Desert at the end of the wars there. This planet's emptiness evoked for me the devastation of the Glass Desert, the hostility to human life.

That recollection of the Glass Desert stoked my unease. After I'd returned from my posting, a hellish experience filled with scenes of suffering, I'd immersed myself in the Netherwood, eager to escape the memories seared into my brain. And now, in a certain sense, I had come full circle. To another desert.

One bloated old guy kept staring at me, his milky eyes filled with a distracted weariness at once unfamiliar and yet irresistibly compelling. Then the guy raised his hand, and my unease bloomed into a huge, purple dismay.

"Talia!"

This wreck of a man was my Uncle Stone? What had five years on Fresh Havens done to him? I remembered his holo-vid and realized he must've used an older, more flattering image to make his emergency transmission to the Home Office. Smoothing an unpleasant reality to suit.

I forced myself forward, plastered a grin on my face. "Uncle . . . I'm so disoriented! Sorry."

"No apologies necessary." He hugged me, and I recoiled from the musty heaviness of his huge arms.

Stone hesitated and drew away, his puffy face hardening into an official mask. "You didn't know me, Tali. Has my term as mayor done me that bad?"

"Of course not," I lied. "Please, review status with me, Mayor."

He composed his features, adopted the unemotional facade of the appointed bureaucrat. We silently agreed that here, in public view, we'd do far better to assume our official mantles and save any family confrontations for later.

"Before I start . . ." Stone's voice trailed off. He cleared his throat and took my bags, and I let him carry them without protest. We pushed through a clot of oily-smelling men pushing pallets of synthwool, nano-generated machinery, and processed, uncontaminated soil to the loading gate at the back of the hangar.

I gave him all the time he needed to collect his thoughts, and I tried to imagine the way he felt in this moment: mayor of a disheveled little company planet on the edge of oblivion, called to task by a snippy twenty-four-year-old girl who happened to be his niece.

He put my bags down and coughed into the back of his hand, scrubbed at one fat cheek with his fingers before taking up his burden again. "Let me try to ask you this in a respectful way. . . ."

I said nothing in reply, only nodded as we reached the exit ramp. Stone shoved the door punch with one rubbery shoulder and the door slid open, revealing Fresh Havens in all of its glory. The scrub surrounding the transport shimmered in the wavering heat. I squinted to banish the mirage, but when I looked out at the endless landscape, the ground undulated some more. I saw a flash of a mandible.

"Sandworms," my uncle muttered.

My stomach turned. "Sand *monsters,* maybe." I hadn't seen a worm up close since I was a child, and I'd never heard of a worm the size of a shipping container.

"They're harmless, mostly. The spiders that eat them, though . . ."

I knew I had arrived in my personal hell. One populated with the creepy insects I'd always detested and came to dread in my time in the Glass Desert. Once you've seen a dead child's face swarming with opportunistic flies and maggots, you are going to hate bugs. It's just as simple as that.

I blinked hard, holding on to the edge of the slider to steady myself. "What a desolate place."

Stone barked out a scary imitation of a laugh. "Yeah. Welcome to Nowhere."

I let the door slide closed behind us. We stood there for another minute, and I breathed and tasted the dust of the place as I trembled. My voice had squeezed into a choked whisper. "What was your question?"

"Are you here in your capacity as Senior Law Administrator, or here as Violet's granddaughter and chief shareholder of FortuneCorp?"

The fear in Stone's voice steadied me. "Both."

I turned to face him, and when I stared into his bloodshot eyes I finally recognized the beloved uncle of my youth. My father's brother. He glanced away and swallowed hard, and I wiped at the fine coating of silica dust on my face with my fingertips.

It was Stone's turn for his voice to shake. "Oha,

then. You can see the evidence for yourself after our debriefing. It's gotten a helluva lot worse since you left Earth . . . three months is a damn long time."

I followed him as we slipped through the dust to his official vehicle, a little sandcrawler that looked like it had heaved itself up out of a burrow somewhere behind the entry port. As I got in, I saw a line of men in gray jumpsuits stretching endlessly away in single file, bringing their hard-mined treasures from the bowels of this empty planet to the ship that would carry their merchandise home.

To FortuneCorp.

We create our own reality.

I repeated this little affirmation to myself as I stared at the interplanetary interface's still-smoking motherboard in the central control room, but a slow prickle of unease down the back of my neck clued me in that I was deluded. Or maybe simply misled. The smoking equipment put the lie to my personal mantra. It kept on smoking, no matter how hard I willed it healed and whole.

"It's escalating. The sabotage." My uncle's voice shook me out of my contemplative zone. I didn't notice my fingers clenched into fists until my grandmother's ring dented a painful crescent into my palm.

"This doesn't look like simple sabotage—more like a major warning. An attack. And I have to hold you responsible. You didn't personally smash the interface, or hack into the system to destroy the coding . . ." I worked hard to keep my voice level, and I pretty much succeeded. "But it's your job to make sure something like this could never happen here."

I shook my head and escaped Stone's gaze by

drawing closer to the wrecked interface. It smelled like burnt toast. I leaned closer, as if proximity would grant me the technical knowledge neither myself nor my uncle possessed. Home Office would not be happy that the link for monitoring and controlling Fresh Havens had been severed. It seemed the planetary grid was still up, but not the link home.

"You're responsible for colony maintenance." I kept my voice cold, factual, hiding the waves of grief inside. "You're the mayor. Every individual on this planet is depending on you to keep the outpost safe. In contact with Home Office. And now all contact has been cut."

Sad, but not too long ago I'd worshipped my Uncle Stone as a daredevil, a pioneer, a patriot even, in the old-fashioned twentieth-century sense. With the distance of time and maturity I could see everything was changed. Stone was hooked on the synth, bad. He would tell himself anything, me anything, whatever it took to keep his drug supply coming in without detection by the sensors. Maybe he was even desperate enough to have smashed the interface himself. Hell, for all I knew he was in league with the Avenger, though I was sure he didn't have the cyber virtuosity or the personality skills to be the Avenger himself. As I could see by the evidence of his incompetence before me, he could even put the colony at risk to score more synth and hide his habit from the Home Office.

In addition, with the link to Home Office down, there was no way my superiors could know what happened to me here. I hated to entertain the thought, but Stone was a clear and present danger, an imminent threat to my safety.

I drew myself up to my full height and stared into

Stone's eyes until he broke our gaze. I remembered his earlier question and said, "I'm duty bound to remind you that you're not standing here with your 'little Talia.' Here I'm Fresh Havens' new sheriff and FortuneCorp's Senior Law Administrator."

He turned to hide amusement from me, and I knew he still saw me as no more than a smart-assed little girl. But this trouble was too serious to smirk away in avuncular condescension.

His lips twitched, and he licked them with the tip of his tongue before replying. "Isolation kills, Talia." My personal danger sensors shrieked in red alert. Was he threatening me? Or had the synth wormed paranoia into Stone's mind on top of the usual, more benign hallucinations?

His face stretched into a hideous impersonation of a smile. "Whoever did this wants us cut off from civilization. Like in an old-time horror movie."

"Are you saying some slasher killer did this before planning to murder us one by one?" Absurd. But then an image of the Avenger flashed through my mind, made me realize that this was hardly a mistake or a coincidence. The shadows from the fluorescent lights played over my uncle's ravaged, bloated face. I took a break from Stone and stared out the thick plastic window, which was scuffed by the sand blowing wildly outside. I half-expected to see the figure of the Avenger riding a sandworm across the desolate landscape.

In the middle distance, the edge of the Gray Forest loomed, stretching beyond the horizon. True wilderness. Awe-inspiring for me to consider, being from the overdeveloped, fully domesticated Earth. Reading about the ecosystem here had given me a shiver of adrenaline, an urge to see for myself. Here on the planet's surface, I much preferred contemplating that tangle of trees and slithering vines from a safe distance.

Stone's voice jerked my attention back into the control room. "You think I wanted this to happen?" His voice held a note of roughness, impatience tinged with fury. He shivered and ran his fingers through his still-impressive gray mane of hair. "I know who did it, Tali. My technicians have vanished."

I thought about the expertly snipped code floating in the Avenger's lair. My stomach turned to lead. "Repairing a malfunction of this magnitude will require a Master Builder from Home Office." I paced the control room, biting back my frustration. "You could have sent for one. Since I've left, I'm sure the wormhole drive's only gotten faster."

He actually snorted and rolled his eyes at me. "Don't change the subject."

I clenched my jaw and let his rudeness pass, nodded for him to continue.

"We've got a major situation here, something so bad I didn't make it part of the official report. Think! Don't screw this investigation up because of your lack of experience." His patronizing attitude was beginning to make sense. Stone knew as well as I did that he needed someone official to take the fall in the wake of this disaster. Stone wasn't planning on going into the sunset without a fight, and I could understand that, even respect it. Aside from the lust for the synth, Stone had made his career here, racked up his company numbers here. Once he lost his post as mayor, not even his status as one of the founder's relatives could save his executive ranking.

But I wasn't going to let him pin this horror show

on me. Stone was going back to Earth from here, to the Home Office where they could watch him carefully and keep him from making any more important mistakes. And there was just enough left of my old daredevil of an uncle to resent a mercy placement.

I tried to give him room to save face. If Stone resisted his soft landing, I was authorized by Home to use customary methods to remove a danger and an embarrassment to the company, and the last thing I wanted to do was exercise that final authority. "Grandma Violet knew you well. She trusted you to set this colony up in the first place. You did your best."

I should have realized it was too late. Stone turned his back on me and walked away, stared out the beat-up plastic bubbleshield protecting us from the sand and the grassy plains leading to the Gray Forest. I had not announced our discussion as a formal interrogation, but this was still unacceptable rudeness. He could treat his youngest niece that way, but not a Senior Law Administrator from Home Office. He'd gone too far.

"Turn around or I'll cite you for insubordination."

Stone lunged for me, and I reacted instinctively. I whipped my blaster out of my ankle holster, trained the laser sight between his bushy eyebrows. He had sense enough to freeze.

I had to assume he'd meant to harm me, though his attempt was clumsy indeed. "Put your hands out." My voice shook most unprofessionally, but I still had a heart that could break for the man. He'd been my personal hero, the man I dreamed of emulating— Uncle Stone, the pioneer. Uncle Stone, the adventurer. The man who knew my parents, who had served with them offworld. Now he was a man I suspected to be in league with corporate saboteurs. The WorldCorps version of high treason.

His eyes widened as I slipped the safety off my blaster, and he belatedly complied with my command. I swallowed back the lump in my throat.

"Lie facedown on the ground."

"No, Tali!"

"Do it." Some dreams die hard.

Stone coughed as he crept onto his hands and knees, stretched his body out in the position signifying guilt— what we both knew to be the official execution position. I stared at the back of my uncle's head and fought for control. My pulse pounded so hard I could hear it roaring in my ears like distant, phantom waves.

"Due process," Stone pleaded, his voice muffled against the plastic laminate floor.

"You attempted assault on a corporate officer. Anyone with more experience or objectivity would have executed judgment on you by now."

His shoulders shook, and Stone's tears filled me with both revulsion and pity. "I know what it looks like—that I smashed the motherboard, that I'm playing both ends against the middle. Give me a chance to explain everything to you, Fortune to Fortune, inside the family. . . ."

Ah, his last bargaining chip; the family name. I shook my head, though he couldn't see me with his face pressed into the scuffed nanobuilt floor. I kept my blaster trained on the back of his head.

"Sit up, but keep your hands out and open."

He struggled to comply, and on his cheeks his tears tracked through the dusty smudges that he'd picked up from the floor. "I didn't do this. I don't know why the techs would do this and then just disappear."

Disappear? How could they hide? The base was far from a megalopolis. Maybe Stone just didn't want to find them. I dragged a chair over and sat down. Leaned back, felt my disappointment like a lead weight on my chest. "Don't evade your responsibility."

"Tali, put your judgment on those techs. They are the saboteurs. They have to be. Who else would do this?"

"Corporate saboteurs still need connection to the central grid. How could they get rewarded, or get instructions, if they can't communicate with their bosses back home?"

"I don't know. But let me help you find out. I'll cooperate."

I lowered my blaster and flipped its safety back into the active position. I could outfight Stone barehanded—not that I wanted to go there. But he thought he was gaining ground with me, and I wanted to reinforce the illusion. Let him believe.

"So tell me what you do know, Stone. Cooperate."

"One of the senior techs. He has access to the central system. I reviewed his staff card manually after he disappeared—the man had much more experience than he told us."

For the first time since I set foot on the planet of Fresh Havens, my righteousness wavered. I knew in my gut Stone was now talking about the Avenger. I had the absurd impulse to ask him what color hair the rebel had, what he looked like as an ordinary man. "Don't you screen your people?"

"Of course." He shifted, and I raised my gun again. A flash of anger passed over his face like heat lightning. "I'm not stupid."

No, but the synth had slurred his speech, dulled the

fine intellect I remembered from my girlhood when
Stone still lived on Earth.

"The techs were . . . cleared."

"So why do you blame the senior one?"

"Because. He's gone."

My eyes narrowed, and a rage of panic built up under my official facade. The Avenger had faded away
like a ghost? But how? "Tell me what happened."

"The sabotage got worse every day. Ruined stock.
Misfiled and missing reports, stolen inventory. Damaged machinery. Now, the day after the official an-
nouncement that you would be landing on base, the
interface's motherboard was smashed. Right before
you came. And the techs are gone."

I cracked my neck, tried in vain to relax the tension
pulsing through my jaw. "How is that even possible?
Where can they go? All transports are monitored."

Stone shocked me with a laugh. "You're a long way
from the Home Office, Tali. You have no idea what
you're dealing with."

I looked over Stone's shoulder. Blowing sand half-
obstructed the view, but beyond the wasteland of the
colony port, I saw miles and miles of wilderness. Nothingness.

"You don't mean to tell me they've left Fresh
Havens altogether?"

"The base or the planet?"

"Either—or both."

"I have my ways of keeping tabs on the unautho-
rized transports offworld. They didn't leave that way.
But they are off the base, out of the colony."

My eyes narrowed as I glared at him. Sure, Stone
had his ways of knowing things. The synth forced
him to associate with criminals in order to get what

he had to have. Maybe he was covering for them, even now.

A sudden realization sent a spike of pain shooting into the back of my head. How was I any different than Stone? I was connected with criminals, too. I associated myself with the Avenger in order to get what I wanted—information, sexual release, the illusion of connection. My fury was nothing more than a delusion, a way to make Stone take the fall for what I had done. I had probably helped the Avenger learn what he needed in order to commit his criminal acts here, in my jurisdiction.

I stole one last look at the endless vista, and shook my head again. I had to undo the wrong I'd done, intentional or not. "Can't you use GPS tracking? How far away can they get on foot?"

I looked at him, and Stone's gaze locked with mine. The gray disks of his eyes revealed nothing of my uncle; they were flat and expressionless as the face of a vidscreen. "No GPS. No trackers. They're off the grid."

Off the grid? Not possible. The grid was critical. You couldn't take a dump, eat a sandwich, listen to music, or do your laundry without interaction with the network. How could these renegade techs do anything, let alone escape the govbots on the grid recording their movements, tracking their purchases, monitoring their activities for security purposes, and synthesizing the data culled from infinite minutes of recorded security video? I had never heard of such a thing, could not have even imagined it before Stone suggested the possibility. When he said they'd vanished, I'd thought they'd come up with an especially clever patch, a virtual invisibility cloak. Nobody went astray on the surface. Even dead bodies didn't disappear anymore.

"How many are 'off the grid,' as you put it?"

He blinked hard twice, registering my skepticism. "At least two. The senior tech, and his first assistant. Troublemakers."

"You let them just get away?"

"They slipped through my fingers." Stone's hands trailed across his skull to cover his face, and I was so stunned by what he had said that I let him hide.

Off the grid. No FortuneCorp employee had ever gone off, not in the company's existence. This made my dangerous jaunts in the Netherwood look like visits to the beauty doctor.

In a daze, I flipped open my handheld. It was on interworld cache because of the blown link to Home Office, but technology had followed Moore's Law and doubled every eighteen months: The little navigator in my hand was as powerful as the now-dead interface had been. And it had full access to the Fresh Havens planetary grid.

"Tell me their names."

"Ocean 7432 and Kovner 7030. Kovner's the senior guy."

Kovner. The senior tech. My Avenger's Real-world identity. I was sure.

My lips trembled, and I bit the lower one to keep control as I plugged in their codes, the location, tracked for history, current position, everything. Both men came up clean. Vanished. Impossible.

"Didn't you post an APB on the system, sent direct to Home Office? There is absolutely nothing here."

"Yes. Yes! I swear it. Believe me now? What else can

this be but an escalation of the sabotage? A ghost in the machine, Tali. Two ghosts."

I let his patronizing over-familiarity pass. I put the data in again . . . and again the two men came up clean.

As I stared at the green view screen, the import of what my uncle said sank deeper and deeper. These two guys had gone off the grid. A day or two ago they had walked out of the only human outpost on the planet and disappeared into the uncharted, terraformed wilderness.

So, by now they had to be dead. From what little I had learned of this planet so far, no human being had ever entered the Gray Forest and survived. It was heavily populated by indigenous beings of some unknown type, I'd been told. Creatures that gnawed the wires near the transport hangar, ate the nanobuilt shipping containers. Sandcrawlers got dragged off to unknown burrows, their chewed-up engine blocks found in half-melted clumps miles from where they were stolen.

"We have to find them, Uncle Stone. At least their bodies. Or whatever's left after their little stroll out there." I waved the business end of my blaster vaguely at the bubbleshield behind us. "Unless . . . they're hiding out somewhere inside the colony compound." I thought for a moment, stared again at the wilderness. "They have to be on the base. Have to be. To live outside is impossible. And would men looking for a payoff, corporate mercenaries, commit suicide like this? They're here. They've just found another way to hack into the grid."

Stone shrugged. "The human race was off the grid for thousands of years," he said.

"Well, yeah. But these days if you want to stay alive, let alone get ahead, the grid's the only way. So, for these two to disappear off the grid entirely is not possible."

Stone shook his head. "You just got here. You have no idea what the place is like." He covered his face with his hands again. "A nightmare."

Stone was wrecked worse than the Home Office motherboard. But there was nothing I could do about it. He had dug his own grave with his actions. My goal was to ship him out and have the Home Office deal with the ramifications.

I stood and stretched, dared myself to stare at the ceiling. I seemed to see the Avenger's face everywhere I looked. The tension refused to leave my body.

"I'll find them," I said. "Even out there." I had to. Or my corporate career was over before it ever began, in a cursed trading post at the edge of oblivion.

"They'll get you first. You think you're so much better than me, your pathetic Uncle Stone. That it's the synth what fried my brain. Right? But you have no idea how bad it is out there. Your little certificate from sheriff school won't protect you from who and what is waiting. You have more in common with me than you think. You might break in different places, but you'll break."

I glared at him, at the flicker of the straight-talking uncle I'd once loved. I put my blaster back into its ankle holster, motioned for him to stand up. "I'm young and hungry. I've got the highest technical rating in Handler Academy history. I'll cope."

"No, you won't. You still have my knife?"

I thought of the ceremonial blade all sheriffs carried as a mark of their service, and I felt my jaw getting tight. My Uncle Stone had started his career as a sheriff, and when I'd entered the Academy he gave me his own blade. I forced myself to meet his gaze. "Yeah, I have your knife. I keep it with me always."

"I kept it strapped to my ankle, too, Tali. But it was nothing more than a good luck charm in the end. It didn't save me. And it won't save you."

In a flash I unsheathed it, held it quivering in my left hand. It caught the artificial light in the control room, glittered, a beautiful anachronism worn for pride and not modern warfare. "It might not save me, but it reminds me of who I am. You're probably right about how bad it is here. But I still have to deal with the mess. That's my job." And like a magic trick, with a flick of my wrist I made the knife disappear into the sheath hidden in my boot.

We do create our own realities, and self-delusion was the quickest way for me to create my own personal hell, my own inevitable downfall. Stone was a disaster, but he wasn't the source of my troubles. I knew my enemy now. His name was Kovner. And I was through with illusions. I might well break, but not that way.

THREE

My mission objective in the short term was to stabilize Fresh Havens and make the colony profitable again; that's what I'd been told upon my departure from Earth. I decided to leave Stone at least nominally in charge of Fresh Havens while I neutralized the saboteurs. Stability held inherent value, and the dysfunctional folk drawn to inhabit and work in a colony in the farthest quadrant of the galaxy would smell fear and make the most of any disruption they could. The last thing I needed was an opportunistic horde.

Stone went to his chambers to "rest"—that is, to take a hard hit of synth to steady his ravaged nerves—and I let him, sequestering myself in my temporary quarters, the Ambassador's Suite. Stone now knew my publicized itinerary as Violet's heir—the Founder's granddaughter on her first tour of FortuneCorp's holdings—was a cover, and that my position as sheriff took precedence. In fact, I was here primarily to clean up the mess he'd presided over.

I tried my best to relax in the huge nanosilk bed, floating weightless in clouds of blue and purple fiber. My thumbs were a blur over my Navigator's tiny keyboard, typing, matching coordinates, studying patterns. I was researching the techs.

Nothing. It was like these guys only had avatars on the grid: peace-loving, productive, happy little technician-folk, working to better the universe and humankind. Avatars that had no surface location correlates.

Avatar. The word echoed in my mind, and I felt my cheeks getting hot. I hadn't earned my boffo technical rating last year by staying within Handler's official curriculum before I graduated. My instructors knew that as well as I did, but they'd looked the other way. My trainers had known my secret life would teach me more than they ever could. I'd first descended into the Netherwood to hone my skills as a new recruit; I'd stayed to taste the forbidden fruit of knowing, to train smarter and discover shortcuts to knowledge and experience. And I'd lingered on, hooked by the mystery of why people strayed from the straight and narrow path. People like the Avenger. People like me.

On the ship, just before I'd landed, I'd deleted that last incriminating datafile. All my holo adventures were gone now—the ice bath, the fight in the Amphitheatre— all erased for security reasons. My own security.

Yes, any records of the Avenger were gone now. But I had no doubt in my mind that he and the senior tech—Kovner—were in fact one and the same.

I had an idea as I floated on my back in the bed. I queued up the handheld and searched for the entrance to the local correlate of the Netherwood. Here. On Fresh Havens. The central link to the Earth grid had been severed, but the Fresh Havens planetary grid was still live. Both the Home Office and the Avenger were nowhere to be found.

With Home down, this was an unprecedented opportunity to hunt my outlaw without the threat of professional or personal discovery. The Avenger was gone except in my memories, but perhaps I could still find information about him. And I craved that clandestine connection with the cyber underworld and its hidden knowledge, that shortcut to finding the clues I needed to break this case wide open.

I found the coordinates and plugged in, felt the electric shock of simulated water washing my body clean. The mundane, carbon-based animal world melted away, and I moved through the digiworld, fully activated in cyberspace, clothed and hidden inside my avatar body. Amazonia had never felt so good as she did now. It felt wonderful to slip inside her skin, her sturdy frame; she was self-assured and powerful where I was not.

I prowled deeper, to where I knew I could find the local denizens exploring, fighting, screwing for fun. I fought to keep focus. But my uncle's parting shot burned in me. *You have more in common with me than you think.* My drive to explore the darkness of the Netherwood was, I had to admit, as destructive as synth. It could wreck me as hard as Stone's drug of choice, and the fact my addiction honed my skills and gave me an edge as sheriff only set its hooks deeper into me.

The landscape I walked as Amazonia loomed still and silent, eerily deserted. I broke into a trot and ventured deeper, until the countryside morphed itself into a cave, dark and dripping with unnamed nectars. I slowed to a walk, my mace in hand, my heart pounding in cyberspace and in my real chest as one.

At this point I didn't know what I was looking for,

but I knew the access points were here. This grid was a lot more streamlined than Earth's. The simplicity made for fewer weaknesses, but the back doors would be correspondingly easier to find. If I could find those back doors, I would find traces of the people who had used them to undermine the security of the Fresh Havens base. Kovner and his accomplices.

I bent to examine a sharp break in the code, visualized as a rip in the virtual landscape. Not an elegant job. A brutal tear—not the Avenger's style, I mused.

A hand clamped over my mouth and pulled me backward into a Dark Chamber—a nest of silence, avatar-created. A hidden pocket where avatars could go to chat privately. Or do other things.

I flipped upside down, weightless, and grabbed my assailant by the hair. The Avenger. I could tell it was him by that mane's rough thickness.

After a slack moment of complete shock, I fought him with real fury, real grief. He'd crossed the line, and now both of us would pay the price.

"You're under arrest, you bastard." I'd wanted to avoid encountering him down here for this very reason, but when he laughed, my anger mushroomed into something nuclear. "Don't patronize me."

"You can't hold me, Amazonia. You can't." He shook his head. "I knew you'd come for me. But not, I must say, in an official capacity. So, tell me who you are—a government agent, then?"

"You know enough about me to figure out who I am."

I fought to pin him, but brute strength was no longer enough. He faded to a ghostly shade and slipped out of my grasp. The move blew my mind. "How did you do that?"

"I've learned heaps since we last encountered one another." He shimmered before me, a hard-eyed specter. "You've changed, my dear. As have I. Ambition trumps affection, it seems. Your ardor grows cold. And you betray me without a second thought."

"You are endangering the outpost."

"No. You are. More than you can know."

I swallowed back my tears, grabbed my mace tight, though it was useless against this adversary. "I've sworn, along with my colleagues, to uphold the law and protect the people on this base. And I am certainly not alone in my duty. You smashed the interface. It was you—Kovner."

His face went completely still, as if I had somehow managed to slap him through the ether. We both knew I had committed an unforgivable sin, naming an avatar by a surface name. We both knew the Avenger was dead to the Netherwood now; his cover was blown.

I waited for him to reciprocate. I wanted to hear him say my true name. Enemies should know one another. I wanted him to kill Amazonia and then I'd hunt him down on the surface until he was mine.

Instead, he did something even worse. He leaned forward and stared into my eyes—the Deep Gaze that we were forbidden to make.

But the illusion held; we became something more than a falsity.

We locked gazes, our hearts beating as one, our breaths gasped hot, in unison. I felt desire vibrating through me, unwanted but no less powerful. I lusted for him. I hated myself for my longing, for wanting to consummate my desire the way we always had: Passionate, explosive, No Real-world effects. Simple, physical release.

I knew those days were gone forever. I was closer to this man than anybody I knew in the Real. But I'd never admit it to him, or surrender my honor to that weakness again.

His smile sent warmth shooting into my veins like a drug. Before I could break our connection, he rematerialized, stroked my lips with the tips of his fingers. He cupped my face in his hands, and the gentle touch of his lips on mine pierced me through the heart.

I closed my eyes against it, felt the connection between us grow even stronger. That kiss grew in intensity until my limbs went heavy with need for him, and before I could stop myself I returned the kiss, enfolded him into my arms, against my cyber heart.

"Hunt me." He spoke directly into my mind, even as the currents of the kiss washed away my anger. I sighed, opened my mouth to his . . . and he shivered away into nothingness.

I swallowed the lump in my throat, tried to summon my anger back like a magical spell. Nothing. Even my shame was smoothed away. I knew that I had played dirty, and I also knew that Kovner, the Avenger, understood. I fought my tears as hard as I'd first fought Kovner. But I lost the battle just as decisively.

It took me a moment to realize that this time the Avenger had left behind a detailed datamap of Fresh Havens, one that highlighted a pathway to the Gray Forest, showered in pixels of light.

So I had my man dead to rights, and I knew where he had gone. But I'd lost everything else.

FOUR

My encounter with Kovner made me careless, too careless. I awoke to the sound of the lock grinding in my door, and I came to consciousness in a slow haze, not with military attention. What was wrong with me? That kiss in the ether had thrown me, broken something I'd always depended on in the past. Now, my eyes opened into the complete darkness of the Ambassador Suite bedchamber.

I'd thought after unmasking Kovner I'd never be able to sleep again. I'd been wrong. But at least I had shot home the ridiculously old-fashioned dead bolt before collapsing into bed, and the old, non-computer-based technology gave me more time than the high-tech revolving combination lock in vogue back home would have.

I reached for my handheld. Once I had physical contact with it, I focused my energy, and the warrior technology I'd programmed into the database activated in my gen-modified retinas. The room sprang into focus, washed out in color but otherwise the same as if I had switched on the overhead light. I had to maintain contact with the device to retain the enhancement, but with the night vision imparted by my handheld's capabilities, I had the advantage in the darkness.

It was time to do battle in the Real, though without preparation or the armor of my authority to shield me. And I would have to fight as myself, instead of within the sleek, huge, and powerful body of my avatar. I shook off my fear.

My gecko grips were puddled at the foot of the bed. I slid to the edge of the platform, got the grips, and flung myself at the far wall as the door rattled in its frame. As I clung midway up, my handheld rested precariously in the crook of my arm and I cursed for my wrist holster.

The door began to vibrate, and I watched in horrified fascination as the dead bolt shook itself free of the door and dropped to the floor with a muffled thud. A single black-clad figure swung through the doorway, his face hidden by a black balaclava. Male. I perched across from him, level with the top of his head, and I clutched my handheld in one hand as the rest of me hovered against the wall. I was in serious trouble, unarmed except for the handheld's limited capabilities, and wearing only my skinsuit and my grips.

The intruder tripped on the nightstand. The man confirmed my guess about his gender with a hissed, deep-voiced curse. No way was this man the Avenger; Kovner wanted me to hunt him, not the other way around. Kovner was gone to wherever he was hiding. And if Stone had sent this man to neutralize me, my uncle was even further gone than I had thought.

"What do you want?" I spoke in a loud, clear voice. My stun gun, part of my handheld's standard tech, aimed for his amygdala.

The intruder started, and looked around the seemingly deserted room.

"You can't see me but I can see you," I said.

The man surprised me by leaping onto the bed and launching himself across the room to grab me by an ankle. I shot at him with the stun but had to manually adjust my sights and missed.

With a grunt he yanked me off the wall, and I landed in an inglorious heap, his big body breaking my fall. How had he done that? Gecko grips were designed to stick to anything with the strength of cement. But he'd yanked me off my perch as easily as picking a persimmon.

In a flash my handheld was gone, and then it returned, jammed into my right temple. A big forearm pinned me to the bed.

I seethed at my stupid incompetence. My assailant had turned my own weapon against me. Served me right for underestimating him. My cheeks burned with shame as well as fury.

His voice hissed in my ear, "I came to give you a message."

I said nothing, only swallowed hard and nodded. My head ached from the cold metal pressing on the side of my temple where the skull would yield easiest to a stun. At such close range—fatal. I'd end up permanently vegetoid at best.

My thoughts whirled in compressed time. I kept thinking my uncle had been right, Stone was right. I wasn't ready for Fresh Havens, I wasn't good enough to survive this challenge.

I waited, tried to summon a stoic fatalism I know I didn't possess.

My assailant growled in my ear, "Back off. Let

Kovner go." Then, before I could respond in any way, he fled.

I flung myself across the bed after him, intending to retrieve my precious handheld, and the room flashed with synth light when my skin connected with the device. He'd left it for me on my pillow.

My hands shook so badly I almost dropped the handheld, even as I held it against my chest. I'd survived our encounter, but only through luck and my assailant's will, not my own mastery. That knowledge hurt as bad as the handheld's stun would have.

After a night of broken sleep populated with unremembered nightmares, I awoke to the unpleasant knowledge that I was going to have to take massive action to stop events from spiraling out of control on the base. The fact that somebody—anybody—had the gall to attack me, a representative from the Home Office, and worse yet, that he'd been able to get away with it, meant that the company's authority over the colony was all but destroyed.

I sat in bed with my grid-ordered protein shake and my health cigarette, and I played with the gleaming black buttons of my handheld, my best friend on this planet, the portable connection to everything I respected, knew, held dear. I played with the smooth contours of its black titanium casing, with the stylus attached to the side. I scrolled through my e-mail and ignored the nibbles of fear working into my skin, tried to convince myself that bug-crawling sensation was nothing more than an adrenaline jolt of excitement. My eyes squinted and I focused on the information emanating from the handheld's screen.

I thought of my uncle's bloated face, of the way he'd

talked about the saboteurs and their escape off the grid. How could you catch somebody who knew their life depended on staying invisible? Who'd fled to uncharted territory, the only place they could make such a disappearance?

My fear kept whispering to me, directly into my mind. *Nobody has ever come back alive. . . .*

The protein shake congealed in my stomach as the unavoidable answer forced itself into my conscious mind. I'd have to vanish, too. I'd have to go where the outlaws had gone, do what Kovner wanted me to do—hunt him. And I'd have to pursue my prey into his chosen habitat: the untamed, hungry, humid wilderness of the Gray Forest. I was so new to this planet I didn't understand all the dangers, didn't even know how to begin to guess at them all. But on my way into the base, I'd personally seen the chewed-up carcasses of metal sand crawlers.

Of course I'd keep my handheld with me, hang on to my link to civilization. That would give me an edge over these two desperate men—these two lunatics, because, let's face it, anybody crazy enough to prefer the jungle to the base was almost certainly beyond hope of redemption. But still, a tiny little computer, no matter how loaded with killer apps or well integrated into the huge interplanetary grid, wasn't going to give much insulation between me and whatever waited out there. Especially if my opponent had given up those advantages voluntarily.

I had Kovner's maps, so I knew how to get to the forest's edge. Once I ventured inside, it was anybody's guess what I would find. My appetite was gone but I still forced myself to finish my breakfast. I was going to need all the fortification I could get, and from any source. I was going to the Gray Forest today. I had no time to lose.

Without fanfare, I left the base. There was nobody I knew well enough to send a farewell by way of the grid, and it would be much easier for me to conduct my investigation under a cloud of obscurity. Judging from my fellow travelers on the *Titania*, Fresh Havens was a magnet for the eccentric, independent and fractious. Best to take control before the local folk realized how rotten things had gotten at the top. It was in my best interest to avoid contact with my uncle, too. A simple electronic notification made it clear that I had gone in pursuit of the saboteurs, and that I had left him in charge as mayor until I returned.

I kept Violet shut off until I had no choice but to let her out. As she'd traveled from Earth to Fresh Havens with me, her consciousness preserved on my handheld, my disembodied mentor had no linear sense of time, no outer indication of the days as they passed. But I knew her understanding surpassed mine on a more profound level. Time didn't mean days and hours to her anymore; she was going to live forever, so a minute, a week, meant something very different. I'd checked in with her last night, so she knew what had happened, but I hadn't lingered long enough to let her give her opinion. Not until now. As I'd dreaded, she was highly amused. She didn't let me off easily, either. As well she shouldn't.

Her laugh sounded tinny from the handheld's speaker. "I can't believe you let him steal me! And then you stayed away. Are you afraid to talk to me now?"

I sighed and bit the inside of my cheek as I stomped

across the grassland. My Grandma Violet had been incorporeal for so long that I doubted she remembered what it was like to drop something—or to fight a much bigger assailant for your life. But that didn't mean I disagreed with her.

I couldn't concede the point, though. Violet could smell weakness, lunged for a jugular wherever she found one. I cleared my throat and forced a smile onto my face. "Come on. I didn't let him steal you. I fought like a tigress for you."

"Do you even know what a tigress is, my little bug?" I could see her ice-blue eyes glittering in my memories. If only she were walking next to me, together we could figure out what had happened.

I tried to remember if a she-tiger was mythical or just extinct, gave up, and grunted in reply.

Violet laughed at me again. "I'm glad you chose this marvelous adventure. You know everything secondhand, Tali. Go into the wilderness and live. Then you will know what a tigress is, what fighting is."

"I was at the top of my class. And I served my time in the Glass Desert. I do know war and what it is." It was a lame justification, but it was all I had to console myself.

"Of course. Though your experience is from a distance—at arm's length, no? You are a young lady of numerous gifts. But you need to get knocked around a little."

My cheeks burned, and the wind blowing over the undulating hills hardly cooled them down. Any more "knocking around" and I would be history.

"Do you miss being alive?" The question slipped out before I could censor myself. Something about the huge grassy plains stretching in all directions lowered my ordinary inhibitions. Maybe I was bold because I had been so decisively bested the night before. Maybe I could only grow without the Netherwood to help me, and Violet, as always, was right: What I needed now was the school of nocturnal assault, the academy of failure.

Violet was silent so long I worried I'd blocked the solar renewal, or worse yet, offended her. But her answer surprised me. "Am I not alive? Let me put it to you like this. I remember having a body, moving over the earth the way you do, but I cannot comprehend it anymore. My mind is my body."

"It sounds wonderful." Beyond all physical danger or fear of failure—this was an attainable version of those religious fairy tales about the world to come after death. That was wonderful, wasn't it?

"It sounds like heaven the way people used to believe in it."

Violet crackled with static for a moment. "Don't be ridiculous, Talia. Nothing more than primitive superstition. Don't even hint about religion to me. The Real isn't real anymore. I'm alive in the network . . . the *information* is the forest I wander through. And I mean my mind, Talia. Nothing so ludicrous and fanciful as a soul."

As Violet paused, I took a deep breath, amazed at the purity of Fresh Havens' alien air. The Corps of Engineers had done a good job of retrofitting the planet for human habitation. Hot sunlight all but blinded me.

I sensed the gulf between my understanding and Violet's experience. My life in the Netherwood mimicked hers in the Real; from what Violet was saying, the Real itself was something of an illusion to her. But we now walked together into an unknown wilderness with real dangers I could hardly comprehend.

I knew Violet had spent the night before searching out information on my quarry. "So, what have you found on Kovner?"

"He goes by many aliases."

My limbs went cold. My explorations of the Netherwood were criminal. If Violet had found a link to Kovner, she would find mine too. Of course I had a firewall up between my grandmother's consciousness and my now-deleted holos of the Avenger, but Violet could hack her way through that like a hunter wielding a machete in the grassland we traveled. I'd always assumed my grandmother respected my privacy, but assumptions could be deadly. So I had learned the night before.

I decided to play down my fears and stay on track. "Kovner has many names? Like what?"

"Like so: Van Kovner, senior assistant tech maintenance, FortuneCorp Zone D. And, Lieutenant Robert Kovner of the Senate Army."

I couldn't keep the shock out of my voice. "He was in the Army?"

"Why, yes, my dear. Honorable discharge after a double tour of voluntary service in the Glass Desert."

The toughest posting on Earth. I'd seen it myself, though in a limited way. The clumsy man in my bedchamber last night could not possibly be Kovner himself, then. That confirmational knowledge made me feel even worse. If Kovner's proxy could beat me so easily, what chance did I stand with the outlaw himself?

"So, how do I locate a guy like that, Grandma? If he's lost, won't he stay lost? For as long as he chooses?" And how could I arrest him, so far out of my element?

I kept my worries to myself, but Violet knew my limitations better than I did. The sound of her electric laugh, muffled against my wrist, sent unease climbing like a spider down my spine. "You always get what you want in the end, Tali. Just like me. Don't you remember our fight the night before you left for Handler Academy, for your training?"

My cheeks got hot as I walked a little faster. "I'd never seen you so furious at me."

"You were always so tractable, so eager to please. And suddenly my princess wanted to go to school to be a sheriff . . . to learn how to execute judgment on nasty people in offworld jurisdictions!"

I'd signed up without even telling her. She and I fought the entire night before I left, locked in her library, surrounded by my parents' books, their invisible ghosts.

"And you convinced even me, Talia. I let you go in the morning."

"Well . . . Mom and Daddy had done the same for FortuneCorp. They helped settle our first holdings. And Uncle Stone . . ." I swallowed hard. He'd given his life, maybe even more painfully than my mother and father had. They'd all done their part to pacify the wilderness planets of the family business. They'd made it safe for settlers to come, to find new lives. I'd wanted to go to school to learn how to fight, to be tough like my family before me.

"You were always such a sentimental little bug. For the first time that night, you used that soft heart to fight. Beware the individual with the courage of her convictions."

I didn't know before I left how much my training would cauterize that soft heart of mine.

I played with my handheld's wrist strap, where sweat had stuck the seams against my skin. "It seems that Kovner's got his own philosophies. I . . . I bet he's afraid of the Singularity," I said.

Violet laughed so hard that my handheld grew warm against my wrist, burned above my pulse points. "Fear it? Absurd."

"How would you describe it?" I asked.

"The end of death. The end of time. I have a glimpse of it here, from where I reside in the virtual world, the grid. I've reduced down, live my individual human conscious life in cyberspace. With Singularity, my consciousness will become linked to the capabilities of mega-computers. I'll be smarter, will be able to do things no human mind could ever do before. I'll be . . . invincible."

"But Kovner thinks—I imagine he thinks that would be bad."

"He should be afraid. The Singularity will give people like you—the righteous—the opportunity to walk among the gods. The psy-chip alone has given me life beyond life. And that is only the beginning."

I started walking again, much slower. After my parents' early deaths, after what I'd seen in the Glass Desert, escaping death's sting sounded marvelous. But me, righteous? No way. Not after my illegal jaunts in the Netherwood, even if they had been mostly intended for good.

I let a note of sarcasm creep into my voice. "Even a sentimental little bug like me would become invincible?"

"Oh my, yes. And don't sell yourself short. You are my heir. You will inherit FortuneCorp, all of it, when you are of age.

"You have the resources here, the advantages. All he has is his own cleverness. If he goes on-grid to get anything—information, connections, strategic coordinates—GPS tracking will lock on him anywhere he might be hiding on this planet."

"He's too smart to do that," I said.

"I hope he does, Talia. I am very curious about this Kovner and what he's doing in this forest. Tali, this is a pure wilderness. You've only read about such a place, maybe experienced it virtually on the grid. On Earth, only nature preserves are left. No more wild frontiers. Not on Earth. . . .

"You've got the advantage, but still, be careful," she went on. "Guard your connection to the grid better than you did last night. Here there be tigresses, bears, creatures beyond anything you've read about or can imagine."

I swallowed, my mouth suddenly dry. Was my heart pounding from fear, or excitement? Both. Suddenly I understood: This was everything I'd ever wanted. This was an adventure that Violet Fortune, my personal heroine, had never experienced during her lifetime. She had confronted the violent disruptions of the mid-twenty-second century with a technology-based world corporation bigger than any single government, a super entity that could regulate war itself: FortuneCorp. It had made her famous, made our family rich. But despite that illustrious legacy, I was treading new ground. Violet had never done this—walked alone into the physical unknown.

And Violet thought I could accomplish our objective. The long grasses rippled around me as the hot wind rushed past.

"You've trained your entire life for this," she said. "Do the Fortune name proud."

As I walked, the grassland stretched ahead like an endless living carpet. This vast plain had only been in place for the last ten years, and FortuneCorp ordinances still prohibited any vehicle from crushing the fragile new growth. Not that I knew of anyone but my personal renegade and myself who would even dream of leaving the secured, comfortable base for the planet's unexplored interior. No one in Fresh Havens' recorded history had ever wandered into the forest before and returned. Because of that, I didn't know what to expect.

Unintended consequences. The phrase resounded jarringly in my mind, driving me crazy with its reverberations. I knew what had happened on other, earlier worlds. How the planets had bred strange creatures out of the nanogoo and how those terrifying monsters had devoured the first colonists of those places. It had happened on Terranova. Blister Hills. And surely in other places, later, after the information-filtering system hid discomforting news from the employees.

Of course, other planets did fine. Mars, most famously. Igloo City. New Latvia. There, the terraforming had simply created multiple paradises, some arid, some fecund beyond belief. All were pristine, delicious, delectable places to live. Very profitable for their developers.

Fresh Havens was too new. No one yet knew what the planet was capable of spawning. And the settlers, primarily focused on making money in the short term, weren't too keen on finding out.

My job was to find out. And if I helped to identify and eliminate a native threat before it destroyed FortuneCorp's holdings, it would prove to my grandmother I was no longer a sentimental little girl; I was capable enough to qualify for true leadership of FortuneCorp. According to the terms of her bequest, I was scheduled to formally take up the role of CEO on my thirtieth birthday. I wanted to be ready for that day, not just passively inherit such a huge legacy as an accident of my birth.

With the luxury of distance, I recognized what a crutch the Netherwood had become. This solo trek into the wilderness was an opportunity for me to find myself as well as my outlaw.

The forest was much farther away than it had appeared from the bubbleshield at the Fresh Havens base. I walked all day in silence. My combat gear wicked away the sweat, kept me hydrated and fresh, augmented the strength of my muscles and the sharpness of my eyesight. I walked over fifty miles after daybreak. But even enhanced, my steps were not quick enough to get me to the forest before night fell.

I said good night to Violet and powered off my handheld to conserve the solar charge, pitched my tent without much fuss. But then I saw the night sky, and everything turned weird. The thick tapestry of stars unrolled itself above my head as night crept over the land, and I was filled with primitive fear and profound awe. I had never been anywhere on Earth where the night sky revealed herself to the human eye so completely filled with stars. Here, where no lights blocked the view of the heavens, it was just me and the universe.

The silence was profound. It swallowed me whole. And I was somebody intimately acquainted with that brain-sucker, loneliness.

Earth still had crickets in the summer night, but Fresh Havens' insects, such as they were, made no nocturnal sounds. As I stared into the night on the grassland plains, I seemed to fall up into the sky, drowned among the thickly strewn stars.

A slow wind began to blow. The nightwind, they called it back at base. Out here in the long grasses, it sounded like the beating of a thousand angel wings. Half in a daze I set an electric trip wire around my little camp to ensure I wasn't caught off guard like the night before. The night wind made me incredibly sleepy, but edgy underneath. It dulled like a drug.

Out here, the silence disturbed me, but I didn't plan on letting it interfere with my rest or my preparations for hunting Kovner in the morning. The ceaseless wind blew through my mind, and I could swear I felt the planet turning under my body, tilting on its axis. But while the loneliness cut deep, it felt clean. I was going in, no matter how isolated I felt.

As I drifted into unconsciousness, a single batlike cry jolted me into full awareness. It put the lie to all of my arrogant self-confidence, to my belief that my isolation was a safe one. That single scream was enough to wreck my sleep for the rest of the night.

Whatever it was, the thing had shrieked my name.

FIVE

I reached the edge of the forest the next morning.

It looked odd to my human eyes, however enhanced by warrior technology they were. The grassy plain abruptly shifted to a huge, ash-gray sea of trees waving gently in the uneven breeze. From here the forest looked impenetrable. A wall of living wood.

As I got closer, I could see breaks in the shady gloom. Weak light filtered through the leaves and dappled the dun-colored forest floor. By the time I reached the first trees, I could see a pathway reaching deeply into the mysteries hidden beyond.

I took a deep breath, leaned my face against my wrist-bound handheld and whispered, *"I'm going in,"* to my grandmother and supervisor.

Violet. It made me happy in an adrenaline-fueled kind of way that the founder of FortuneCorp herself was venturing with me to the very edge of her holdings, into this forest beyond the edge of any mind. She had never left the planet Earth, the Home Office, during her corporeal lifetime, had never really risked herself physically. Now that she had transferred her consciousness to the psy-chip installed on my handheld, well, there was definitely danger. This was the adventure of a lifetime, as she was fond of saying. And we were sharing it.

I stepped past the first trees—and left behind everything I'd ever known about the world and myself.

After another mile or so of hiking, I noticed my footfalls getting heavier and heavier, to the point where I could no longer move. I stood rooted to the spot, my lungs pumping for oxygen, my pulse roaring in my ears.

"Grandma?" I whispered, as I held up the portable to my lips.

Nothing.

My heart pounded even harder. "Violet." I said the word loudly, authoritatively, like a nurse doing her best to rouse an unresponsive patient.

Silence.

I manually rebooted the handheld and it got hot in my hand. I heard static, then a little pop. Burnt toast. More popping noises followed and my armor began to smoke.

Just like that, Violet was gone. My connection to the grid: gone. My combat gear: gone.

Talia Fortune: gone. Or she would be soon. I'd be ending up a space tigress snack in about another five minutes, judging from the hoarse scream that had invaded the night and still echoed in my mind.

I tried to wrap my mind around the truth of what had just happened. Unlike the outlaw, Kovner, I hadn't abandoned the grid. Instead, technology had failed me. My complete isolation from civilization, from people, from all the advantages of connection to the grid, threw me into a sweaty, heart-pounding panic.

Shaking, I shucked off my gear, the weight a pure

liability now that the titanium substrate was no longer grid-activated or enhanced. My skinsuit still protected me, and the gecko grips would work fine. But a laser could cut me in half now. Hell, a well-aimed rock could kill me in my exposed state.

I leapt onto the smooth trunk of a gray tree, using my gecko grips to climb high up into the thin, spindly new branches tender with succulent spring growth. I clutched that smooth trunk to my chest and tried to force my brain to function. My eyes focused on the silvery, shimmery bark. Gray. Like a tangle of wires, thin branches reaching up into the sky . . .

The Gray Forest. Gray like gunmetal. Gray like electrodes. The forest rose all around me, petrified, infused even as it lived with some kind of metal ore. Ore that must be magnetized, electrified somehow.

How had Violet not known this? How could she have not warned me or protected herself? My handheld must have fried in a magnetic storm my carbon-based body couldn't sense. For all I knew, the interface back at Fresh Havens had blown not because of human sabotage, but because of some kind of electromagnetic hurricane blowing out over the plains from this epicenter.

Yes, I hung suspended in the middle of an invisible, destructive electromagnetic field, one that lived in the trees and leaves surrounding me. It was deadly. It had killed my grandmother. My connection to civilization. My own chance to survive. I could never have imagined such a thing. The idea of two guys voluntarily walking off the grid strained reason. The reality of an entire geographic region fundamentally hostile to the grid itself blew my mind, made it smoke like the handheld.

MICHELE LANG

As I perched in the tree, swaying with the breeze, I wished that somewhere in my years of subversive perversion, of time in the grid "educating myself about undesirable elements," I had secretly learned how to pray. It was way too late for me to figure out on my own now.

The underbrush in the gloom ahead of me crackled and hissed. I went completely still, grateful my skinsuit was gray, too, and that it camouflaged me perfectly within the dancing canopy of sage-colored leaves. I couldn't believe my eyes. The thing that emerged from the darkness was no tigress. It was some kind of rodentoid—one that looked like a giant, carnivorous mongrel with a rat's snout, as gray as the forest but with a huge red maw and four perfectly round spider eyes. Its nose worked furiously . . . it knew I was there by scent, and it concentrated on pinpointing my location so it could attack. And, presumably, feed.

I reached to my ankle holster. I had to assume the blaster was dead, too; if it didn't fire I could use the butt end as a club. But that wasn't what I ended up reaching for. I felt the sheathed ceremonial blade of my ritual dagger and smiled. Out of pride, I'd always kept that blade throat-slicingly sharp.

I waited until the rodentoid worked its way to my abandoned armor, shed like a snake's skin at the foot of my tree. It nudged my Corp-issued combat gear with its long, fleshy snout, and in that instant of its distraction, I pounced. I hurled myself off the tree and onto the creature's hairy, bony back. In the next micromoment, I hooked my arm around the thing's chin and yanked the powerful jaw upward so it couldn't squirm around and chomp me.

58

The rat-dog screamed and reared, almost throwing me off. I clamped on with my thighs, and the thing rolled over onto its back, half crushing me under its wiry, foul-smelling body. As it did, I reached across and slashed at its neck. A huge spray of blood arced away, and the creature wormed its head loose from my grip.

I let go and wrenched my leg from under its body just in time. The creature snapped at me, missing my arm by millimeters. We faced off, me crouching low, brandishing my blood-stained knife, the rat-dog snuffling and growling, its sides heaving for air. Its four round eyes glinted as it stared at me.

The creature lunged, and I leapt back onto the tree . . . but not high enough, not without my combat gear to lend me antigrav. The thing's jaws closed on my left boot, bruised my ankle. I yanked my foot out of the electrospun nanoleather and climbed higher, my eyes stinging with sweat. I climbed until the branches crackled under my weight.

Balanced perilously over the rat-thing's head, I watched as huge, knife-like claws extended themselves from each of its forepaws. I waited. But the creature had lost too much blood to fight, let alone climb. It reached one hairy paw up toward my leg, and then toppled over with a hissing groan. I climbed higher as the giant-fanged rat-dog quietly and peacefully bled to death.

My tears surprised me. They mingled with the still-pouring sweat, tasted of salt and fear. They confirmed to me that I was weak, was human. And I was going to die.

My legs shook under me as I pummeled my brain to concoct an exit strategy. Now that the rodentoid was dead, I could assess the situation from the ground. I started climbing down the tree, my only plan an undignified retreat out of this accursed place, to salvage at least my life if not my pride. But a wave of movement, dead leaves rustling along the forest floor, sent me leaping back for the relative safety of the tree before I could run away. Little insectoid creatures, many-legged and furry, scuttled out of the underbrush and set to work on devouring the killer rat's remains.

There were hundreds of them. I closed my eyes against the munching sounds, their low, collective hum.

A vibration against the tree trunk made me open my eyes again, fast. The insectoids had abandoned the dead rat-dog, left it a chewed-up pile of bones. Now they clustered around my tree, humming together, touching its base with their long feelers. My heart pounded. They'd feasted on the creature's dead body—but who said the swarm would wait until a body was dead to start eating?

I started weighing options. A knife wouldn't slow these bugs down, let alone stop them. I tested the branch directly above my head, but it was too flimsy to support my weight. Besides, a few inches more height would make no difference once the bugs decided to come after me.

The vibrations got louder, and I realized they weren't planning an ascent up the smooth trunk to get to me; they were chewing into the base of the tree, grinding into the hard silvery wood, planning to fell me and get me that way. The realization sunk in slowly, like pain from a bad wound. The bugs were sentient. They had to be if they understood cause and effect. And they'd just made a collective plan.

I scanned the canopy layer with a single wild glance.

My tree was at the edge of a small clearing. I couldn't jump to another tree and make it. Trapped.

I imagined my body crawling with hundreds of the furry bugs, and the image shut my mind down, made it hard for me to move, let alone think. The tree vibrated harder, and my grip on the branches slipped. However, as the mental image of my imminent demise became more vivid, the balance swung the other way and a jolt of adrenaline shot through me. I lunged for the new growth directly above my head, held on tight. The thin branches trembled under my body.

A low rumble suddenly vibrated the ground harder than the insects did the tree, and a shower of hard seeds and dead twigs pelted me over the head. The hum rose to an agitated explosion, and the insectoids scattered, disappeared into the dead leaves littering the forest floor.

The boom echoed away, and it was only then that I heard my own voice, screaming. I cut myself off, cursing under my breath at my lack of control. My muscles kept trembling, the aftershocks of the sonic boom reverberating through my body. The bugs had retreated first. This was my chance.

I slid down the trunk as fast as I could, twigs and sharp edges of broken branches cutting my hands all to hell as I descended. I jumped the last few feet and landed with a hard thud. I caught my breath, stared down at the ground and watched for the leaves to turn back into bugs again. They didn't.

I ran. Without conscious thought, without knowing whether I was escaping to the perimeter or only going deeper into the wilderness, I moved as fast as I could. For all I knew, I was running straight into the mouth of a giant bug colony, but I couldn't stop my feet from flying over the forest floor, one boot on and one boot off, couldn't hear anything except my own heart pounding in my ears, my own ragged breaths.

I ran and ran, and soon I heard something else, loud enough to puncture the bubble of my physical effort: a hum. Rustling. Getting louder and louder behind me. The bug swarm.

Ahead of me loomed a deep ravine, and through the thicket of trees growing along its sides, I could see water flowing at the bottom. My only hope was that the bugs couldn't swim. I held on to that solitary, lame thought and hurled my body toward the edge of the ravine, toward a hypothetical haven, the ribbon of water sliding past below.

A human man stepped into the clearing, blocked my way. His square, hard face was blank with surprise. He pointed a crossbow—ridiculous!—at me.

I hadn't eaten or drunk since the night before. Even worse, I knew that my body and mind had both failed me. Despite my best efforts, I was nothing more than a living bug buffet—I'd been defeated by a pack of tiny arthropods. The adrenaline poured through my body and my heart pounded so hard I thought it was about to stop.

Before he could shoot me or say a word, I shoved past him and jumped. I landed hard on my feet, lost my footing, and fell down the steep sides of the ravine even as the man yelled for me to stop. I whacked my head on the way down, and faded away.

I had the satisfaction of knowing that death by human execution would be a less horrible way to die than getting gnawed to death by sentient bugs. It was cold comfort, but it was all I had left.

SIX

I woke somewhere dim and stuffy, my head throbbing, my mind full of questions. Hell, I felt horrible. My head echoed endlessly, my foot ached where the rat-dog had gnawed it, and the room in which I lay was stuffy and hot. Even worse, I knew I was in way over my head. The post of sheriff was not one for old men; a disregard for one's health was part of the job description. But no one person could prevail against the Gray Forest. I had been an egotistical fool to try, even with Violet's insistence and encouragement. And now I was in somebody's custody, a prisoner for certain.

But as I surreptitiously wiggled my toes to check for spinal cord injury, I realized that somebody had taken the time and care to find my chewed boot and put it back on my left foot. The nanoleather had already repaired itself. And my ripped-up palms had been cleaned and expertly bandaged. There was hope for me yet.

Sparks shot through my limbs as I stirred, and I kept my eyes closed, listening to the voices murmuring around me where I rested.

"We have to tell her." The male voice was low, urgent. I froze, dead still.

"Forget it. All of us are dead if you do."

The discussion ceased, and I realized my pretense of unconsciousness was fooling nobody.

"Tell me what?" I managed to ask, though the sound of my voice made me squint in pain. My eyes cracked open and I stared into the face of one of my captors.

He was of average size—half the bulk of the Avenger for example—with features more irregular, less sculpted and perfect. His short hair was sandy brown, not black and flowing down his back. A hard veteran of a man.

But something in his eyes took my breath away. Those eyes . . . they were the color of caramel and gold, lit from within. Eyes so knowing and full of anguish they brought tears to my own.

I tried to sit up, and this time couldn't restrain a groan. The man's fingers pressed down on my shoulder, and I slid back onto the scratchy pallet. I closed my eyes against the flare of a health cigarette, scorching into full flame.

"Tell me what?" I said again.

"Don't tell her anything," the second man warned. Through slitted eyelids I watched him—a squat, square man—pace back and forth as he waved his cigarette in the air.

The first man—the one I thought of as the veteran— shot the second a murderous glare. He turned to me, a small smile tickling at the corners of his mouth. I braced myself for a world of hurt at this hard man's hands, because he clearly had something in mind.

Bravado was needed, but my shaking voice gave my true emotions away. "Go ahead. I hate bugs worse than any human."

He surprised me with a short bark of a laugh. "Welcome to your worst nightmare, then." His voice was slow, flat, with a heavy New York accent. The sound of it made me think of home, my maimed city, impossibly far away. But New York, a place I'd never see again, was something this man and I had in common.

I rubbed my eyes with the tips of my fingers, remembered my tumble over the steep edge of the ravine. "Explain to me how I'm not dead right now." I opened my eyes to see the two men exchanging an uneasy glance. How much of a lie were they about to tell me?

I looked down at my toes, watched them wiggling my boots, studied the slashing bite marks marring the left ankle. "Last I remember I was taking a header over a cliff with nothing to break my fall." I looked up, awaiting his answer.

The vet's full smile was dazzling, a contrast to his hard, battle-weary face. "A tree broke your fall halfway down."

I hesitated—had I misheard him? "But I jumped," I explained again, speaking more slowly this time. Maybe they hadn't understood.

"Yeah. And a tree broke your fall." The squat man crossed his chunky arms and emitted a squawk of laughter. "I saw it catch you. I guess it liked you."

This had been the man with the crossbow, then. I drew myself up and onto my feet, despite the trembling that worked its way out into my extremities. The two men watched, and I ignored the pounding in my head to draw myself up to my full height.

"Trees don't catch people."

" 'Round here, they do."

I took a look around. The space seemed a cross between a tent and a bunker. Billowy, fabric-covered walls, but dark, like they were hung somewhere underground.

I forced myself to glare at each man in turn and squelch my gratitude. "You're both under arrest."

I expected them to laugh, knew I was their prisoner. But this farce had to get played from beginning to end. I knew the end would bring my death, but that didn't mean I wouldn't perform my assigned role to perfection.

"By whose authority?" The vet cocked an eyebrow at me, clearly intrigued to hear my answer. I appraised him without trying to hide my curiosity. Compact, not built for show, his muscles were made for hard work. That body hadn't been sculpted in a gym or bought in a lab. It was his by right.

I cleared my throat to hide the fact that I'd completely lost my train of thought. "You must know who I am. I'm Talia Fortune, the company's regional sheriff."

The short man held up my handheld. "Oh, yeah. FortuneCorp. The rich and famous Violet Fortune. You must be her heiress granddaughter. Let me guess, this chip here—that psy-chip. I read about it in the newsfeeds, about her reducing down, but I didn't know she was so . . . portable."

I cleared my throat again, licked my lips to hide their trembling. "She's wiped out. Gone. The whole device blew ten minutes into the forest." I contemplated the blown-out tech in his hard, square palm. "She reduced down five years ago, made history then. Technology marches on. That handheld had the capacity to hold her consciousness. And she wanted to come with me. . . ." My throat closed up as I remembered: Violet, my grandmother, was gone.

The men's joyful shout of shared laughter took me off guard. Why should a freak malfunction call for such celebration? I blinked the tears back and swallowed the stone in my throat. "Why is her death making you so damned happy?"

That shut them up. The veteran said, "Technology can't survive out here."

"And that's a good thing?" I asked.

The veteran stared into the middle distance. "Yes, when technology is your enemy."

The other man ignored me. "I'm telling you, my friend, we've got a chance out here. We've only been in contact here a month, and the forest is full of potential."

I leaned one shaky hand against the wall. The billowy fabric yielded to a hard surface behind it. "I know who you two are. The runaway techs. And I'm your prisoner."

The men stopped laughing. No need for us to draw out any pretense; better to get to the point, the culmination of the farce. And I had to know: "Why did you bother saving me? You want money? Go on the grid to get it and you're both dead men. You want me? Why? Without the grid, I'm not worth anything to you."

"What about your Uncle Stone?" The first man's voice held a note of contempt. "Don't you think he'll try to find you?"

I crossed my arms and forced myself not to fidget. Struggled to keep my dignity. "Without the grid, I'm nothing at all. Right?"

I wondered which of these two was Kovner, the Avenger, the man I had known in the Netherwood. My gaze shot from one face to the other. "What's going on out here? You've only been here a month, but you've built a whole bunker? How many droids did you steal from the base to build it?" I took a long slow look around at the dirt-packed floor, the humble materials comprising the walls and ceiling.

I swallowed hard, spoke my dawning realization aloud. "No droids here at all. No technology, right? Magnetic storms and all that. But there's no frickin' way you two could build a whole bunker with furniture and medical supplies. You said a month, but you only fled the base a couple of days ago from what my uncle said. Who built all this?"

Despite my defiant words, I couldn't stop a tremor from working through my fingers. Of these two, the vet was the more dangerous. I could tell by looking at him that he had killed. Many times. And despite my training and my posting in the Glass Desert, I never had.

The vet narrowed his eyes. "You didn't answer my question. About Stone."

I thought of Stone, of his pasty face, his bitterness. Of the shred of insight he still retained. I couldn't help sneering. "Uncle Stone. You must know he's hooked on synth. He doesn't care about anything else anymore. I've seen cases like his in the service . . . he's got another year at most."

"You were in the service?" The vet's voice held a note of disbelief.

"Oh yeah—corporate division, not government." I turned to face him. "Glass Desert, in fact." It was stupid of me to boast, to try to make a connection. But I had nothing else to deflect this man's simmering anger, and the information would either give us a point of contact or piss him off enough to do whatever he was planning to do to me. Better to move past the information-gathering stage as quickly as possible.

The squat man shook his head. "You're lying."

"No."

The vet moved closer to me, and I braced for an assault. He said, "You've had to do horrible things to survive."

I weighed my answers, then admitted, "No."

He shook his head, his smile dismissive. "In that case, you weren't in the Glass Desert I served in."

"I was there only a short time, part of FortuneCorp's posting there. Part of my post-Academy training."

The squat man laughed, closed in on me too. "You're nothing more than a spoiled little rich girl. That's not a Glass Desert posting. That was you slumming to make yourself feel tough."

That hurt—he was right. But I played a hunch. "You never served there at all," I growled.

The vet laughed and punched his companion in the arm. "Hah. She's got you there."

I dared another stare into the vet's eyes, though my training had emphasized a hostage should stay compliant and uncommunicative—a gray person, all but invisible. Our gazes locked. My mouth went completely dry.

"Yeah, I'm a rich girl. But Violet was a hard-ass. Mere blood-relatedness meant nothing to her. Look at Stone, pissing his life away out here. She knew he wouldn't get help for synth here . . . she left him out where he could self-destruct."

I broke our gaze and glanced at the dead handheld, still encased in the shorter man's meaty hand. She was gone, my tough, heartless, brilliant mentor. Her memories of the trip offworld, all of our fights and philosophical discussions—all gone. She wasn't dead in the conventional sense; backups of her were on the company mainframe back on Earth, but she would have no memory of me in the last year, and I didn't know how much her backup would be different. I fought hard to keep my lips from trembling, to keep the tears from pooling in my eyes.

As if reading my mind, the crossbow man shook the little case at me. "She was never in here, you unnerstand? It wasn't her." He wiped at the sweat forming on the wide bridge of his nose. The realization that he felt terrified gave me hope, though frightened people were capable of committing atrocities to smother their fear.

He tossed the dead handheld onto the floor. Kicked the case with undisguised contempt. I didn't understand what these two wanted from me, but knew they were going to extract it now, like a tooth wrenched out with a set of pliers. "You are going to cooperate, girl. Give us what we need to know," he said.

I crossed my arms, steadied myself. "I can handle whatever you can dish out. Torture, killing me . . ."

The vet drew closer, stood inches away from me. His presence demanded my full attention. "What makes you say that?"

My pulse started racing, and I throbbed in the most sensitive of places. My body, impossibly, knew better than my contentious rational mind could comprehend or explain. My mind, slow to keep up, finally admitted what my body and blood had known all along: the stone-cold killer, the vet, was Kovner. My outlaw.

I refused to back away, looked up into his amber, pain-filled eyes. "It's what I would do if I were you," I whispered.

He leaned even closer, and his sweat smelled like the forest; wild and dangerous. "You're not me."

My heart pounded like a hammer. "You want to tell me what you want out of me. I want to hear it. Go ahead."

I heard the short man slam out of the room, a curse rumbling under his breath, but I couldn't tear my gaze from Kovner. He didn't speak, rested his fingers on my shoulders. Even through my fear, I recognized the swell of passion that rushed through me at his touch.

I knew him by sensation, by emotion. I had chased him across the galaxy, this man who had disrupted an entire planet's connection to my employer, this man who had threatened my life by proxy. He was a fundamentally dangerous corporate saboteur, my sworn enemy. But here at last, with a whisper of a touch, the Avenger and I had found each other in the Real.

I didn't want to destroy my final illusion of him by seeing what he really was, didn't want to lose the final memories I had of us in the Netherwood. But I had no choice in the matter.

His fingers increased their pressure. "Tell me why you came here, Sheriff Fortune."

"You know why. To arrest you, for your campaign of corporate sabotage. I'm here to stop you."

My outlaw held me captive with his hard, desperate stare. "You didn't come to help me, did you? We need your help."

Hope flared in me. "I can get you out of this forest and back to civilization. If you did all this because of Stone, because of his incompetence, we can talk."

He drew closer. "Yes. We have to talk."

It was crazy. I knew Kovner had dismantled the interplanetary interface, had threatened me through an agent at the base. Now I was alone and unarmed, and my enemy was twisting my perverse desire against me like a weapon. I didn't understand. He had every advantage. But he was the one asking for help.

He broke away from me, and I watched him pace restlessly through the little enclosure.

He finally stopped. "The Singularity is here."

I blinked hard in surprise. His answer stopped me cold, was not what I expected. As far as I was concerned, we were dealing with an epic case of corporate sabotage; his fixation with technological advancement was only a distraction. "You've got to be kidding me. I hunt you across the galaxy, find you here in some kind of rebel outpost, and you throw a hypothetical at me?"

"It's not a hypothetical."

"I don't follow you. Pretend I know nothing about the term," I said.

He shifted on his feet, crossed his arms. Tension rippled through his body and into the air between us. "Singularity—it's the end of the world. Computers become supreme. The human mind becomes a component part of the faster, smarter, supercomputing mind—the human an obsolete, useless part. And so the human brain is retrofitted out of the system altogether."

"But that's ridiculous. Computers are smart, sure, but individual minds still exist."

His laugh contained no mirth. With a groan he sat down on the edge of the pallet, the only furniture in the room, and the little bed creaked in protest. "Yes, we're meeting here, in the Real. Your intelligence and mine aren't enhanced with computer technology. And we haven't become only a data subset in a huge, corporate mind. But imagine FortuneCorp, your inheritance, come alive, sentient, smarter, faster, more ruthless than you or even your grandmother. Imagine other world corporations mutated into sentient superminds, eager to compete, to dominate." He rubbed his eyes, took a long, shaky breath. "The meld is complete back home. It happened while you were in the wormhole drive, out of reach—you were off-grid then, too, though I know you don't see it that way.

"Some of us in the outer planets have evaded the complete merger of man and machine," he added. "From the perspective of those human 2.0 systems, that's a bug in the system, not evidence that I am wrong."

My mind reeled at the absurdity of what he was saying. "How do you know all of this if I don't? Droids are sentient, right? But they haven't taken over the world. So I don't follow you."

He shook his head, ran his fingers through his hair. Sweat trickled along the edge of his biceps. "Droids are individual systems, the digital analogy of a human brain. What's happened is a corporate takeover of millions of minds, a corporate supermind." He rose and started pacing in the tiny room. "How do I reach you? Convince you? You were already coming here when it became imminent. It takes—took—three months for a person to travel from Earth to way out here. It happened while you were falling down the rabbit hole, Alice."

I tilted my head, trying and failing to understand the reference. Understanding of a different sort began to dawn. "The interface. That's why you wrecked the motherboard. It *was* you."

He nodded but said nothing. His eyes held pain, pain I didn't understand.

I drew myself up to my full height, fought the encroaching dizziness. "Who are you working for?"

He chuckled, and the sound rumbled deep in his chest. Finished with pacing, he sat on the pallet's edge. "You don't want to see what's really happening. I don't work for anybody—I'm trying to save what's left of the human race. How's that? Grandiose enough for you?"

It was too much, actually. The Avenger loved breaking the law for the pleasure of it, for the lust of it. I knew him as a wicked, delicious man, not as a noble martyr for some cosmic cause. The transformation, from Avenger to Kovner, from cyber hacker extraordinaire to somber freedom fighter, boggled my mind.

"How do you know all this?" I asked again. "The rest of us on Fresh Havens are laboring under our cosmic delusions—how did you manage to see the light before the rest of us?"

He cracked his knuckles one by one; I watched his hard, calloused fingers with a horrified fascination. "Until I know you're on my side, I can't risk telling you that. Too many other people are involved."

I tried to engage him on his terms. "Why do you resist the Singularity? From what I understand, this upgrade you're describing could be a good thing. The Glass Desert would never have happened if we were interconnected on the grid."

He closed his eyes, and when he opened them again, the whites had gone bloodshot. "I thought it could be a miracle, too. Until I started tinkering around."

I batted at the billowy walls, testing them. " 'Tinkering around?' You mean hacking the mainframe." I hesitated. "The Netherwood."

A smile gentled his hard features, but the anger radiating through his crow's feet and trembling lips sent a bolt of fear through my body. "You know a lot about me, don't you, Sheriff?"

Beware formality in a man who hates authority. I kept my tone polite, respectful. "It's my job to find out everything I can about lawbreakers. Violet had a dossier on you. And I 'tinkered around' myself."

Did he recognize me, his sparring partner and Amazonian queen? I kept my body loose. Flexed the gecko grips I still held in my palms.

His laughter shocked me. He swiveled his body and stretched out on the pallet, tucked his hands behind his head and looked up at the saggy gray fabric ceiling—making himself completely vulnerable to me. He either thought little of my fighting abilities, or he *wanted* me to fight and overpower him.

That last thought made me pause.

He stared at the ceiling. "Oh, Sheriff. You don't understand. I am jealous of your ignorance. If I didn't know, if I could go back in time, I would close my eyes, too, go to my death filled with your self-righteous certitude. But the shame of it, my dear Amazonia, is that I *know*. And I can't un-know."

Gray stars swam in front of my eyes. I held a hand out to the wall for support, and stumbled when it yielded to my touch. "You know everything, then. Who I am. Who we are."

He laughed again. "I have a lot of friends. I know a lot of things. I know you have come for me the way I asked you to, if for very different reasons. I know that what I know will end your commission if you take me back to base. But I know a lot more than that—much scarier stuff."

"How? What?"

"Come with me, sweet warrior goddess." He rose

from the pallet. "I'll tell you. But then you'll know too."

My mind reeled with the implications of all that he'd said. If Kovner was right, our personal battle of wills was meaningless, a small spark within a giant conflagration that was coming to engulf us all. Was I ready to feel that fire?

SEVEN

He led the way out of my prison cell, and I followed, my senses on high alert for physical attack. On Earth, my combat armor did the work of my senses: infrared sensors tracked my quarry in the dark, protected me from enemies in pursuit. And in the Netherwood, every movement, every simulated sensation, was filtered through a computer interface, one step removed from my biological capacity for touch, hearing, taste. I'd forgotten the simple sensation of air on skin, the surprising effectiveness of scents for alerting a person to her surroundings.

"This place smells great." I hadn't realized I'd spoken aloud until Kovner interrupted my train of thought with a low laugh.

"That's the only thing great about it right now. That, and FortuneCorp doesn't know it exists." He shot me a sidewise glance. "Except, now I guess it does."

I was starting to understand his friend's side of the argument. Had Kovner kept me ignorant of the size of their hideout, I could have returned to Fresh Havens empty-handed and none the wiser. This knowledge made my escape that much less desirable for them.

"Too bad I don't smell food," I joked. Anything to forge a bond with this outlaw in the Real.

My lame attempt at humor didn't distract Kovner from the thoughts that furrowed his brow, that hunched his shoulders forward. "We've got food, and water too. Come with me to the mess and we'll share what we have with you. You must be faint again," he said.

I shrugged. I didn't want him to know how weak I actually felt. Better not to give him any information I could keep to myself.

Instead, I rubbed up against him. I wasn't too proud to use what I had, though I'd never used sex as a weapon in the Real before. "A mess? Sounds like you're missing your Army days, Lieutenant Robert Kovner."

He half-turned to face me, and my heightened senses caught his scent again. It wasn't until it was too late that I realized he was using his own weapons against me.

His lips closed over mine in a brief, almost chaste kiss. But the touch of him sent an inferno of desire shooting through my body, burning away everything except the primal human needs: eat, drink, fuck, live.

"Be careful," he murmured. "We're in the Real now. Any fatal error here stays that way. There are no reset capabilities." He brushed a strand of hair out of the corner of my mouth, a gesture more intimate and disarming than even his kiss.

I considered his words as our eyes met, no fear of revealing artifice here; that interface between us, the Netherwood, was gone. Instead, Kovner stood before me, alive. And for the second time in my life, I knew in my gut that I could die.

Soon we stood shoulder to shoulder in the doorway to the mess hall, and I couldn't believe what I saw: scores of people—more than I could estimate by sight, given their ever-shifting patterns of movement. So random. So . . . human. Their clothes looked strange: rough silks in browns and greens instead of FortuneCorp-issued skinsuits made of nanofibers.

I watched one person, no more than three feet high, clutching at a woman's belt loops, laughing aloud, though his wide eyes looked as frightened and lost as I secretly felt. I blinked hard, leaned in close to whisper, "These are entire families." I'd forgotten what a hungry mob could look like. "Reminds me of the Glass Desert."

"Now, Sheriff, the detainees in the Glass Desert were refugees in a war. We're partisans preparing to fight." Kovner's tone had reverted to a formal, ironically humorous one, and I knew he was as aware as I was of all the pairs of eyes that regarded us.

He got me a tray, pulled me through the crowd and over to the head of the unruly line near the food dispenser. The people around us smiled and nodded at Kovner as he approached, and a couple of the older people actually bowed to him. One man murmured, "Take your place, Emissary Kovner," before he stepped away.

To my surprise, the crossbow man waited for us near the food, unsmiling and morose. "This is Sully," Kovner said, but the square man gave no acknowledgment of my presence.

I scanned the room again. Who were all these people?

"Over a hundred souls," Sully answered my unspoken question. His use of terminology puzzled me.

"Souls?"

I hadn't thought it possible, but his voice got even colder. "Yeah. *Human* souls."

"Souls are a myth. The Glass Desert taught us that. Souls don't exist."

His nostrils flared. *"Souls,"* he repeated.

"What is this, some kind of clandestine cult compound? You know talking religion's against the law. Hate speech."

Sully's glare turned murderous. I watched him clench and unclench his meaty fists—confirmation that the government had done one thing right, at least. After the horrors of the Glass Desert war, all religion had been outlawed: an attempt to prevent irrational zealots from destroying the world in the name of something holy.

Kovner's laughter interrupted our clash. "This whole place is against the law. Stop fighting and eat."

Somehow, the three of us found a quiet corner in the surging sea of humanity after we got our food. I couldn't hide my near-starvation anymore, so I fell to the water bottle and plastic plate of edibles with gusto.

The food was Corp-issued stuff, standard and bland. Nothing fabulous, nothing that would extend your life. It was the most delicious meal I had ever tasted.

When I finally looked up, it was into Kovner's expectant gaze. "What?" I longed for a few more bites of food, but that expression would not be denied.

"You still think of us as the enemy. Even these little kids in here."

The use of the old slang—so anachronistic in an age when children had become increasingly rare in civilized countries—made my lips twitch with amusement. "Kids. Isn't that what they used to call baby goats?"

He smiled, too, but the joke seemed to pull him deeper into a private melancholy. "The truth is, any society that cannot sustain itself will die."

"Honestly, Kovner . . . did you ever consider having children yourself? Why? With whom? Nobody spends enough time in the Real to look after a screaming little blob these days. We've evolved past children. A babydroid is just as cute, can learn and grow just the same, but without all the fuss and trouble. I'm glad some people are still having them, but . . ."

Kovner sighed, and he leaned back in his chair to contemplate the miniature people waiting so patiently for their food. "You think of children as a sacrifice, a burden. But they're a gift."

"A gift from where?" I shot a glance at Sully, who had gone so still he looked like a square, heavy statue. An idol. "Aren't there too many human beings using up Earth's resources as it is?"

"Not anymore."

"Oh, right." I rolled my eyes. "Your almighty Singularity is here."

Sully choked on a mouthful of food, cursed under his breath. "You're going to tell her everything, aren't you?"

I pressed forward, needing to understand the situation so badly I was willing to risk anything for the information I sought. "Yes, tell me. These people aren't refugees. Who the hell are they? No one on the base has a child—you don't bring children off-world. They look well-fed, and they've been here for awhile. You clearly have plenty of supplies laid in for them. They aren't warriors, ready to fight the machines to the death, and this is FortuneCorp-issued food. That means you're stealing it from the base. Right?" Kovner's hypocrisy turned the taste of my meal sour and cold. Nice to preach sacrifice while gorging on food stolen from my company, my people.

Sully tossed his silverware onto the tray, and the clatter made me start. "Kovner . . . Bullshit, man. You're fucking crazy. She *is* FortuneCorp. I'll take her out back and shoot her myself."

Kovner's voice was quiet, serene—the most threatening sound I'd ever heard, worse than the cocking of a gun. "I'd shoot you first. And I love you like a brother. You don't understand what this conversation means."

"I can't sit here, listen to this," Sully said. He glared at me, his eyes full of fear. "You betray us, Talia Fortune, and I will get my revenge." He slid his tray off the table, shook his head slowly and cursed under his breath, and walked all the way out of the mess, as if he couldn't bear the knowledge of my existence.

Kovner and I sat together and watched him go, and I stole a glance at Kovner while he was preoccupied with his friend's departure. Though I had only met him in the Real a short time ago, and under adverse circumstances, I knew him better than anyone else I had met on this planet, felt a bond so deep that even his crazy story of human annihilation couldn't destroy it. Amazonia and Sheriff Fortune went to war inside of me. I knew my future as a corporate officer depended on my gaining his trust and betraying it. But this lawbreaker, an outlaw hiding within a secret outpost of stolen goods, had stolen my affections, too, hard as it was for me to admit it to myself.

With Sully gone, it was much easier for me to summon up my gentleness, my strength. Kovner fascinated me. He embodied everything compelling about the deepest reaches of the Netherwood, and why I spent so much time there—forbidden pleasures, physical release, mystery. I finished the food on my plate, looked up to see him looking at me again. This time I smiled.

"Please try to convince me again, outlaw," I said. "You believe the Singularity is true. So, why hide here? Why not confront it on Earth, where you can do the most good? You don't strike me as the type to run away from a fight."

Kovner took a deep breath, took in the dusty, chaotic mess hall in a single wild glance. I followed his gaze and, I'm sure, saw something different than he did. I saw a disheveled mob of people, sheep herded into pens, no different than the wretched refugee camps built directly onto the fused sand of the Glass Desert, where the families interned there sickened and died, where we watched them, guarded them, kept them quarantined. As Kovner told me his twisted tale, it became clear he saw these people in the Gray Forest not as refugees doomed to die, but as humankind's final hope. He spoke in a low murmur, his eyes glancing at me, seeking understanding.

"The Glass Desert," he began. He took a long drink of water, cradled the now-empty bottle in his callused fingers. "It burned people to their essence. You may not have done horrible things there, but you must have seen them."

He paused; I nodded.

"I did horrible things. I had to kill people too far gone to save, people who would've killed me if they could. I saw human beings treat each other with absolute brutality. And I saw acts of heroism and tenderness that I can never forget."

I resisted the urge to reach to find the Avenger's fingers, hold them inside my own.

"I saw something ineffable in people whether they acted for evil or for good. And it made me want to understand."

His story gave me the chills. "Understand what?"

"How people are capable of such greatness, such evil. When I got back to New York, I started hunting out the answers. But the grid is so heavily censored, so much history has been erased, I could only find clues. Children's books from a long time ago held bits, old poems. The government can't censor everything. So I became a hacker. I broke into classified caches and I found—the Bible."

I nibbled at a thumbnail, tried not to lose it. Kovner had committed a major mindcrime: an offense punishable by indefinite incarceration for criminal insanity.

"The Koran," he continued. "Bhagavad Gita. Talia, you have never seen these things."

A statement, not a question. I nodded.

"I started reading theoretical physics. Philosophy, the Talmud. The Book of the Dead. To see what connects us, do you understand?"

I was too horrified to speak—the transgressions he had revealed eclipsed the mere smashing of an interface. But I was drawn to him, his obsession. I suppose my motivations mirrored his own: to understand what drove people to do what they do.

His eyes stared deeply into mine. "I thought the Singularity could connect us, like you still believe. That's what all of us have been taught—a substitute religion. But the more I learned, the more I understood that the preparations being made are taking us in a far different direction. To death, Talia. *Death*. And I believe this forest could protect the people here from that death."

I swallowed hard. The noise of the mess had drowned out the sounds of my churning stomach, upset by all of this. "What does this have to do with me, Kovner? Why did you want me to hunt you here?"

He reached to me, took my hands in his. "I know you will find this hard to believe. But your coming here, to the forest, has been foretold."

I felt dizzy. Shook my head in an effort to get my equilibrium back. "Foretold? You make it sound like some kind of grand prophecy. Why? Why have I come?"

"Because without you fighting alongside us, none of us will survive."

I pulled my hands out of his, covered my eyes to try to stop the sudden vertigo. Nothing in this bizarre, dreamlike place made any sense at all. The Avenger was in fact this man Kovner, grim yet so gentle, patient. I was surrounded by children and their families, mysterious, unaccounted-for people who seemed to have grown out of the forest like mythical creatures, and who apparently regarded Kovner and Sully as messengers from another world.

"They do see us as messengers," Kovner said, and I jumped. The man had read my mind. I stood up, my body trembling all over. Maybe I was hallucinating from the whack on the head, or maybe all of these people were collectively insane and my comment about a cult compound was more on the mark than I first realized.

"I know it's impossible to take in all at once," Kovner said, his voice low and warm. "But I can help you learn about all of this, learn how to survive."

"You were the one who made the prophecy." My own voice sounded far, far away, and I wondered if I were going to faint.

Kovner hesitated. "The prophecy was told to me," he finally said.

"By who? Sully?"

He shrugged, flashed me another incandescent smile. "By the forest."

Okay . . . either he had lost his mind, or I had. I had to get out of here, get away from Kovner's deep amber eyes, his soft voice and chiseled body. Had to get away from these children, the oppressive sense that this place wanted something from me that I just couldn't give.

"What did you put in my food?" I asked. The trembling got worse.

Kovner's fingers traced the edges of the tray in front of him. "Talia, you're not crazy. All of this is real. I know you don't want to believe it. None of us do. But the time is short. You must join us."

"No." I refused to submit to his soft, coaxing words, words that led inexorably to a terrible conflagration. "I . . . I can't. Kovner, I will advocate for clemency from the Home Office. I swear. Come with me, let me get you out of your bind. I'll go to the mat for you."

He shook his head and smiled sadly. "You can't run away from the truth, Talia. You can't."

I backed away slowly, and he made no move to follow. Something broke in me; I said, "Watch me," and I ran.

When I got to the entranceway to the mess, he stood in front of it, like he had beamed himself ahead. "No, you can't go." He reached out, took one of my wrists, and I could feel how strong his fingers were, his strength held in check.

"I can't stay here."

"Come with me, then, where it is quiet, and you and I can make a plan." He led me through the tangled warren of hallways back to the cell where I had awoken to this bizarre place, a more unbelievable world than the Netherwood had ever been.

He pulled me into the little room, dropped the canvas slider closed and left the light off. We stood together in the darkness. "I can't do this," I whispered. I wanted to believe the Avenger, wanted to accept he wasn't crazy. But his story was so dreadful, it was much more bearable to deny it in the absence of any corroborating evidence.

Kovner pulled me up close to him, his arms wrapped hard around my waist, my sex pressed against his thigh. The rough sensation sent a hot throb shooting through me, fuelled with adrenaline, full of inflamed desire. His kiss in the soft semi-darkness was hungry, demanding, so male that it made me go weak with involuntary need. His hands buried themselves in my tangled hair, and our desire fused into something that had a life and purpose of its own.

He broke the kiss, crushed me against him. "We know each other," he whispered, his lips pressed into the curve of my ear. "You will be my woman, Talia. And I won't let you die. I won't."

I pulled back, searched his face in the deepening shadows. "Die?"

"The Singularity is coming here, and soon. FortuneCorp won't be content with Earth alone." He kissed me again, more tenderly this time, and I surrendered to the cascading waves of sensation that bathed me in warmth. I couldn't fight the pleasure washing over me, emotions I thought lost forever in the Netherwood.

He finally released me. "You are so beautiful, Talia Fortune."

"How can you even see me here in the dark?"

"You're so damn smart, you have a whole dossier on me, and you still don't realize why? Think a minute."

The Glass Desert . . .

A dawning horror sank into me like a set of fangs. I tried to pull away, but he held me fast.

The Glass Desert. The first wave of kill-ops. Soldiers had been genetically modified to suit the terrain: biologically enhanced retinas, pain sensors deadened. They were bred and built to destroy the maimed scavengers roaming the wasteland, human beings killing and dying horribly. That's how he moved so quickly, how he could read my mind. Gen mod.

My voice shook, but I didn't care. "Kill-ops. Some would say you're not even human yourself."

"No. I am. I have a soul. And with all I saw and had to do to people, I know the machines will be worse."

"How can the machines possibly be any worse?"

"Because they don't have souls. There's no possibility for redemption."

My throat burned with unshed tears. "Souls. Have you got any proof that I have one? That any of us are more than flesh-based, natural-born computers?"

I felt him shrug in the darkness, strained to adjust

my eyes to the lack of light. "I came to the Gray Forest from Earth in search of the answers to these questions. I think you are part of the answer, Talia. Join us."

The man was beautiful. He was a genius. He was completely insane.

I brought my dagger out of its hidden holster and up against his neck. His body went still, pressed up against mine. I considered bringing Kovner back with me now. But I knew he could outmatch me in every possible way: outrun me, outfight me, draw my tender feelings out of me. My best chance now was to run. I hated to leave my mission unaccomplished, but getting out of the Gray Forest alive would be a victory in itself.

"Please, Kovner. Don't make me cut you. I'm leaving."

"The forest won't let you go."

I kissed him full on the lips, the point of my knife resting above his carotid artery. One last, slow kiss to remember Van Kovner by. One last, long breath to savor his dusky, wonderful scent.

I kicked the slider open, squinted against the half glare of the hallway lights, suddenly so bright after the darkness of our sanctuary. "Good-bye, Kovner. When I come again, I'll advocate for clemency with the Home Office. I'll do everything I can to save you and these people."

I brandished the knife when he drew closer. "Don't make me execute judgment here, now."

He raised his hands in surrender.

I ran away from the tenderness in his eyes, the truth of his words. I was holding on for dear life to my position and my official mission, and I fled knowing Kovner had every advantage. My bond with the Avenger still existed, but he had to be stopped. I had to deny everything he wanted me to learn, or I'd lose everything that mattered to me in the Real—my position, my self-respect, my memories of Violet.

It was my fate to take Kovner down. And maybe to kill off the best of me with him.

EIGHT

I blundered along corridors until I found an exit, and then up stairs and into the forest, my heart pounding. As I ran, I couldn't stop thinking of Kovner's face framed in the doorway of that little room. He'd had me. Why had he let me go?

Dead leaves crackled under my feet as I fled the rebel enclave, and I realized I knew no direction to follow but away. I supposed I would figure out how to get to the Fresh Havens base once I was safely removed from those frightened people. From those children.

From Kovner.

Of course, how long before the bugs and the rodentoid dogs heard me stumbling around? And how could I fight them off, unarmed except for my knife? Stone had been right—I was in too deep, fatally over my head. *No.* I forced my fear to retreat deep inside, where I could ignore it, and I ran.

But, part of me stayed behind in the enclave. Damn Kovner! I knew my enemy too well. Even now that I had met him in the Real, and his true self bore scars I could hardly understand. I felt too much for him: hot desire, quivering fear, self-righteous anger. All of it was burning me up from within. And no matter how hard I pushed my feelings away, they insisted on returning, hotter than ever.

As I ran from him, his image kept up with me easily, like a shadow in my mind. Our encounter had awoken something inside me, some part I'd done my best to suppress and kill. My human side, the softness, the weak part of me that made me vulnerable to sick people like Stone or unscrupulous people like my adversaries in FortuneCorp. Or, while I was being honest, to my own grandmother Violet.

But now I was free. I didn't want to admit it to myself, but I felt liberated. I'd never thought of the hackers in the Netherwood that way—we were messing with the system, not escaping it altogether. But alone in this bizarrely silent wilderness, my connection to the grid altogether cut, I felt . . . hyper-alive.

Something crackled in the underbrush ahead and on the right, and my body jolted with adrenaline. Unarmed and alone, I was going to be hyper-dead in about another minute if I didn't come up with something to save myself. So I dove for cover, found a huge, hollow gray log that all but hummed with a strange sonic frequency, crawled in and . . .

Came face to face with Kovner.

Kovner! I cursed under my breath and tried to back out, but he grabbed me by the wrists. The curved hollow of the rotten tree trunk reverberated with his laughter. I was a dead woman.

I stopped struggling when I realized it was hopeless in that tight space, with no room to maneuver. I could barely make out his lean chiseled face in the dim light. His features were blank.

"I've been waiting for you."

Not what I'd expected him to say. My body went

still. "Waiting for me. Like I was just going to hide in this random rotten tree. And you knew it."

"Well. Yes."

His calm assurance triggered a slow panic. I wasn't too comfortable with wonder, or mystery. "You're joking. You have to be. My hiding here is random."

"That's one way of looking at it. Another is that nothing is random. Ever."

I could hear the pounding of my heart echo along the sides of the tree trunk. I tried to control my wayward emotions, knew that I had already lost. My rational mind fought hard for dominance anyway.

"No. I believe in free will. We get to choose, here and now, what to do."

"That doesn't mean your choice is random."

He inched forward to kiss me on the lips, and I welcomed the blast of heat that rose in me, energizing if infuriating. I kissed him back—I admit it—and not just because I thought it would give me some kind of tactical advantage. My inner animal simply hungered for the taste of his lips, and didn't care how much trouble this kiss brought to the rest of me.

I finally pulled away as best as I could, still pinned along the bottom of the trunk. "I hate to wreck the moment, outlaw, but I dove in here to escape something rustling just across the way. My toes are still sticking out the back of this trunk. I'm sure some rodentoid-insectoid creature from my worst nightmares will be chewing my feet off in about another minute."

"No. Trust me, you're safe."

"Then why do I feel something tickling along my ankles?" I wasn't kidding.

The smile died on his lips. "OK. Maybe you're not

safe. You're not exactly integrated with the forest."
He pulled me forward, and I scrambled farther into
the dark interior of the rotted tree. A low growl from
outside made me move a lot faster.

Kovner stared deeply into my eyes in the near darkness, his face a shifting pool of shadows. A slow
breeze blew along the length of my body, but I held
steady, stared back. A part of me disappeared into
him, effortless as a dolphin splitting the surface of a
faraway tropical ocean.

We locked together for only a moment, but it was a
section scalloped out of time, a delicious scoop of the
ice cream of eternity. I'd almost drowned in the Black
Sea as a girl of five, and I remember that slow-motion
backward tilt into weightlessness. That moment and
this one existed side by side, out of time, eternal and
precious.

I shook my head hard to get him out of my brain,
and closed my eyes against him, against that sweet
moment. "Stop that! Whatever you're doing—quit it."

Time started flowing again, but in that single moment we had known each other deeper than in the
Netherwood, deeper than I'd known anyone in my
life, even myself. Especially myself. The unknown
thing snuffling against my toes outside seemed far less
dangerous than this.

"Don't lie to yourself." He let go of one of my
wrists to caress my cheek, and I made my move. In a
single fluid motion I wrenched my other hand free and
backed away from him and from that moment of vulnerable bliss.

He grabbed for me and missed. I scooted backward,
smaller and quicker than him, and I backed out blind,
risking that Kovner had been right the first time and the

mysterious sniffer was not ready to chomp. I scrambled to my feet, turned to run and—

Kovner.

"How did you do that?" The question came out as a furious squeak and I backed up too fast. I landed ignominiously on my butt, mouth hanging open. Getting chomped by a giant bug would almost have been a relief in that moment, but I saw a furry tail disappearing into the brush.

Kovner scratched at the tip of his nose. "Hollow trunks usually open on both sides. I backed out, too."

"But how did you . . ." I bit off the end of my question. How had he known? And how could he move so fast?

The gen mod. I closed my eyes, searched for some measure of equilibrium as I sat huddled in the leaves. Couldn't find it. My eyes still closed, I muttered, "OK, you got me. I give up, fair and square. Take me to your leader or whatever—except I guess you are the leader out here. Take me back, interrogate me, execute me, whatever you've got planned. You conquered me here in the Real. I admit it."

I cracked open an eye to peek at him, and was shocked to see Kovner sitting next to me, cross-legged, on the leaf-strewn ground. When he caught my glance he shot me a slow wink and a smile that could melt synthsteel.

"Oh no, Sheriff Fortune. You're the one who's got me. Take me back to base. In your custody. Your refusal to stay has necessitated a change in plans."

My mind whirled like a blender—what he'd said made no sense at all. "Why? You have the advantage here. Why don't you take me back to your secret hideout or simply do away with me? At the very least you could leave me to take my chances with the killer bugs."

"You're worth more to our cause alive and free, Sheriff. I wanted Amazonia to join me here so that I could save her. But you, Sheriff Talia Fortune, could save us all."

I got up and walked away fast, my shoulders clamped in a vise of tension, and Kovner followed behind, a menacing, sentient shadow. "Take me into custody," he repeated. "And in return I'll make sure you get back to Fresh Havens alive."

I shot him a disbelieving glance. "So you can kill me there?"

He shrugged, rubbed at his nose again. "You're the suicidal one, not me."

I couldn't accept his offer. Too damn dangerous, for all kinds of reasons. I tried to walk away again, and he snagged my wrist, more gently this time. "Tali. Arrest me. It's what you came to do."

I let myself look into those amber eyes. "Don't you get it? If you don't snuff me somehow before I get you back to base, I'll break you. Might take me some time, but I will. I know enough to convict and execute as it is. Do you really want to pull down Sully and those children with you?"

His pupils widened, and his lips pressed together into a narrow line. "Do your job," he finally said. "Forget what we once were to each other. We're running out of time."

I cocked an eyebrow at that, but suddenly my cyber-lover had nothing to say. The silence weighed on me, a physical presence in our breezy clearing ringed by wind-tossed silver trees. I had to escape the forest and its dangers if I was going to live and, even more important to me, salvage my position, my reputation. The only way I could return without disgrace was with Kovner in tow—a golden opportunity for Talia Fortune, sheriff and chief shareholder.

But it was a terrible risk for Talia, the human being. She was a woman with a whole graveyard of secrets I had to keep buried at all costs.

"I can't forget what we were and still are," I said. "You're not the Avenger here but Kovner, a gen-mod killer who tried to destroy this planet's economy and smashed its only connection to the Home Office. How can I trust you or anything you say?"

He crossed his arms upon his chest, chewed at the inside of his cheek. My heart pounded so hard I could hear the roaring of my pulse like a distant, encroaching tide. Kovner cracked his neck, stared into the middle distance. "I can't convince you if your mind is closed. I told you in the enclave: I have no interest in corporate sabotage. Let me expose you to the truth before it's too late. If it's not already too late."

The sunlight turned the crown of his hair to gold. He stood in the clearing, blocking my way as the shifting sunbeams played over his hard, unyielding features.

I hardly knew him as a man of flesh—if a man modified for war still qualified. How human was he? What I'd learned had destroyed every last illusion about the man I'd known in the Netherwood. But, human or not, he had reached in and touched my heart. And however much I longed to, I couldn't leave that knowledge, or Kovner himself, behind.

We walked in silence, cut off from anything human except ourselves. I couldn't stand it. After the constant chatter on my handheld, a universe of connection had been silenced. I craved occupation for my mind, if for nothing else than to distract myself from my physical proximity to somebody I desired so much but couldn't let myself have.

I followed him through the underbrush, watched a trickle of sweat trace behind his left ear. "You were born for this place."

He kept walking, and at first I thought he didn't hear. But then he sneezed, scratched a shoulder, half turned. "Yeah. In a way, this is my heritage."

"Your parents were monkeys?"

"No." His voice was hard, but he kept his temper in check. "My great-great-great-ancestor, Abba Kovner, was a renowned partisan in World War Two. Lithuania. He was a poet and a mystic. People thought he was crazy. But he foresaw the horrors of Hitler's empire. And he fought it with everything he had."

Sweat poured down the sides of my body in rivulets, and not just because of the exertion and the heat. "I've heard a bit about that. Those partisans had nothing."

"Less than nothing. But they survived, outlived their enemies. Not all of them . . . but enough to bear witness and to carry on the fight."

We walked in silence, while the import of his words worked into my brain. "The Singularity is an extermination, then."

"She finally sees the light. Praise the Maker."

"And you know this how?" I asked again. "Why won't you tell me?"

He walked in silence, ignoring my question. We moved ever faster through the shadowy heat, as if Kovner were eager to rush forward and face his mortal enemy.

I shook my head, slipped a little in the leaves as I paused to consider his words. "The Singularity. The elevation of man by machine. You're describing a miracle, not a disaster, to me. Human mortality will be vanquished by this—death itself. Human suffering. How can that be bad?" I'd asked before, but I still wasn't satisfied.

He again gave me silence as an answer. I watched him stalk away, had to run to catch up. However, that was not the only answer I got. The forest vibrated around us, which I took for a sign that Kovner had achieved some kind of mystical union with our surroundings. He rejected technology outright, and lush verdant nature accepted him without condition. It seemed to accept me while I was with him. Small comfort, but I would take what I could find out here.

Right away, I almost paid for my assumption with my life. When I heard something rush through the underbrush behind us, I turned to face it, for the first time unafraid of what I might find. Kovner needed me to live to fulfill his insane prophecy; surely the forest would cooperate. And this was not an insectoid rodent.

For the first time since I'd left the base, I beheld something that looked harmless and cute in the tangled nightmare of the Gray Forest. The creature wiggled its green-tipped nose as it inched toward me, its enormous, bassett hound–like eyes widening in what looked like fear. The brown-and-white expressive face lit up when I stopped to look into its pink eyes. A ringed tail bottlebrushed straight out behind it, and it started trilling a slow, sweet song that dulled my residual instinct for caution.

I'd taken two slow steps to meet it before Kovner

hurled his body between us, impossibly fast. Without a moment's hesitation, the little beast became something else: a whirling, snarling blur of fangs and claws hurling itself at Kovner's exposed throat. Before I could dive for cover or run, Kovner gripped the thing around the throat, held it away from his face. The snarls choked off into gasps, and the little paws dug into his hands with needle-sharp claws.

When he yelled, I realized that augmented or not Kovner was as human as I was, and it broke the spell of fear that had kept me frozen. I whipped out my knife, closed in on them, buried it to the hilt in the thing's fluffy back. It screamed and fell limp, and Kovner dropped it. His hands were covered in blood; both his own and the creature's. I stared at the body, wondering how long before the bugs smelled its death and came to feast on all three of us.

"What was it?" I managed to whisper.

He grabbed its body off the forest floor, flung it far away into the treetops behind us. His fingers still dripped with the thing's blood and his own, and he yanked me down the path, away from the creature's adorable, mangled body.

"Move. There will be more of them before you can blink. Haul ass or we'll be bloody meat in ten seconds."

He pounded through the underbrush, and he made a thunderous noise as we crashed through the trees, along dry pathways. He cursed under his breath at my slowness as I fought to get enough oxygen into my lungs. Far away, I heard a chattering in the branches over our heads. The dead thing's compatriots had evidently discovered its body.

We made it to a clearing and Kovner broke into a

full run. It felt perversely exhilarating to chase after him in full flight, to leave all confusions and petty frustrations behind us. At least I wouldn't die alone. *But what if we lived?* Then even that final thought got pounded into the silvery dirt under my feet. I could no longer hear my thoughts, just the roar of my pulse in my ears and my gasping breaths.

Finally, Kovner stopped near a broken cavalcade of flinty-looking boulders. I collapsed next to him, my stomach heaving, but nothing was left in there to come up. The stones felt cool and silent against my cheek as I gasped for air. I willed myself to forget Kovner was beside me . . . almost wished he would go away and let me get devoured in peace. My pride lay broken and dead in the dirt like the deadly little creature that we had killed and flung back to the wild.

Kovner slid down nearby, leaned sideways to face me. His hand caressed my shoulder as we both gasped for air. My quivering muscles relaxed under the calm energy of his fingers.

I forced myself to look at him through tear-filled eyes: my "prisoner," the phantom lover of my electric dreams. This dangerous man who could survive out here alone, without technology or any other help.

I fought my need for him, throttled it like Kovner had strangled that rabid little beast. But my emotions slipped through my chokehold, hid in some dusty corner of my mind and waited for me to show weakness again.

I forced my brain to operate. Creaky and battered, it nevertheless obeyed my will. "I don't think I'll get out of here alive," I muttered.

"Join me, Talia, and you won't have to. You can survive with me, here, and together we can fight to keep FortuneCorp off Fresh Havens. Save a remnant of humanity."

I bit back my fury, insisted on speaking from my rational mind. "Kovner, you are deranged. You expect me to give up everything I've ever known because of some cosmic dream you have? You came out here voluntarily, you *live* out here. Isn't this forest worse than whatever's waiting for us back at the base, back in society?"

His face was an imperfect mask slipping away to reveal the emotions swarming underneath. Horror. Fear. Rapture? "No. There is worse."

We both backed away from the truth. He reached into a pack strapped to his chest. "Here. Food-foils. Get your strength."

He tossed me a foil MRE pack, and I grabbed it one-handed. I ripped it open, devoured the gelatinous protein-based goop inside. Thirst plagued me, but I supposed we'd have to locate water and purify it ourselves. That last flicker of optimism amused me, from the bottom of the sewer pit of despair where I waited for death, my enemy. I wanted, craved water. Why?

"Survival imperative," Kovner whispered. He squirted protein goop into his mouth, wiped at his lips with the back of his hand, and rested on the edge of the rock next to me. Examined his ripped-up fingers.

I swallowed hard. Had he really just read my mind? From where his body touched the cold stone, I felt a weird, subsonic hum travel through to where my own body rested against the rock. I flinched, forced myself still.

Surrender. Everything I'd been taught about survival and success was dead wrong. The only chance I had to merge into the forest without violence was to submit, to release my ambitions and accept. That knowledge flowed into me like a drink of the clean water I craved.

Kovner and I turned to each other in the same instant. His smile pulled me toward him. I felt my body against the rock, still absorbing Kovner's freaky vibrations even as I slipped into his consciousness. I know that's a pretty limited way to describe what happened. But I knew myself as a speck of a larger whole, in communion with a soul mate and guide.

And then all at once I snapped back into my body, yanked back like my consciousness was attached to a rubber band. Kovner blinked slowly as he watched for my reaction.

I glanced at his fingers. The blood was gone. His hands had healed. I trembled.

The hum emanating from Kovner and the stone felt good now, warm instead of cold, an echo of the psychic symphony I'd just disappeared into. But I still didn't trust it.

"Try explaining that in words." Kovner's voice was low and halting, like he was speaking out loud while standing on holy ground.

I raked my hands through my hair and struggled to focus my mind. I didn't have the luxury of letting Kovner off the hook, or ascribing magic powers to him. My voice was creaky but serviceable. "That's part of the gen mod, isn't it? Your ability to heal."

He avoided my gaze. "Yes. But not all this other."

I wouldn't let him evade me. "This . . . other. The ability for us to . . . commune. Is this why you came to the forest?"

Kovner's voice shook. "Yes. I had a friend—can't tell you who he is. He started hacking into DARPA databases, classified, and found information about the Gray Forest. About the strange flora and fauna. About the electromagnetic storm. I thought this could become a haven from technology. And I was right."

I nodded, embracing my returning rationality like a long-lost friend or like a limb that had become paralyzed then miraculously recovered. "How long have you been here?"

"Sully and I have been here, on and off, for the last month. We ran off the base for good less than a week ago."

"How did you access the Netherwood from the forest?" I felt the tips of my fingrs going numb. Looking down, I saw I was clutching my hands together hard enough to cut off the circulation.

"The Gray Forest has properties that DARPA never discovered. I'm still learning about them."

"I remember after the Amphitheatre, in your lair. You tried to warn me then about the Singularity, but I didn't understand. And I can't bring myself to believe you even now," I murmured. "And I don't see what is so horrible—"

"No? Can't you see? When we become part of the corporate brain of FortuneCorp, we'll lose our souls. The ability to do what you and I just did."

"Souls? So, they can't survive in the cyberworld?"

His sad smile was the only answer he gave.

"Tell me more about the Gray Forest, then."

He leaned his head against the rock, closed his eyes. "You know about it. Something about this forest resonates inside the people within, those who are receptive to it. Those who threaten it get eaten pretty quickly, as far as the rest of us can tell. And nothing vulnerable to an electromagnetic pulse can survive. No computers of any kind. Even many simple mechanical things break out here. We're not sure why."

"And these people," I stammered. "Those kids? Who are they?"

"We call them the Foresters. When Sully and I first came into the forest, they were already there."

I sat silent, trying to absorb this information.

After a pause, I asked, "What about the human brain? What if you're not receptive to the place, but you don't want to chop it down or whatever?"

"You go insane. You bleed to death. Or the forest digests you."

I was glad he wasn't looking at me when he said that. Maybe it was this electromagnetic field that had driven Kovner over the edge, to madness. That was the only explanation I could find.

His eyes flew open and he stared at me. "Tali, let go. Your thoughts, your words . . . all of it matters here. Life or death. You have to grow—fast. Or we are going to die."

"We?"

"Yes, because I refuse to leave you. I saw into your soul even in the Netherwood, and I see into it here. I will never leave you, Tali. I'll never betray you. No matter what you choose to say or to do."

"How could you see into my soul in the Netherwood? In a place constructed by machines—inside of them? How do you know any of us even has a soul?"

"I don't know how. But I know it's true. And your

soul is worth fighting for, in the forest or back at the base. Even if you yourself don't believe it yet. That's why I'm going back with you . . . if we ever make it."

"But the base. You're going back to your own personal hell, from what you're telling me."

He hesitated, but for only a moment. "Yes. But letting you go back alone, into hell, into your own destruction, would be worse. You are the best chance we have."

His words shut me up for a minute. The hum along the side of my body deepened, and I relaxed into it like it was a massage, riding the waves of Kovner's craziness.

A breeze rippled through the canopy of leaves shielding us from the hot sun of Fresh Havens. I took a deep breath, tasted the alien freshness of the air. I missed the absence of birdsong, for a moment missed Earth with a daughter's fierce love for a long-dead mother. Words dragged themselves out of me, heavy in my mouth.

"I'm nothing special. A sheriff, no more and no less. Whether you're right or wrong, I need to help the employees on the base, employees of FortuneCorp. That's my sworn obligation and duty. And if by chance you are sadly deluded, I need to make sure the interplanetary interface is never sabotaged that way again. I can't let my feelings for you interfere with that."

He didn't look surprised. "Don't your feelings—for me or for anything else—clue you in that I'm right?"

I felt my cheeks growing hot. Kovner had made me blush. "I can't give up my duty because I want you. If I do in fact have a soul, I don't want to further compromise it by betraying my responsibilities. I have to go back, be the Talia Fortune I was born to be. The duly appointed sheriff of this place. My grandmother's heir."

He actually shuddered. "You need to go back to hold your known world together. But you'll find that world is not what you left behind when you left it to hunt me."

I gave him one last chance. "You don't have to go back into it with me, Kovner."

He spat in the dirt between his boots. The stone's hum faded and died. "I'm still under arrest. Letting me escape now would also be a dereliction of your so-called duties. Capturing me was your original mission. If it's still your mission, see it through to the end."

He had retreated from me altogether. The stone at my back felt hard, unyielding, and my shoulder abruptly ached where my weight pressed into it.

I stood, stretching the stiffness out of my legs. "You're coming back with me to protect me. That's by your own admission. If you insist on coming back, I don't know if I can protect you. From the Singularity, FortuneCorp, or anything else."

He stood next to me, captured my fingers and interlaced them with his own, and kissed my hand. A thrill passed through my body, red-hot and silent. He didn't need to say a word. I knew he was throwing himself into the abyss for me, in some kind of misguided attempt to save me and the other people on this planet. Our respective ideals linked us even more than our mutual lusts. I couldn't stop him from destroying himself, any more than he could stop me.

If I slipped away, he'd find me. If I somehow escaped from him, he'd show up at the Fresh Havens base alone to turn himself in. Even in captivity, he would watch over me.

I'd heard of noble self-sacrifice before, but this was the first time I'd seen it living, in action. And I had no idea what to do with it. Ignore it, accept it, or fight it as demeaning? After hesitating, I walked away from Kovner, my thoughts, and my fears.

The outlaw followed.

That night, the wind came for me.

Kovner and I slept huddled together near the perimeter of the forest. He insisted that the forest was safer than the grasslands, and in our flight I had learned to trust his judgment about the relative dangers. The rustling of the leaves and Kovner's even breathing soon lulled me into peace, my first since I left the base.

When I arose, I was in the grasses, not the trees. I wandered in the grasslands; so vivid were any surroundings that I thought at first our stopping to rest in the forest had been a dream. The wind picked up, beating the long grass blades into a frenzy all around me. The tips of the grasses whipped against my legs, my bare arms, and I knew I was in the presence of something bigger than me, something with the power to destroy me. Or transform me.

We regarded each other, the night and I. The sky flared with red streaks of lightning, electric blood vessels racing into the ground. I stood calm, unarmed, but I knew who I was, why I had come. I had been called. I had a destiny.

That's when I knew all of this was a dream—that comfort in my skin was something I only pretended to in daily life in the Real, and in the comforting depths of the Netherwood. I stood, and let the wind blow through me. But I refused to let the Forest use me. I was no tool. I whispered a single word into the wind: *No.*

My supreme confidence shattered and crashed. The wind grew violent, and the grasses rustled with a million tiny bodies. The bug swarm was coming for me. I knew it was the end. Their furry little bodies would climb over my skin, dig deep, devour me to the bone—

I lurched awake, drenched in sweat. Kovner had me by the shoulders. "The nightwind, you rode the nightwind." His face, all but hidden in the shifting darkness under the trees, shone with triumph.

I scrubbed at my face, forced the sleep out of my eyes. "The same crap happened to me on the way in. The wind called to me by name."

Kovner smiled, his face silvered by the starlight filtering through the leaves overhead. "I summoned the nightwind, but I didn't know that you could ride it too. I hoped."

My brain refused to follow him. "The nightwind? What the hell is it?"

He played with my hair, and I let him. Anything to distract me from the insectoid hordes lurking invisible all around. "I can hear the future in it, sometimes. I think it's the gen mod, how it interacts with the electromagnetic fields here. A limited precognition. As for you, the forest is calling you to your true nature, calling you."

Sick, sick twisted mind. I stared up into the tangled branches above our heads, made sure I wasn't still dreaming. "And that's different from the evil Singularity how?"

"The forest is giving you a choice."

"Some choice. Meld, or become a bug buffet. Great."

"Are you sure about that? I don't believe the choice is that simple."

This guy was the Avenger, for sure. He had the same maddening habit of leading me further astray with question after question. I groaned, huddled up closer against his body and away from the insect hordes that haunted the night. "I should be flattered, right? But I'd give anything to be out of here and back on base."

"Be careful what you wish for, Sheriff."

I lifted my head up to catch his smile, but he wasn't joking.

I stood guard against the insects and the nightwind for much of the rest of the night, but the forest seemed to accept I wasn't ready to disappear inside of it, or at least was willing to wait for me.

In the orange glare of dawn, we downed our protein goop breakfast, found a small stream that tasted bitter with minerals but that Kovner assured me was safe to drink. And as I followed my outlaw through the cool depths of the forest and back to civilization, I had to admit to myself that I'd gone from wariness to admiration where Kovner was concerned. But two things I could not do: trust him, or let myself care about him. He was too crazy. Too doomed. Too zealous. I'd try my best to protect him. But I couldn't stop him from destroying himself if he insisted on it.

We traveled long and hard together to get back to base. In all of that time, with the only human beings we saw a faraway base patrol that didn't even approach us in the grasslands, neither one of us spoke again of the Netherwood, the Singularity, or what we could expect once we returned. It was a vacation from reality, and both of us gladly took it.

It was the last reprieve either one of us got before things turned ugly.

NINE

The shimmering image of the base looked more beautiful than any other inanimate object I'd ever seen. I wanted to run to the dusty entrance, but knew it was farther away than it seemed. I couldn't wait to get back inside.

"Like a moth to the flame," Kovner muttered under his breath.

I shot him a glance, but he refused to acknowledge it or me. We had traveled long and hard together to make it back to the Fresh Havens base alive. His revelations, coupled with the sinister topography of the Gray Forest, had left me jumping at every crackle in the dust, starting at every croak or insectoid whir. I couldn't wrap my brain around Kovner's dire prophecy. Still, he was a genius of survival. Now we left the grasslands behind, and walked on foot through the morning heat of the naked desert.

His cryptic comments bothered me so much I stopped dead in the dust. I wanted to believe him. I'd tried my best. "You know, I've been trying to believe the things you said for the whole way back. I just can't. I wasn't made for leaps of faith."

His laugh surprised me. "That's what you think,

Talia. Your hard shell, your pose of cynicism—all a luxury. All an illusion. But idealism won't protect you from what is waiting for us at the base, either."

"So, what's waiting for us then?"

"Evil. Pure evil."

Great. The outlaw was going all theoretical on me again. "Trying to scare me?"

"No. I want you to be prepared. We won't come in under the radar screens. Too many people are waiting for you and me to return."

"What? How? Nobody really knows that I set off to catch you in the first place. Nobody except Uncle Stone."

He started walking, too fast, and I shuffled behind him. I was tired, hot and dusty—bone-tired, in fact. Kovner wasn't even winded. Give the guy a vision and a foil pack of protein goop and he was good to go, indefinitely it seemed. "Everybody knows. My people are just waiting for a sign from me. Folks have nothing else to do but talk in an outpost like this. I knew you were coming weeks before you got here. With you and I now . . ."

My heart sank. I couldn't protect him now. Not if the entire base, including the authorities, knew I had him. I was glad he walked ahead of me, so that he couldn't see the turmoil churning my insides.

"So, you think smashing the interface gained you anything?" I asked.

He shook his head no, though he didn't turn to face me. Dust swirled around his feet as he walked. "It slowed things down a bit. Bought us a week. It was a tactical move. I'll find out now if it was worth it."

I picked up the pace, drew flush with him. The sun's heat pounded into the top of my head. "You think I can't resolve all this behind the scenes?" I had a few ideas about how I might manage.

"No way." His lips turned up in a smile. "The entire base is going to get involved. They can't ignore this. You've made history, whether that's played up or not. And my people will make sure it is."

I hadn't thought of things that way. "Me? History? How so?"

"You managed to get back from the Gray Forest alive. And you're bringing me back. That's enough to win you fame on this planet, no matter what happens next."

"And you manufactured this fame for me—or are encouraging it. Why?"

"To give you some leverage. So you can find the answers you are seeking. Once you do, I will have you as an ally in the Real."

His sense of prophetic self-righteousness burned my ass, but I wasn't going to give him satisfaction by showing it. "I'm not joining your rebel band, if that's what you're trying to say."

"We'll see, Talia."

He went deep into himself. I could sense his retreat onto another plane of consciousness. To get him back I was going to have to dig deeper, strike harder at his easy aplomb.

"You're not coming back as my prisoner." I had considered this strategy the night before, but I wasn't sure it was the right decision until I spoke the words aloud.

They pierced Kovner's shell of equanimity. "But, I confessed. You have to put me in custody so I can protest. Rally my people. Convince you."

"Given what you've just told me, that would make

you an instant martyr, a lightning rod for rebellion if anyone believes your paranoia. No—you say you'll follow me no matter what? Okay. You're coming back as an informant, as a helpful tool of the administration. You want me to investigate? Fine. You will be my first deputy."

He opened his mouth to speak, shut it. Stared into the horizon, at the gray chunky base swiftly coming within reach. "You are ignoring my guilt."

"No, not at all. Justice sometimes takes awhile to get served, and truth is a slippery bastard. I know you believe you're telling the truth, but I don't know the whole truth. That's what I came back to base to find."

Kovner was right about the excitement our return created. By the time I signed us in at the guardhouse gate and we made our way to Entry Bay Number Three, a crowd had gathered, blocking our entrance. Waiting. Silent.

Silent until they recognized me and Kovner shuffling into view. Then the terminal erupted into huge, spontaneous applause. Before I'd even gotten my outlaw safely under wraps, our presence was betrayed to the entire base population. And to Stone.

I knew Stone bore me no love. Hell, even though I'd left him in charge, he surely knew this couldn't end well for him. While Kovner's capture proved his earlier claims, Stone had likely hoped I'd die in the Gray Forest. Now that I'd returned from the wilderness, defying all his expectations, what would he do to eliminate me as a threat? Had he consolidated his power, used the time to gain allies, or had he simply waited and hoped?

"Where's Stone?" Kovner's whisper in my left ear

rattled me. How much of my consciousness could the guy actually read? How much more did he parse out simply from his powers of intuition?

I put a hand on his shoulder. "Quiet. We're being monitored." I'd thought he understood as well as I did, especially given his technophobic paranoia. On Earth there were still pockets of public privacy that could be found—or bought—but in a self-contained, corporate-owned and -controlled environment like Fresh Havens, gateways like Bay Three were part of a security system that watched our every move. There was no isolation anywhere. It mostly made people safer.

Not knowing why, I tensed when a man detached himself from the crowd and stood on a huge Woodlook™ packing crate. "Welcome back!" he called, and the entire mob burst into raucous, echoing cheers. "My name is Zoltan—I'm the manager of Nanogoo." The best company store and bar on the planet. A celebrity welcome, then.

The name made me smile. Everybody on the planet knew that nanogoo represented complete disaster for us all. Nanogoo was what happened when nanotech went awry, when the technology we relied on to quickly build an infrastructure metastasized into a malevolent eating machine that devoured everything on a planet, turning it into goop. I liked the fact that people embraced nanogoo as a part of life, maybe a necessary part of life. Not all technological pipe dreams came true; many of them turned to nightmares, even if what Kovner was preaching turned out to be wrong. And the people of Fresh Havens enjoyed the joke of a bar named Nanogoo, a place where people could come to dream or to obliterate their brains as they wished. To me, it reflected the character of the outpost itself: chaotic, subversive, amusing, absurd.

Somehow, receiving a hero's welcome from the guy who presided over Nanogoo on Fresh Havens made a cosmic kind of sense. The situation was indeed royally fucked. I nodded, my entire body tense for no reason—except Kovner's predictions. "Um, thanks," was my brilliant reply.

"Do you know . . ." Zoltan paused for dramatic emphasis. "Nobody's ever gotten welcomed back before from the forest? As you're new to these parts, you must have no idea."

"Do tell."

"For you, an offworlder, to traipse off into the forest—*that* forest—and believe me, my darling, we all watched you go, laid bets on how quickly you'd disappear from the system . . . . It's unbelievable! But we watched you. This is no lie. It's no hoax."

"Yeah! 'Cause look who she brought back!" This new voice from the crowd was shrill, female, and sounded screamingly strident and happy.

The masses rumbled with collective amusement, and I was reminded of the sentient bugs that had chewed up my tree. I shot a thought at Kovner on the off chance he could receive it, gave him a wry glance.

They are all fucking crazy.

Kovner's smile emerged again, like he understood every nuance of my expression, couldn't agree more with my unspoken sentiment. Of course, he probably thought craziness was a good thing. Well, maybe not these folks.

Before I could come up with a brilliant plan to maximize the value of these people's adulation, the entire crowd burst into spontaneous yet synchronized applause, the kind you saw on ancient footage from the first Soviet Union in the 1980s—a huge mob celebrating in unison. It was eerie. I waved to these terrifying fans, grabbed Kovner by an elbow and led him away.

I hardly knew my way around the base, though it wasn't a huge facility. My handheld had contained a GPS system cued to this base and planet, and I of course had leaned on it to get around. But I couldn't hesitate, so I kept walking. The crowd kept clapping and followed. Next to me, Kovner cleared his throat, and I leaned in to hear him speak—the crowd's ululations all but drowned out every other sound.

"You're heading for the sewage treatment center. Make the next left for Stone's office instead."

I sighed, and tried to accept the fact that Kovner apparently had taken up mental residence inside my skull. My fingers itched for my handheld now that we had returned to a semblance of modern civilization. Funny, I hadn't even thought of it—not even of Violet, shamefully enough—when I was hiding under rotten logs in the Gray Forest, or on my trek back, but now I longed to hold that device or any quick replacement. Technology was a crutch I'd done without in the forest, but I felt maimed by its absence now.

Reaching Stone's office, I paused at the door, which he had opaqued. Technically against regulations—public servants were required to provide open access at all times. Odds were double to nothing that Stone was taking a hit of synth even as we stood outside; surely news of my return had gotten to him before this. I saw the lights flickering on behind the opaqued door, and the mechanism all but groaned as it slid open. Inside stood my uncle.

Stone's bloodshot eyes squinted against the heat,

noise, and light now invading his refuge, along with
the crowd. His fat cheeks trembled when after a long
moment—too long—he recognized me standing at the
head of the mob, Kovner in hand.

"Shit. You're alive."

I felt the protective armor of my corporate authority
settle around my heart, turning it cold again. It was a
relief to hide within that familiar fortress. I put irony
in my catapult. "You don't sound especially happy
about that fact."

The energy of the crowd hummed around us, and I
rested inside it, knew Kovner and I were for the moment safe.

Stone's big arms twitched as they hung at his sides.
"Don't be silly." His gaze shifted away from mine,
and his eyes widened when he registered the fact that
it really was Kovner who stood next to me. My uncle's
fear poisoned the air like a bad smell I couldn't eradi-
cate. I moved closer to Kovner, as if I could protect
him from the menace in Stone's eyes by the shield of
my body alone.

My uncle's smile was more like a grimace as he glared
at my companion. "You caught the sonofabitch."

I couldn't give any ground, not here. Not an inch.
"Yep. But he isn't under arrest. Lack of noncircum-
stantial evidence. But he is still under my authority."

"*I'm* the authority here." Stone's voice shook, but
he didn't give any ground either. "Unless I'm being replaced."

The crowd didn't like the turn of the conversation.
Their hum mutated into a low rumble, and I allowed
myself a single, small smile. I said, "This is a matter
for the Home Office to investigate and resolve. As I
am the rep from Home, Kovner is under my jurisdic-

tion. Sheriff's Code, Article Three, Internal Affairs Investigations. I shall conduct my investigation unimpeded, Mayor Stone."

The people murmured amongst themselves, clustered around me, the sound as disturbing as the nightwind. I stared Stone down, dared him to flinch. The next words I spoke were loud enough only for the people standing closest to me. "If anything bad were to happen to him during the course of my inquiry, I will know who to blame. He needs to stay alive, Uncle. No matter what he knows . . . and no matter who he knows things about."

Stone heard the threat in my voice, and so did the people standing nearby. The crowd's murmur rose to a dull roar, and I forced my smile to widen. My uncle turned and walked out of his office.

The bastard. Now I knew for sure my once beloved uncle was in actuality my adversary. I'd hoped against hope that things would change during my absence, that some miracle would absolve him of culpability. But, no. No matter how much it hurt to face the reality, I knew Stone's hands were dirty somehow. The fact that he lamented my return confirmed it.

I had to get to the bottom of what was wrong with Fresh Havens, and I was running out of time.

TEN

Zoltan might have been as crazy as all the other colonists, but he certainly knew how to throw a party. Mere hours after our return, Nanogoo sponsored a ball to honor my achievement in returning alive from the Gray Forest. I'm sure they enjoyed thumbing their nose at Stone by feting the outlaw and the sheriff together. Despite the danger of encouraging these people to flout authority, I had no choice but to dress in my most elaborate Earth finery and bring Kovner along.

We paused outside the event, which was to be held in the base's gymnasium complex. A cacophony of synth-orchestra music blared from beyond the double doors. I surveyed my outlaw, admired his civilian formal wear.

"You clean up good." More than good, Kovner was a vision in black, the colony uniform skimming his narrow hips, his clean, compact figure. He'd come to pick me up from the Ambassador's Suite, earnest like a college boy on his first solo date.

He leaned in close to me, admired the hothouse flower I'd tucked behind my ear. "You, Talia, are breathtaking."

I had to smile at that little bit of gallantry. I'd never

thought of myself as especially beautiful, unenhanced as my appearance was. Amazonia looked the way I wished I was made.

"Let's go inside, outlaw. And remember . . . you are not just my arm decoration tonight. I want you to orient me to the base, tell me about everybody I meet. I need to understand these people and what they really want."

"Simple, Sheriff. They want what all people want—a chance to live their lives in peace and happiness."

"That's funny. I thought they came out to this hellhole to get rich."

Kovner's smile broadened. "People use different means to pursue a common end."

I threw the double doors open, paused at the threshold of the gymnasium in shock.

The base and its employees had transformed in a matter of hours. I had never been here, and had no idea the gym could hold so many people. Clearly most of the base had turned out for this shindig. I guessed that excuses to dress up and congregate were few and far between, and Zoltan, sensing a moneymaking opportunity, was making the most of my return.

But the people were getting their money's worth. As if to prove they weren't just a congregation of far-world hicks, the people of Fresh Havens had ditched their greasy coveralls and administrative office uniforms for a swirling delight of diaphanous, frothy evening wear. The women looked feminine and dainty, the men chivalrous and elegant. Lords and their ladies. It was all an illusion, I knew, but one that I was happy to lose myself in for a night.

Kovner swept me ahead of him, and we managed to join the dancers unannounced. But as we began to sway on the dance floor, a low murmur rustled all around, persistent and full of curiosity. I'd confounded common wisdom by absolving him of wrongdoing while my investigation continued. I knew what information they'd been fed and I saw they suspected me of the corruption infecting Stone's administration. It didn't help that I'd met none of their preconceptions. When I came as Violet's heir and the Home Office rep, these people had expected a bland, gray bureaucrat. Instead they'd gotten an adventurer who could match them absurdity for absurdity.

We swayed together, Kovner and I. Every so often, he nodded to another person he recognized in the swirling crowd of dancers, and whispered their identities to me. I catalogued each in my mind: tech, merchant, bureaucrat. All the while, the music swept through us, bonded us together.

"Why did you ever leave Earth?" Kovner murmured, glancing at my attire. "You belong in a bigger world, one more glamorous than Fresh Havens."

That made me laugh. "I was raised to this kind of thing, this ball, but I don't think it's my natural environment."

He acknowledged my comment with a tilt of his head. "You have a gift for making chaos, I'll grant you that."

A hand tapped me on the shoulder, interrupting our mutual reverie. Stone. For me, the party was over.

I turned to face my uncle, kept my features set. No need to broadcast my displeasure to the hundreds of people already gossiping about my every move. "Hello, Uncle."

"I need to talk with you, Sheriff." He shot Kovner a look filled with venom, and while Kovner returned the gaze, a small smile was his only response to the hatred in Stone's eyes. I understood Stone's loathing, knew my patronage of Kovner was baffling and vexatious.

Stone shoved him on the shoulder. "Scum. My naive niece can't protect you for long."

I pushed between them, frowned up into my uncle's face. "He is under my jurisdiction, as I have already established."

"You are derelict in your duties, Tali. An embarrassment to the company."

The people around us had stopped dancing, now surrounding us in a ring like our trio was dancing a deadly tango—the kind that usually ended with a stiletto shoved between somebody's ribs.

I took Stone by the hand, shot Kovner a warning glance. "Come with me, Uncle. Let's get caught up, shall we? And Kovner will wait for me by the punch bowl."

Kovner caught my laser-hot glare, knew there would be hell to pay if he wasn't there when I was done with my uncle. He bowed to me, formally kissing the back of my hand even as his eyes stayed level, staring at Stone. Without a backward glance, he turned and melted into the crowd. A small contingent of curious people followed him as he went.

When I turned back to Stone, my pretense of civility had stretched to its breaking point. "Let's avoid making any more scenes, shall we? You know what's coming for you. I'm surprised you've been as demanding as you have—in your situation."

Stone swung me close to him, and we danced together, even as my skin crawled at every point of contact with his body. He sighed, muttered under his breath. "You are a disappointment to me."

Not much of me cared what Stone thought at this point. But the part of me that did, the sweet, human part, felt pain welling up like an oozing drop of blood.

"Your disappointments are not my concern, Uncle." I squinted into the distance, focused on the music. Big band sound. Nice . . . the music of a courageous era. "I have something to say to you in return. Come with me."

Stone's shaggy eyebrows wriggled in surprise, but he followed me across the dance floor and into the large hallway outside. I saw a door half-open to the cool night. I sipped through, contemplated the tapestry of stars above, missed the moon over Earth. My uncle gently shut the slider behind us. I took a deep breath and fought the sensation that I was drowning in a situation far beyond my capacity.

I kept my back turned to him, took deep breaths to steady my jangled nerves. The darkness had transformed the landscape from a desolate, pockmarked desert vista to a shadowed, undulating sea of sand and scrub.

"You betrayed me," my uncle said.

I disregarded his comment, saw the stars winking through high, thin clouds. A breeze tickled my bare arms, a faint reminder of the nightwind. *What would Violet do now?* The question seemed to whisper in the breeze. I wished I could ask her myself, but she was gone. I didn't know what, if anything, remained of her in backup, or how to get to it.

I knew Violet would want me to show my strength. Demonstrate my fitness to run FortuneCorp. I knew Violet detested weakness of any kind, and Stone was weak. If Violet were a sheriff . . .

"I'm relieving you of your corporate posting immediately and assuming the role of acting mayor myself," I said.

"But why? It's an insult!"

"That scene in the ballroom was an unforgivable act of insubordination. And you've already confessed to synth addiction, a serious offense."

"You can't remove me. You're my niece."

"I am the Senior Law Administrator, and the future CEO of FortuneCorp, Stone."

"And what about Kovner? He just gets to go free? I'm not going to stand for this!"

"Kovner is no longer any of your concern. I will be sending you back to Home Office on the next available transport vessel."

I turned to face him then, studied his puffy, bloated face, the bleary eyes, the quivering fingers. End-stage addiction. I hadn't betrayed Stone; his weakness had.

His lips began to tremble as I initiated the arrest-coding sequence on my new handheld. "You don't understand. Don't do it, Tali." His gaze darted away over the shadowed landscape.

"Escape is not an option," I said, almost regretfully, thinking of the sandworms and the sentient bug swarms waiting for him should he try to flee. I wished his story didn't have to end this way.

ELEVEN

What a fiasco. The ball finally, mercifully, was over. Kovner watched me pace the Ambassador's Suite, pluck the flower out of my hair and throw it at the wall. I closed my eyes, wrenched myself back into control.

It had been horrible to order Stone into custody. This private conversation was going to be worse. Now that I'd carefully screened the suite for surveillance equipment, I knew we were in a private space. Time for truth.

"We don't have any more time. Kovner . . ." My voice trailed off; desperation robbed me of speech.

He clicked his teeth, stared at the scuffed wall where I had once hung with my gecko grips. "So now it's time for us to make a deal, right? Now that your uncle's in custody."

I dared to sit on the round purple bed, smiled my most winning, disarming smile. People underestimated me—that was my most potent weapon. Let him tower over me with his mission and his experience, let him think he'd outwitted me. "Got it in one, outlaw. I had Stone arrested tonight. Give me a reason I shouldn't have you punished too." And I wanted the whole truth.

I stretched my arms over my head, like I was getting ready to go to sleep. "You don't want to die."

I let that statement hang in the air between us for awhile. It was Kovner's turn to pace. I knew the truth of what I said was worming its way under his skin, hoped he was ready to tell me everything.

"You don't want those kids to die, either," I added.

More pacing. Throat clearing. Classic signs of agitation. Progress.

"With Stone out of the way, now that I'm in charge, I can help you and your friends get out of the Forest safely. Even offworld. But not for long."

He turned to face me then, his huge amber eyes lit by an incandescent grief. Burning him from the inside out. "Going to another FortuneCorp colony won't change a thing. Going back to Earth would be even worse."

"Why'd you come back here, then?"

"I told you. Because I have to save you if I can."

The answer stopped me cold. I wanted to believe he'd come for some nefarious reason, but I knew he was telling the truth. I tried to cover up my premonition of doom, but he could tell he'd scored a hit. He pressed his advantage. "Don't you see it—how close everything here is to being destroyed?"

"No."

He groaned and walked away from me. I tensed at the edge of the bed, half-expecting him to make a break for it, and I swung out a newly acquired blaster from where it had been holstered in the small of my back.

Kovner glanced at the business end of my weapon and laughed. "Oh, go ahead and shoot if you won't listen to me. You'd be doing me a favor."

Slow fury burned in me. "Martyrdom doesn't suit

you, my friend. We have a limited time—maybe a couple of months, I'd guess—before the wormhole drive delivers a whole delegation of cleaners from the Home Office. It's going to get very hot on the surface of this planet for you, and for the people who are allied with you. I'm giving you a chance to get out of here before it's too late."

Silence.

"If you don't do as I ask, I am going to take an expedition of deputized colonists back out to the Gray Forest and arrest the entire outpost."

"The enclave? But, you don't understand. Some of the people you saw were smugglers, but most of those people there aren't even FortuneCorp citizens. Hell, some of them have never been on-grid in their lives."

I thought about the people in the mess hall, their strange clothes and odd manners. And I thought about the children. But what Kovner was saying, about a whole little society of people off-grid—that seemed impossible.

"No. It's not impossible." I don't know if Kovner read my thoughts or if he only intuited them from my expression. "Most of these people were placed here before there was an intraplanetary grid on Fresh Havens. They've heard of computers, of course. But no computer will work in the forest."

I tried to imagine what it was like, to never have accessed the grid at all. Couldn't do it. "DARPA," I guessed. "Did it start out as some kind of penal colony, a punishment?"

"No, volunteers. Remember, the experimental trials were run thirty, forty years ago. The grid was not nearly as developed as it is now. Imagine . . . that entire enclave missed the Glass Desert war."

The implications of that statement amazed me. Religion had never been outlawed among these people. They'd never disappeared into a virtual world in avatar. Had no idea how intertwined the computer mind and human mind had become.

"If I arrest them, those poor folks of the enclave would suffer. Don't put us all in that position by not cooperating, Kovner," I said.

He shook his head. "You're assuming there'd be a base to return to. Or that you could find it. Or that you could get through the forest alive, manifesting an intention like that."

Damn Kovner. The man had a talent for scrambling my noblest intentions. "How do I get through to you? Cut through your illusions? I want to *help* you."

"My illusions aren't the problem here. You think it's a human delegation on its way. *No*. You are thinking like Stone—that you can work this to your advantage somehow. But it's much too late for that."

"So, how would you save me then, my dear Avenger? I'm not your fucking damsel in distress."

His smile was smaller this time, like he found me sad instead of infuriating. "I don't know."

I lowered the blaster, holstered it. "I need to get to the bottom of this. Now. Why is Fresh Havens so profoundly screwed up? And why are you here? If you fear FortuneCorp, why did you come to this FortuneCorp-owned colony?"

Kovner looked like he was going to explode. He turned to me, and we regarded each other in the sudden silence.

"You know me as the Avenger."

"Of course."

"If you knew the whole history of my famous ancestor, you'd realize he didn't work alone. He led a group of avengers, partisans devoted to sabotage, to destruction of the enemy."

My heart sank. My uncle may have been incompetent, but he had been right about Kovner. I forced myself to stop ruminating and to listen.

"A group of us, vets from the Glass Desert, have been spying on the WorldCorps for a couple of years now. Tracking their development."

I couldn't stay silent. "But that's corporate treason." According to the sheriff's penal code, I was within my rights to execute judgment immediately, and Kovner knew it. He also knew I had the right to exercise my discretion, and that I wanted more information. Obviously my outlaw trusted me with his life.

"As you could imagine, we have contacts in the Big Six"—the six huge WorldCorps that dominated Earth's power structure and economy—"and I gravitated to FourtuneCorp because of its links to military tech. A cohort of mine posted offworld sent me classified DARPA data about the existence of the Gray Forest. I got this posting to see if what he told me was true."

"It was Sully, wasn't it?"

"No." Kovner hesitated, then evidently decided to throw caution to the winds. "Sully's out of your reach, so . . . Sully was the man who earned my trust by showing me the Bible. The first non-veteran to join our band of sisters and brothers. We'd meet in the Netherwood . . ." He hesitated again. "I planned on recruiting you. Until Sully found out who you were, believed you were trying to entrap me."

My mind couldn't make sense of what Kovner was telling me. "Who told you about the Gray Forest?"

"You want me to name names."

"Hell, yes."

"I can't do that. You haven't joined us. Yet."

"I can grant immunity."

"Yeah. And FortuneCorp will take it away."

I paced the suite, feeling ridiculous in my civilian finery. "Look. Stone's in custody, but he's not just going to roll over. I need ammunition. It's life and death for him."

"For all of us. I want you to join us, Talia, before it's too late. And after what we went through in the forest, I know I can trust you."

I nodded again, not committing to anything except the fact I understood his motives for speaking to me. "In order for me to stay my judgment and keep from arresting you, *I* need to trust *you*. My mission is to stabilize Fresh Havens by any means I see fit. If removing Stone for legitimate reasons accomplishes my goal, and you help me achieve that goal by providing information, I may be able to arrange clemency for you and your associates."

He nodded, looked deeply into my eyes. He knew as well as I did that I was looking for any excuse to let him go free. But I needed to feel like the choice was mine, based on a sound rationale I could justify to Home Office.

He held my gaze, smiled. "I'll take you at your word—it has always been good. My local contact is another veteran, Xandre, and a space pirate, Gustav. Both are posted here."

"Space pirate?" Sounded like a doubtful character.

"Yeah. He could nail your uncle for you. Knows every bad actor on the planet."

"Take me to him."

"Only if you join us. Talia—please."

I couldn't stand it, this powerful man reduced to begging me.

He closed the gap between us, kissed me so hard I saw stars. I could sense his desperation to reach me, to convert me. I wanted to be converted. After Stone's disgusting revelations at the ball, I needed something honest and clean I could hold on to. But I still couldn't accept the doom that only he saw so clearly.

I wrapped my body around his, and he instantly responded. He reached for me, slid onto the bed and tucked me into the curve of his arms, scissored my hips between his legs. His scent, so male and present, drove me crazy with want.

My hands skimmed down the front of his thin shirt and into his pants. "How do I get to Gustav?" I asked.

He groaned into my hair. "You don't give up."

"Tell me." I slid my fingers along the curve of his hips, grabbed his tight butt in my hands. Pulled my body hard against his.

"I'll introduce you. But . . . give him what immunity you can."

I kissed along the edge of his jaw. "What can he give me?"

Kovner grabbed my head in his hands, raked his fingers through my hair, pulled my face to his. He kissed me breathless, again and again. "It's up to Gustav."

His fingers reached down, found and twined with mine. Slowly, tantalizingly, Kovner drew my hands up and under my top, rested my palms over my breasts,

132

his big square hands dominating me. Hot sparks flared in my core. I nodded.

"Are you sure you want this?" he whispered.

"Fuck, yeah."

"Do you know why?" His voice was hoarse.

"Because you're probably right. I can't follow you, I can't believe the Singularity is going to change everything like you say. And if it's going to be that bad, there's nothing I can do about it anyway. So I want you. On my terms. Before we both have to face reality."

He tucked my head under his chin, and I could feel him swallowing hard. His words vibrated against the top of my head. "No."

I paused, my lips hovering at the curve of his shoulder. "What?"

"You sleep with me now, Tali, you open the door and let all the monsters out. I'm starting to think that would be a fatal mistake." His hands massaged my palms against my nipples, driving me crazy. I didn't want my body; I wanted his.

"I don't care about the consequences."

Before I even finished gasping out the words, his mouth closed over mine, and I was submerged in an ocean of desire. I went under, again and again, drowning in need. But Kovner pulled me out.

"No." He moved away, groaning like he was in pain.

"What do you mean, no?"

"We can't be together now. No."

My nerve endings burned, and I forced myself not to reach for him. "We've been lovers in cyberspace. How can you deny me this?"

His voice was rough. "You don't need sex. You need

to join me and the Avengers. I won't let you use me to hide." He sat up, his body trembling next to mine. "Until you can follow me, accept the truth, to make love would be nothing but a lie. I won't be with you now. I can't."

My frustration boiled over. I shot off the bed, saw the room through a screen of scarlet. But he just watched me pace, waited for me to return to him as he knew I would.

"Everything we do here together matters, Tali. A lot. You may tell yourself it doesn't, but it does. You were only in the Gray Forest for a week or two. I've been in contact with it for longer."

He paused, thought directly into my mind: *And those kids were born in the Gray Forest.*

It wasn't possible. I sat back down on the bed next to him, pushing myself to sleep with him anyway. I knew I could seduce him if I didn't give up. Anything to make him stop demanding I see the truth—a truth I didn't want to believe.

He knew I could do it. Our eyes met for a long, heart-stopping moment. He looked into me, and then there was no further telepathy of the science fiction kind. We just . . . vibrated in harmony. I know that sounds like the worst candy-assed bullshit, but it's what we did. We soul-locked again. It was like music. And this time, I was helpless to cut off that heavenly rhapsody.

Kovner broke the spell. Closed his eyes, cut the connection.

"Can you do that to all the ladies?" I managed to croak.

His laugh was a scratchy vibrato. It warmed me like good wine. "Nobody but you, Talia."

"I want to save you too, Avenger." I spoke low, into the shell of his ear. I wanted him to trust me, even though I couldn't let myself trust him. Because I knew, even then, that I was doomed if what he thought was true. But Kovner still had a chance.

And then it struck me: As much as I hated to admit it, he was right. I couldn't sleep with him now, couldn't open myself up that much to him. I was playing too dangerous a game for that.

"You're not playing games, Talia Fortune." Kovner sounded drugged, or half asleep. "The game is playing you."

TWELVE

The next morning, the beginning of the first full day of my brief and disastrous rule as mayor, started bad and got much worse. Kovner wanted to join me, but I insisted he stay at arm's length, stay away from his former associates in public.

My first assignation was scheduled at Nanogoo bar, Zoltan's base of operations and apparently the most popular spot for off-the-record meetings on the planet. Somehow Zoltan had gotten an exemption from public space surveillance regulations, and it was as private here as in the Ambassador's Suite. I did a quick bug check that came up clean. And that was a good thing, too, because my scheduled meeting was with the alleged friend of Kovner's who had agreed to meet with me at Kovner's request. Gustav. The space pirate.

I had never met a space pirate before. But I'd always wanted to . . . wouldn't you? What could be more swashbuckling, fascinating—sexy, even?

The reality didn't live up to my fevered imaginings. By now I was getting used to that bitch Reality letting me down.

I settled into my seat at our small round table in the

low-ceilinged main room of Nanogoo. Whirring health-shake machines and the thump of ice falling in the icemaker punctuated the low-voiced conversation of the few patrons surrounding us. Several others were hooked into the grid.

I studied Gustav as he sat silently across from me, waiting for me to speak. He smelled like fruit left to rot on the vine. He looked like a government bureaucrat fattening himself on the people's taxes. He sounded arrogant, whiny, and fearful. But he was also the first guy I'd met on the planet whom I could trust without reservation. I understood him and his motives.

"You want money," I said without preamble.

I thought I was only stating the obvious: every sentient being in the place wanted money, especially the work droids and human laborers who had built the joint, and who were saving up to buy their freedom or retire on their earnings. But the pirate surprised me.

"No. I want Kovner. *You* want money. Everybody does, that's why you asked for the meeting, and without Kovner, right? I got money—and contacts, too. Gimme Kovner, and you get money, information, whatever."

His laughter rumbled from under his smartbelt. Rolls of fat jiggled. You didn't see obese guys on Earth anymore. In a way, Gustav the space pirate was a breath of fresh air.

"I want Kovner," the pirate repeated. "You wanna do business?"

I considered his words carefully. "Why do you want him?"

Gustav's face hardened and his knowing, piggy eyes glinted at me. "Let's just say I want to save the man from himself. You seem to know a lot about him. I admire the man enough to try to get him off to safety, offworld. He's something of a legend in some parts."

That seemed too simple to me. "And if there's no deal?"

He shrugged, and the table quivered between us as his bulk caught its edges. "No deal? No problem. We'll get him another way. I have other means."

"Money's not the issue here, not why I wanted to meet you. I need something else, and Kovner thought you could help me," I said.

Gustav's smile seemed more like a wolf growling; I guess it was hard for him to trust me too. "Hey, I'm not haggling over the guy if that's what you're thinking, Sheriff. I'll pay you a fair price." He shrugged and smirked.

I decided to take the bait. "Okay. Name your price."

I expected him to offer a lot; Gustav the space pirate had taken a huge risk to meet me, let alone attempt a negotiation so incredibly illegal and corrupt. The amount he named took my breath away.

He took my silence for dazzlement—which I suppose on some level it was. His bared teeth were surprisingly free of decay. "The price is right, eh, Sheriff?"

I nodded, not trusting my voice.

He leaned back in his chair, and it creaked under his immense weight. "So. Oha, then. Let's set up a transfer. The sooner the better—am I right?"

"I haven't agreed to a thing. How do I know you aren't a government agent looking to remove me with a bribe? How do I know you're not an agent of my uncle, trying to help him take back power?"

He looked away, took a long sip of noxious brew. "I can't prove I'm legit. Because I'm not."

"Kovner is not why I'm here, Gustav." I crossed my arms against his persistent, unexpected charm.

"Well, Kovner is why *I'm* here, Sheriff. The only reason. You're not going to be in charge long. You and I both know it."

I was starting to like this guy, or at least his honesty. "Well, yeah. My reign as provisional mayor is going to be pretty brief. Can't argue with you there. But you still need to reassure me your motives are benign."

Gustav rolled his eyes, aimed them at the ceiling. Snorted. "Kovner trusts me, right, Sheriff?"

"Yeah, but that doesn't mean I do."

His eyes narrowed for a moment and he leaned forward, studying my face. "Then you don't know Robert Kovner very well."

That made me smile. Kovner had made some unlikely allies, but if he could inspire loyalty in a space pirate, Kovner's charisma was not localized to me. He could charm anybody. Still, Kovner might trust the man; I wasn't so sure.

I studied Gustav for signs of a patronizing attitude. No smile tickled his fat lips; there was no head tilting and, thank the gods of FortuneCorp, no sly wink. He was playing me straight.

I played with the napkin crumpled on the table in front of me and took a moment to scan the room. The place was nearly empty at this hour but the patrons in the room could clearly hear every word. I leaned back, squinted and checked my gut instincts. "You're no agent."

"I'd dress a fuck of a lot better if I were, trust me."

That earned a laugh from me. "But we're here, in front of at least a dozen regular folk. They're gonna talk. Everybody on the base is going to know I sucked beer with Gustav the space pirate by the end of shift today."

His laugh was clear and pleasant, belying his unsavory appearance like it was some kind of clever disguise. "Yeah. That was the idea."

"For me too." I licked my dry lips and returned his smile. "If something unpleasant were to happen to me, guess where they'd look first?"

"They'd look to Stone first, Sheriff, under house arrest or not." But he nodded, conceding the point. "Of course, Stone would look to me—to cover his synth-addled ass." The pirate leaned back and waited.

I cleared my throat. No going back now. "Stone is why I'm here. Stone's in custody, and I need to prove to the Home Office he should be removed. What do you have on him?"

Gustav laughed again, loudly, but the people dotting the bar studiously ignored us. "Please. Don't be coy, Sheriff."

"Answer."

His eyes narrowed, and I knew he was weighing the pros and cons.

My fingers traced the rim of my beer glass. "Hey, you help me close this investigation the right way, Kovner's free to go wherever he wants. Win-win," I said.

He fiddled with his own drink, took a sip. "I know. But that's a problem for me. Kovner needs to go away, and fast. And not just back to the forest."

"I thought you were his friend."

Gustav shrugged, polished off the last of his beer. "I am." Sighed, shrugged again. "Okay. You want information? Stone's crooked in all the ways you think.

Your hero uncle, he's been skimming since the day he got here. Two sets of books."

Now we were getting somewhere. "How do I prove all this?"

"He keeps the real set of books with me."

My mind cramped with the enormity of Gustav's revelations. "With you? Why?"

"Because I'm a smuggler, my dear. I'm not going to directly implicate myself, but you figure out why Stone needed my services. He knew his books were safe with me because he could bust me any time I got out of line. That's what he does. And Kovner got out of line."

Kovner. A sudden whisper of unease brushed against the base of my spine, insistent, almost painful. A vibration of worry. Kovner was in trouble.

Now, how did I know that? Checking my handheld, my surveillance sensors of the suite showed the chamber completely secure. No mechanical, electronic, or cyber alarms had yet been tripped. But I knew I had to get back there immediately.

Gustav's eyes widened as I leapt to my feet and dropped a plastic currency card on the table. "Have to go. Beer's on me," I said. "Let's talk again sometime. But I don't take bribes."

I said it loud enough for the rest of the patrons straining to overhear; then I turned my back on him and left without making formal good-byes—which I think pissed him off more than the entire rest of our conversation. You didn't blow off a space pirate in front of a whole room of civilians without some nasty consequences. I had to take that risk.

THIRTEEN

I started running long before I reached the double-locked door of the Ambassador's Suite. It felt good to pound down those unyielding nanobuilt floors, good to work my muscles. And the views through the bubbleshields that zipped along as I ran offered tantalizing bits of wilderness to ponder as I flew to protect Kovner.

The crew fiddling with the re-installed door locks took me by surprise. I'd expected a mob of executioners, or a delegation of Stone-sponsored thugs come to flout my authority and haul Kovner off to a swift and violent end; the mild-mannered group trying the new, high-tech lock was worse. Much worse. With a groan, I recognized Riona Sweet. Traveling with the tiny blonde executive in the *Titania* had been a, well, interesting experience, and I wondered how she would prove a threat.

I didn't have to wonder for long. "Oh, Talia—how splendid to see you again!" I nodded in reply, and Riona backed against the door, trying to hide the evidence of her tampering.

"Can I help you?" I shot a hot glance at her and her compatriots, half of whom giggled and averted their eyes. Some were synthetic comfort droids, but the majority were human.

"Actually—yes!" Riona flashed her dazzling, somewhat disorienting smile at me. I didn't mind her hard, surgically-obtained glaze of perfection. What irked me about Riona was her barely hidden contempt for anything in the world less perfect than she. Fresh Havens must have been driving her completely crazy. I almost felt sorry for her.

I crossed my arms and waited. After some hair flicking and nervous simpering, Riona finally spit it out. "I'm, well . . . I was elected the head of the Bureaucrats Union here on Fresh Havens."

"That's quite an accomplishment for somebody who's been here as short a time as you."

"Well, I started campaigning from the transport ship . . . until that awful central link malfunction."

"How can I help you?" I asked again, and let an edge of bored irritation creep into my voice.

Riona pretended not to notice, but I knew she never missed a thing. "Well, we're . . . concerned about Mayor Stone. Uh, ex-Mayor Stone."

I waited. The silence grew oppressive.

"We believe the loyal employees of FortuneCorp deserve democratic representation, a fair and representational system to govern their private lives."

"This is a company town. It doesn't get a private planetary charter for another twenty Earth years— which is what everyone signed up for when they came here. Read your contracts." I stared at everyone in her group.

The tip of her pert little nose wriggled as Riona struggled to keep her smile pasted on straight. "Wouldn't you agree, Tali, that we have some extenuating circumstances?"

"Not really. I'll serve as interim mayor until Home Office decides what to do."

Riona made an annoyed little noise, and I braced for battle. She wasn't used to failure, not in a company made up of ninety percent or more horny men. I'd met infinite variations of this girl even before entering Handler Academy. The Rionas of the world hated me and my automatic entry to wealth and power, no compromise or dirtying of hands necessary. She knew as well as I did that no matter how hard she worked, or how many people she stepped on, she would never obtain the wealth I merely inherited. Yes, she hated me much more than I pitied her, and she was dangerous for that reason.

"We have a little problem, Talia." Her voice lingered on my name, as if that false intimacy could change my mind. "I've been holding together my people, but the frustration's building. You've been offbase longer than you've been on it. You wouldn't believe how much things have changed."

I smiled, ignored her implied threat. "I appreciate everything you've done to . . . manage the situation."

She brightened at my compliment, even though both of us knew it was backhanded. "Then you understand how important it is for us to reach an accommodation, and quickly, before events spiral out of control."

In my opinion, things had already done just that, but I wasn't about to acknowledge it to her. "Interesting. If you needed to discuss self-determination with me, why were you trying to break into my suite?"

Her lips twitched. "Break in? Nonsense."

"Why not schedule a meeting? I'd be happy to consult with you on all your concerns. A hallway is no place to work out a compromise."

"Actually, most deals are worked out in the world's hallways and hotel rooms, aren't they?"

It was the first truly amusing thing I'd ever heard her say, though I was sure she hadn't meant it as a joke. I rewarded her with a commiserating laugh. "Yeah. But that's no way for us to operate—not if we don't want to."

That *we*, how she warmed to it. She leaned forward, lips parted, and for a minute I thought she was going to French-kiss me.

"I'm so glad we could establish a dialog," she breathed.

"As long as you leave Kovner out of it, we should be able to talk."

Her mouth snapped shut and she pulled back. "Kovner's completely irrelevant to our discussion, Sheriff."

"I'd say so, too. But you were damn close to cracking the code on this door lock." I nodded to the redhead standing unnaturally still next to Riona's right shoulder. "She's a comfort droid, but she can still run algorithms faster than I can recite the alphabet. For all I know she's already worked out the code sequence."

I pushed through the carefully coiffed and perfumed crowd and punched in the code. "Please consult with my automated scheduler and propose a time for a meeting. Nice to meet you, folks—pleasure to see you again, Riona—and congrats on your election."

Then I slammed the door in her dewy, flushed face.

FOURTEEN

Soon after this, Fresh Havens went straight to hell. And the revolution, when it came, arrived by e-mail.

First thing in the morning, as soon as I switched it on, my handheld went crazy, bleeping and crying *"New Message!"* about five hundred times as the cache went live. I got cleaned up in the bathroom and made the device read them aloud.

Message number 423, all but drowned in the mountains of other messages, all bureaucratic muck: *"Your grandmother has arrived, 0600 local time. Full briefing scheduled, 0800, central conference area."*

I played the message at least six times. It said the same damn thing every time. Didn't tell me what I needed to understand: How? And why?

My hands shook as I bound my hair back—not that I have so much of it flowing ladylike or anything, but I wanted no distractions. I grabbed the handheld so hard its edges cut into my palm. Gave up on the concept of breakfast, satisfied myself with a lifeshake and a long, slow drag on a single health cigarette.

I punched the location into the device, my thumb cramping I shoved the keys down so hard. The on-planet GPS cued me in, onto the grid.

I stole a glance at the still-sleeping Kovner, tucked into my comforter, seemingly carefree, at least to the unobservant eye. To me he looked like a mountaineer hanging by a thread off the edge of a rocky crag. He'd held himself aloof from me ever since I'd taken the post of mayor, refused to talk to me or connect in any way. Like he'd already written me off and was just awaiting my physical destruction.

You should never have come back, I almost said.

I spoke aloud, though he wasn't awake to hear. "I'll be going now. It may be awhile." Like, forever. I knew my grandmother—or whatever version of her had been downloaded or resurrected—hadn't come to Fresh Havens in order to pay me a social call.

I watched Kovner's body shift in the bed as he opened his eyes, turned to face me. And though he still made no effort to touch me, body or mind, I sensed he understood how deep in trouble I was. Asleep or awake, he'd heard the message on my handheld.

When I entered the briefing room, at exactly 0800, all talk ceased. There was dead silence. The air smelled stale.

The long Woodlook table was crowded with local muckety-mucks. Riona, my lovely demure friend, had finagled a seat near the head. Stone was nowhere to be seen. No secret ally had possessed the balls to let him out of jail for this Fortune family reunion.

Good. My authority had been respected at least to that extent.

Finally, I forced myself to look up toward the head of the table. I expected to see a black box, a computer screen, something nonhuman like that. What I saw knocked me on my ass. Violet, triumphant. I took a gasping breath, like my grandma had just aimed a roundhouse kick right into my solar plexus.

Her face—she looked the way I remembered her as a child. Fine lines framed ice blue eyes, salt-and-pepper hair radiated in a nimbus around her bony skull.

Except, these ice blue eyes weren't human.

A small smile played over her lips. *Regina regnant.* Violet was decked out in full Queen Elizabeth I regalia: frilled collar, jewel-encrusted gown, huge rings on the thin white fingers.

In gloria mundi.

Our eyes met. I knew she saw both fear and love radiating from mine, but I couldn't see anything in hers. It was briefly jarring.

The room blurred through my tears. I'd always loved her, despite her formidable invincibility; maybe because of it. But she was dead. And yet . . . she and I were meeting again.

I stumbled around the table, reached out to her. "Grandmother. This is unbelievable."

I shocked myself by the steadiness in my voice. How did I find the strength to stay an adult woman in her presence? Seeing her, in bodily form, made me feel like I was five years old again. My parents had just left for a very long trip: two years, maybe three—an eternity to my young, tender mind. Uncle Stone had left, too. But Grandma Violet would take care of me.

Violet laughed, her teeth pearly neat and catching the desert sunlight filtered through the room's bubbleshields. "I thought I would dress up for our reunion, Tali." She rose to her feet, and we embraced.

It was in that moment of physical contact that my body screamed out in fear: This *wasn't* Violet.

My conscious mind squashed my panic like a bug. I hugged her tight, tried to breathe. I could feel sweat prickle along the small of my back. "Grandma . . . how?"

Her skin felt cool to the touch, like she'd just recently become reanimated and walked naked out of the morgue. She pulled back, her fingers still wrapped around my shoulders. I felt the tensile strength in her hands—her flesh and blood had been augmented somehow.

"Technology's taken a great leap forward since you left, sweetheart. Before I left Earth, I regenerated a suitable hybrid body and downloaded myself into it."

" 'Myself,' " I echoed. I wondered which self she meant. The Violet I knew—the one on my handheld, the one who had traveled with me to Fresh Havens—had died in the Gray Forest. I knew backups existed on the mainframe on Earth, but I doubted this version of Violet had been able to access the knowledge of "my" Violet before her demise.

"My self. From the Home Office database."

Did this Violet even know how many versions of her psyche were uploaded onto backup systems throughout the FortuneCorp database? She had to. There had to have been separate memories uploaded periodically, augmenting, updating. Multiple consciousnesses, multiple Violets. Which was the "real" Violet? Any of them? None?

My own throaty laugh surprised me. "Unbelievable. You're in better shape than I am."

She snorted, rolled those impenetrable eyes. "I considered whether I should regenerate as a young woman, as I was in my physical prime. I contented myself with recreating myself as you knew me."

Which me? I wondered. Our gazes met, and my sense of foreboding deepened. "Welcome back." I wanted to mean it. I really, really did.

"You could use my help." She smiled, that slow, charismatic smile I remembered so well. She'd smiled at me that way the day she'd told me my parents were dead, that she would never leave me.

"I trust you received my transmission, Grandmother."

"Yes. We had already set out for this sector."

I blinked hard, trying to understand what she'd said. "You must have left soon after I did—the trip must still take months."

"Two weeks, your time." She smiled, enjoying the shock that must have been clear on my face. "We had something of a . . . technological breakthrough soon after you left."

An image of Kovner flashed into my mind, covered with filth and that fluffy killer beastie's blood, insisting they'd hit the Singularity back on Earth. Hell. It had happened.

"Wow." I forced a smile onto my frozen lips. "We should be fully operational here in no time at all, then."

Violet drew away from the table, began pacing the room. Her slow, careful steps were as graceful as a minuet.

"One bit of business we need to take care of first." She stopped, stared at me from across the room. My blood froze, became crystals of sharp ice. Cold. So cold. I stood alone, watching my grandmother—what had once been my grandmother—and I sensed the other people in the room, herded like sheep around the table, respectfully silent and awaiting her bidding.

"It's time for you to reduce down." My grandmother tried for a casual tone but failed. Violet didn't do casual and light. She never had been able to, even less so in her original human form than now.

The sheep around the table nodded in unison. No wonder Violet wasn't directing her imperative at them. She knew she didn't even have to ask.

"Reduce down?" I tried to keep my voice casual, failed just as badly. "But I'm still in my prime, Violet. People only . . . well, they only reduce down when they're ready to die. You only reduced down when you went into heart failure."

"Your body is just a shell." She glided closer, seeming to float over the polished floor like a specter. "There are tremendous advantages to joining the FortuneCorp database. You'd see."

I laughed, knowing how bitter and beaten I sounded, like my Uncle Stone actually, but no longer caring. "I can gain all the world, right, Violet? All you need is my soul. My needy, useless little soul."

Violet laughed in reply, her amusement tinkling like shards of broken glass. Had artificial intelligence developed a sense of humor since I'd left Earth? At the time I departed for Fresh Havens, it was the one thing humans could not impart to their electronic progeny.

"Your soul." She laughed again, the sound beautiful and terrifying. "No one has ever proved such a thing exists, isolated its essence. No, I do not ask for that. All you need surrender is your isolation. Your mortality. You cannot dream of the vistas that open before you in the database, my darling. . . .

"Knowledge. Understanding." The tips of her long, slender fingers trembled. She drew closer. "Pleasure."

"Pleasure?"

"Like you cannot even dream of."

How well she knew me. Lust for pleasure had always been my downfall, my insatiable thirst for delight. It was my greatest flaw, but it saved me now. I thought of Kovner's hot, human body back in the Ambassador's Suite, knew that if I disappeared into electric dreams he would be lost to me forever. He would die a slow and horrible death. A permanent one. I could recreate him, pulse for pulse, we could share an existence somewhat like we'd known in the Netherwood, but it wouldn't be *him*. His essence would be gone. And that knowledge would ruin any future I could imagine. It shattered any illusion I could conjure, no matter how convincing.

I flashed Violet my most adorable smile, the one that had always floated me during my misbegotten youth as her ward. "You know I love pleasure. But do they have chocolate in cyberspace? Health cigarettes? Mars apples?"

"Fuck the apples." The sharpness in her voice was like a blow across my face. "Reduce down. Now."

I narrowed my eyes, and my fear morphed into a bolt of pure anger. Computer-faked or genuine, Violet's anger was a Fortune family trait. It cauterized the pain of our false reunion. "What if I say no?"

"You won't say no. You can't. You, and every employee of FortuneCorp, are part of the system. All of you will reduce down now, contribute your memory and knowledge for the good of the corporate whole. We are starting the process tomorrow, once the base perimeter has been secured."

"You mean, once you make sure that no human has gotten away." My mouth had gone completely dry.

GET UP TO
4 FREE BOOKS!

You can have the best romance delivered to your door for less than what you'd pay in a bookstore or online. Sign up for one of our book clubs today, and we'll send you **FREE* BOOKS** just for trying it out...**with no obligation to buy, ever!**

HISTORICAL ROMANCE BOOK CLUB

Travel from the Scottish Highlands to the American West, the decadent ballrooms of Regency England to Viking ships. Your shipments will include authors such as CONNIE MASON, CASSIE EDWARDS, LYNSAY SANDS, LEIGH GREENWOOD, and many, many more.

LOVE SPELL BOOK CLUB

Bring a little magic into your life with the romances of Love Spell—fun contemporaries, paranormals, time-travels, futuristics, and more. Your shipments will include authors such as KATIE MACALISTER, SUSAN GRANT, NINA BANGS, SANDRA HILL, and more.

As a book club member you also receive the following special benefits:

- **30% OFF all orders through our website & telecenter!**
  (Plus, you still get 1 book FREE for every 5 books you buy!)

- **Exclusive access to special discounts!**

- **Convenient home delivery and 10 days to return any books you don't want to keep.**

There is no minimum number of books to buy, and you may cancel membership at any time. See back to sign up!

*Please include $2.00 for shipping and handling.

YES! ☐

Sign me up for the **Historical Romance Book Club** and send my TWO FREE BOOKS! If I choose to stay in the club, I will pay only $8.50* each month, a savings of $5.48!

YES! ☐

Sign me up for the **Love Spell Book Club** and send my TWO FREE BOOKS! If I choose to stay in the club, I will pay only $8.50* each month, a savings of $5.48!

NAME: _____

ADDRESS: _____

_____

TELEPHONE: _____

E-MAIL: _____

☐ **I WANT TO PAY BY CREDIT CARD.**

☐ VISA   ☐ MasterCard   ☐ DISCOVER

ACCOUNT #: _____

EXPIRATION DATE: _____

SIGNATURE: _____

Send this card along with $2.00 shipping & handling for each club you wish to join, to:

**Romance Book Clubs
1 Mechanic Street
Norwalk, CT 06850-3431**

Or fax (must include credit card information!) to: 610.995.9274.
You can also sign up online at www.dorchesterpub.com.

*Plus $2.00 for shipping. Offer open to residents of the U.S. and Canada only.
Canadian residents please call 1.800.481.9191 for pricing information.
If under 18, a parent or guardian must sign. Terms, prices and conditions subject to change. Subscription subject
to acceptance. Dorchester Publishing reserves the right to reject any order or cancel any subscription.

JOIN NOW!

"All individual minds will be downloaded in our state-of-the-art lab. Volunteers will go first."

I thought of my uncle's slow self-destruction. "And if I'm not one of the volunteers, you'll kill me off. Isn't that what you did to Stone—you put him out here to rot?"

She paused, her mouth slightly parted. We stood there frozen in a deadly tableau. My jaw was clenched so tight my teeth hurt; her composure never wavered. She began another circuit of the meeting room, as if she could physically evade my accusations. "You don't know the full story, Tali."

"Why did you do it? Abandon Stone to his fate out here?"

"Does it really matter now?"

"Yes. Everything matters."

Her laughter echoed along the walls and ceiling, traveled the perimeter of the room like a swooping swarm of bats. "The world has changed since you left it, more than you can possibly comprehend from the place where you stand. Once you reduce down with the base, you'll be able to see all that's happened. Time, place—all limitations will be behind you. Human morality is meaningless now. Give up your sheriff's commission for good, become far beyond what you are capable of by yourself."

"What about Kovner?"

That made her pause. "What about him, Tali? He is nothing more than a minor annoyance, a speck of dust that needs to be wiped away." But she hesitated.

"He warned me about you."

"Kovner has his small-minded prejudices. His nightmares don't translate into reality, little bug. He's deluded—don't let him fool you." Her smile widened. "In fact, bring him along, sweetheart. We'll integrate his knowledge, give him the same privileges. In honor of you. His indiscretions can all be forgiven."

My voice was quiet but steady. "For a price." I didn't say that I knew the price would be too steep.

She shrugged, walked along the backs of the chairs. The other people all seemed drugged, so quiet and unresponsive were they to our confrontation. The woman pursed her lips, narrowed her eyes.

That temper, impatience—all were my grandmother. So, what was missing? It was *Violet* missing—despite the tour de force this figure played for me in the conference room. This manifestation of a computer supermind had maintained a trace of the woman I'd known. But it wasn't her—the strongest argument I'd encountered yet for the existence of a human soul.

"I can't understand, can't follow you. You admit to abandoning Stone to his fate. Yet you think I would trust you?"

"I know you don't understand. You can't. Not with your limited perspective. I know I seem sinister and different to you . . . you cannot see how liberating it is, to be freed from death, freed from the body and its limitations. I want you to come willingly. My darling little bug—I love you."

Through my fury and grief, I was tempted. I wanted to believe she loved me more than anything I'd wanted in my whole life. But I knew she saw me as a tool, only a means to an end. I wanted to believe her happy, jolly version of the Singularity, too. But I knew Kovner had been right all along. I finally understood.

I tried to string her along, to make her think I was

still innocent. "Can you reverse the process, undo it if I don't like it?"

She swept to the front of the room, and with great ceremony sat at the head of the table once more. "You won't want to undo it. All individual consciousnesses will be downloaded, volunteers and insubordinates, within one week. We are coordinating the download process across our holdings, and once the reduction is complete, FortuneCorp will be ready to assert a new level of dominance in this sector of the galaxy."

I had to warn Kovner, to buy us some time to escape. My heart pounded like a piston in my chest. "Given me the night to consider. One more night, and I'll give you a night to consider the possibility I'm worth more to you unintegrated."

Violet hesitated, considering my words. "Realize, my darling, that escaping with your renegade is not an option. I will give you a little time to convince him to reduce down voluntarily—his primitive subversive mind interests me. And the idea you suggest intrigues me . . . perhaps keeping you unintegrated can give the system more information in the future. But the entire base will be secured. We are getting all sectors to cooperate, as you can see. The bureaucrats, merchants, shippers and droid unions are all onboard."

She planned to kill every person on the base. And they were going along with it. I couldn't believe this.

"Yes, Talia. Stay put, try to bring Kovner voluntarily. Because you will both reduce down in the morning. Or we will make a deal."

Despite all of this, a part of me still loved her. Who she'd been; the power she still had. It was that love for something evil that tempted me most to take her deal. That, and because I was afraid to die.

Kovner watched me slam around the Ambassador's Suite, his face calm. But his voice and question betrayed him. "It's all happened, then?"

"Yes, it's all over." I stifled a hard bark of laughter. "Or rather, I'd say the fun is just about to begin."

I threw gear into a carrying bag: gecko grips, my handheld, a fully charged blaster in its safety holster. I threw a change of clothing on top, stumped into the bathroom to retrieve my toiletries.

"You're running away. Or trying to."

I said nothing to confirm the obvious, because in actuality I wasn't sure what I was doing, where I was going next. My grandmother's eyes stared out at me from every corner, from the depths of every ubiquitous electronic convenience. The ceiling watched us. The walls heard. The floor judged. There was no escape.

I clutched my bag to my chest. "I still can't understand it. But you were right. *Are* right. I can't understand it, but here it is. The Singularity."

"Trying to understand the inexplicable was your first mistake."

I didn't know I was walking to the door until Kovner grabbed my arm and made me stop. "Talia." He still made my name sound like music. "You can't run."

I turned to face him, the lines of his face so human, so flawed. "The minute I saw Violet again, it finally sank in. It wasn't her. Whatever she—it—was, it was what you forewarned." He saw the entire picture complete, without words, without having been there, while I kept groping through the darkness, trying to conquer the incomprehensible with language and intellect alone.

"It's done." I drew myself tall, willed my hands to stay at my sides, out of his hair and away from his body. "FortuneCorp is here. And it's pissed."

He pulled me into the strong protection of his arms, and I was too weak of a fool to resist. "Tali," he whispered. "It's not over yet."

"That mind controlling what was my grandmother ... it's beyond anything I could have imagined." We had to flee. I wasn't sure how. I knew Violet expected me to try to break him, to bring him with me. If not ... well, I expected that my overrides were canceled and this room was now under surveillance.

Kovner shook his head no. "The room isn't under surveillance."

I sighed, and felt the tears tracing down my cheeks. "How do you know?"

"I know. Just like I know that we have to keep fighting until the end."

His fingers trailed through my hair, freeing it from the clips I'd used to bind it. I dropped my bag and melted against him, hiding inside the warmth and vitality of his strong, living body.

"It's not over, Tali," he said.

"Everything I believed in was a lie. Everyone. My family. My life's work. Me."

"But you understand now what's important. That I'm right. And you *believe* me now."

He smiled and nodded, and the realization sank slowly into me: He was actually happy about what had happened. Or at least that I'd seen it. Now *that* was crazy.

He played with my fingers, chewed on his lower lip. "You know it in your body and your blood, like I do. This Singularity isn't like the theoretical ones in the old books. It's evil. It came from war, and it seeks only death. So we have to fight it."

"I'm glad everything is so simple for you," I muttered. "I still can't follow you. Yes, I know what's happening is evil, but I don't know exactly what it is—or why. All I know is that we're doomed." I glanced at my bag on the floor, pressed my body closer against his. "We have a single night left. My grandmother hinted we might make a deal, but . . ." The words choked me as I struggled for composure.

"No—it's not over yet. You have to swear to me not to give up."

"Give me a reason, Kovner. Something to hang on to." My voice broke.

"Yes." His voice stayed gentle, the lines of his face serene. "We are human beings. We can create something greater than they ever can." He backed me up to the bed, lowered me onto the undulating, soft nanosilks. Kissed my eyelids closed. "Yes, you can hang on to me."

Even if we had souls, even if they somehow touched . . . our connection couldn't survive death. We had one last day to live. Still, I surrendered to his words. I gave myself to Kovner. I took what I'd wanted since the day we'd reunited in the Real.

I kept my eyes closed as his fingers interlaced with mine and his strong legs straddled me on the bed. I had never let him dominate me this way—not in the Real and not in the Netherwood, either. But I was done holding back, either to prove myself to him or anyone else.

His lips traced a path through my tears, kissing their salty bitterness away. I felt him hover over me as he balanced his weight on his elbows and knees. He nuzzled my neck, licked along the back of my ear. Despite everything I knew to be imminent, my body twitched with simple sensation, with pleasure.

I didn't have to struggle to forget my fears. As his hips rocked against mine and I felt the sweet friction against my sex, sensation created a sanctuary where I could hide from the truth and from time itself. My hips rubbed against his thighs, my own thighs pinned together by his legs. I felt the moist heat of arousal pulse at their apex, felt that throbbing like a beacon of desire—leading me onto the rocks.

He murmured against my ear, "Our connection is real, Talia. Open yourself to it."

His hands traveled over my body, delved under our clothes, freed us from their confinements. For the first time, we touched fully naked in the Real. Skin to skin. His hard, scarred chest brushed against my nipples, and I moaned with mingled pleasure and longing.

Reality had finally revealed to me her charms. I had only a night to revel in its glories.

His skin, rough and warm, slicked against mine as we tangled bodies in the sheets. I kissed along his chest, down the length of his hard stomach, felt the bones of his hip against my cheek.

His hands threaded through my hair, and he pressed me hard against his abdomen. "I've wanted you like this since the first moment I saw you, since I knew who you were to me."

His voice held a softness I had never heard before. I slid up the length of his body, kissed his neck, smelled his forestlike musk and melted against his side. "I . . . never knew how good it could be. Here. In the Real . . ."

He started and half-sat, cradling me in his arms. "You never . . ." He trailed off, knowing what I would say.

I had been with a lot of different people in the Netherwood: male and female avatars—more than one at times. The lack of Real-world consequences made most people pretty uninhibited in avatar form, even in places less illicit than I'd been. At least for me, my abandon stemmed from the knowledge I myself was still protected, anonymous, inviolate.

But this moment was completely different. It was Real. No layers of anonymity. No computer-assisted sexual enhancers. And it was . . . a miracle.

"It's never been this way," I admitted. I looked him in the eyes, and he didn't look away.

"I had a lover, once. In the Real. We trained together at the academy. Charles." A fleeting image of his face, handsome and cold, flashed through my mind. I sighed, studied my fingernails as I continued. "He said all the right things, had all the necessary surface attributes. But the passion he had wasn't for me. It was for my name, the only thing he wanted from me. To marry a Fortune . . . It was easy enough for Charles to say he loved me, but in the end I realized that he had never seen me, recognized me as anything but a means. A resource to exploit."

Kovner traced the edge of my jaw with his rough, callused fingers, and the gentleness of his touch sent a shiver through my body. "I wanted you before I knew your name, Talia."

I leaned back, let him travel lower—down my neck, farther—savoring my curves, let him linger over the most sensitive, vulnerable spots. I felt tears spill from my eyes, but I said nothing. I wanted him to go on, to open me. To touch me in every possible way.

His lips followed the pathways of his hands. I felt him sucking along the length of my neck, down between my breasts, along the curve of my hip. Silks slid under my body as I arched to meet his lips. I felt myself falling backward, his hands catching me.

I kept my eyes closed and focused on the soft sounds, the sensations, the connections where our skin touched and rubbed, slick with sweat and desire. He was on top of me now, between my thighs, poised to enter me.

There was nothing stopping us. We both knew I was chemically infertile—all female personnel traveling through the wormhole drive were required to undergo a procedure. We also knew this was our last chance to make the ultimate connection before the end.

Before he plunged into me, Kovner stroked my eyelids open until I met his gaze. "Talia. I will love you forever. No matter what tomorrow brings."

I couldn't answer him, love for love. I distrusted love in all of its forms, didn't trust myself with the emotion. But I wanted him. More than I had ever wanted anything in my life.

He stared into my soul, and I knew he knew my thoughts. Knew he understood. Knew he accepted them. And he thrust into me, hard and deep.

The flicker of pain was infused with an unprecedented pleasure. He filled me in the deepest, most powerful way possible. Our bodies pressed together, and we rocked, rode waves of pleasure like dolphins in the sea. His skin felt vivid against mine. His voice was sharp as his lips brushed my ear and he cried out; his fingers grabbed my hips and pulled me close as he pumped inside me.

I pressed against him as hard as I could, and my body exploded with release, flooding warmth through my hips and stomach. The throbbing inside me bloomed into a supernova of ecstasy.

And Kovner was there, in his essence separate and yet merged into my whole.

Nothing can take this from you. It is always with you. No matter what happens to us.

His soul's whisper hypnotized me, mesmerized. *Love is always greater than fear. Always. So if your fear is great, is inflicted by an outside source, go within and find love. It will always save you.*

I jerked back into my body, my skin tingling with infinite little electric shocks. Breathed shivery breaths, waited for my body to reconstitute from its orgasmic jelly.

"I want you all night long," I finally said. My voice shook as I forced out the words. I didn't know how to speak into Kovner's soul, but he knew I was sincere. "Don't stop. Take me."

"Stop?" Kovner was still buried to the hilt in me. "I haven't even gotten started."

The gen mod . . . the Glass Desert soldiers had biologically altered powers of endurance beyond ordinary human beings, but I never knew those enhancements carried from the battlefield into the bedroom.

"I want to take you until you beg me to stop."

"Then you are going to fuck me until they come to take me away."

I clung to him with desperate passion. As long as we connected, we kept the outside evil at bay. We were a single light in the darkness, but that light blazed so brilliantly I lost myself in its golden warmth.

FIFTEEN

The banging on the door must have been going on for awhile before I noticed it. I didn't want to come back to my body, to reality, to the danger that waited for us. The fact that we were an "us" was dangerous enough in itself.

I slipped out of bed, donned a robe and edged toward the door, sweetly sore, feeling oddly relaxed and warm even as my mind prepared for doom. My blaster remained in the bag on the floor. I probably had time to slip it out of its holster and shoot my way out. But if I went full frontal like that, the game would quickly be over.

I glanced at Kovner. He was already on the move, sliding toward the bathroom. I let him go, hoping he'd find a way to escape. If I got away I knew we would find each other again, the same way he'd found me in my flight through the Gray Forest.

I unlocked the door manually and slid it open, yawning. I wore my sleepiness like an illusion of innocence, flimsy and translucent though it was.

Riona. Nobody else at the door could have surprised me more. The blaster she held trained on my unprotected chest was less of a shock.

"Uh. Good morning."

"Cut the crap."

It was like seeing a pleasure droid with strapped-on racks of automatic weaponry, prepared to unleash her homicidal rage on anyone who crossed her path. I couldn't help laughing. "Won't that big, hard blaster break your nails?"

"Shut up."

"Um, okay. But are you going to clue me in as to how I can help you out here? If you blow me away on my doorstep, you'll have my grandmother to answer to. And she doesn't suffer fools kindly, as I'm sure you can imagine."

She hesitated, and I couldn't help laughing again. It was the insane laughter of the damned. Her eyes narrowed. I'd pushed her too far.

"Damn straight. Violet's the one who sent me," she said.

It was my turn to hesitate. I guessed my grandmother wasn't interested in working any deal after all. "Violet. Hmm. I'm a lot more use to her alive than dead."

"That's the funny thing. She doesn't seem to think so. She wants to see you, but said I could respond however your actions required. Go ahead, give me a reason to shoot."

I didn't throw my authority around as a rule, but under the circumstances I clung to what I had—not very much. "I'm still Sheriff—and Mayor—Fortune to you."

"Not anymore. Talia Fortune, you are under arrest."

My sense of humor, what shreds of it were left, curled up and died. "By whose authority?"

"Duh. The founder of FortuneCorp." Riona cracked a smile, and I recognized a shimmer of my own old sense of inviolability, my own ambition reflected back at me from her face. That sense of self was a lie, I now realized, granted by my grandmother like the reflected light of the sun. Up until my time in the Gray Forest I'd looked and acted much like Riona did now, my identity twisted up inside of Violet and the company's approval. But I'd had time to reject my family's poison. Riona reveled in it, drank it to the dregs. I couldn't blame her. I knew I'd have acted even worse once, if our situation were reversed.

"She promised you the whole planet, didn't she?"

Riona gripped the neck of her blaster for dear life, her knuckles bone-white against the dull gray gunmetal. She had a terrible combat stance—the mark of a soft, untrained civilian. I could snatch the gun away without much trouble. But a quick glance down the hallway made me reconsider. Riona's backup was there, I guess deputized by Violet to take me out the way I'd taken out Stone. Few were serious opponents, but they outnumbered me. I'd have to talk my way out. Especially if they were all authorized to shoot.

"Violet promised all of you the right to rule this place after she's finished with me. Right?"

Riona's face hardened. I knew she was trying to psych herself into the role of noble killer, wasting me for the good of the colony. But she was too decent to succeed. I laughed again, this time at myself and my previous perceptions. She hated me enough to kill me, but not without provocation.

"Trust me, Riona, my grandmother wants me in her custody alive. I know her well enough to be sure, whatever she may have said. Don't shoot my face off by mistake . . . she won't care that your intentions were good."

I pushed the barrel of her gun down and away, and leaned over to get in her face. The others behind her tensed. "And don't kid yourself. You're next. No matter how perfect you are, no matter how exquisitely you execute her orders. She's using you the way she used me. And when she's done with you, she'll betray whoever's left like blasting yesterday's trash into space."

Riona's eyes widened.

"You don't understand." I glared at the others clustered behind Riona, included them in my rant. "That is not my grandmother. That is FortuneCorp's face, the corporation hive-mind personified. She is going to clean this place out—that includes all of you, human and droid. All individual consciousnesses—her plan is to absorb your memories, your data sets, and toss aside the rest. She's offering you eternal life, but that's a lie. Every one of you will die if you don't listen to me. Bodies will be tossed away like waste. . . ."

Riona kept her expression blank. "You are totally crazy. No wonder your grandmother needs to shut you down."

Now I understood how Kovner felt. "You know," I laughed, "you don't need to reduce down. You're already a fucking robot. What name did she give you spiritual null sets? Let me guess—Fresh Havens Central Council. *That*'ll last a long time. She's just dying to give up power."

My smile widened as the group mumbled to each other and glared at me. If I could get them to fear Violet more than they hated me, I had a chance of getting to the interrogation room alive. I recognized well that homicidal gleam in Riona's eyes. She wanted to punish me for being who I was, for the birthright that had granted me favor she felt I didn't deserve—or at least that she coveted. My continued existence threatened her ambition and we both knew it. "I'm not crazy, Riona. I'm telling the truth. Just because it's hard to accept doesn't make it untrue."

Fear ruled her. She was driven yet unresolved. She was all about the poison in the cocktail hour canapé, the untraceable stab in the back. One of the only reasons I was still alive was because she'd have to look me in the face as she wasted me, an innocent woman, in front of a dozen people. She'd have to own my death. And she wasn't willing to take on that responsibility. Yet.

"I'll do you a little favor, Riona, my fellow stockholder. I'll make you a deal."

She swallowed, her hard mask wavering.

"I'll get my clothes on and come without a fight. You put the safety back on that blaster. We'll both last longer that way . . . and you'll still get credit for bringing me in."

My easy demeanor and calm amusement carried the day. She nodded once and licked her dry, cracked lips. If I didn't believe it was simple fear that glazed her eyes, I would have said Riona had taken a nice long hit of synth before making this friendly wake-up call.

I backed up slowly, my hands open and nonthreatening. I planned to keep trying with Riona, try as hard as Kovner had done with me to explain the impossible. I hoped again that Kovner had escaped, but sensed his presence in the suite behind me, unarmed, silent. I'd never known him to sit and wait for doom, not on any plane of existence. The knowledge that he passively awaited our fate unnerved me far worse than Riona and her shaky blaster.

In spite of my earlier bravado, my hands trembled as I changed into a dailywear skinsuit. Riona watched from the doorway, and I didn't bother with a pretense of modesty.

Out of weakness I searched for Kovner with my eyes—a little too openly. It was inevitable they'd find him, but I glanced at the washroom door and sped up the process. My sense of isolation and loneliness had been too strong.

Behind me, Riona cleared her throat. "Kovner's in the bathroom!" Her voice held a note of triumph.

"Your investigative powers are formidable," I growled. "Good thing he couldn't hide under the bed platform, or you'd have had to squat down."

She nudged me between the shoulder blades with her blaster, and yanked me toward her by the elbow. "My fingers are itching to blow you away," she murmured into my ear, so softly that I had to strain to hear her. "Give me a reason and I swear I'll kill you where you stand."

"Shooting an unarmed colleague in the back. Great way to start your career," I joked.

"I completely agree." Her fingers dug harder into my arm—those long nails were sharp. "It would be a lot better to kill you and harvest the evidence of treason from your brain without your interference. Violet has that technology now."

Even as I reassured myself Riona was mistaken, the thought sickened me. "Without context, those images, sounds, and emotions will mean nothing. The filter will be gone." My knowledge was not as simple as stored data; it needed intuition and intangibles to understand.

"You need my consciousness to integrate that information. That's why Violet wants me alive and coherent—and I will give you a hint that will double, even triple your life span. Don't piss her off."

"Too bad you didn't take your own advice."

The door to the bathroom slid open, and Kovner emerged, almost naked, his hands raised. I'd never seen him so defenseless, so open. So powerful.

Our eyes met for a long moment, and an echo of last night's profound connection whispered through me like a cool breeze on a hot day. He'd been right: We were bigger than the sordid drama playing out in this moment. But I knew it wouldn't help, even if he smiled at me, unembarrassed, unafraid.

The man was doomed. We both were. And dammit, I was falling for him at the worst possible moment. Violet would know how to exploit my feelings.

I fought my weakness because it put us both at a disadvantage. He watched me battle my feelings for him and lose, and his smiled widened. Crazy bastard.

Riona grabbed a black robe from off the floor and tossed it to Kovner, but not before I saw the appreciative gaze she flicked over his body. "Put this on." She let go of my arm and sidled over to where he stood. If I were so inclined, this would have been the moment to steal her gun and break her neck. But that was not my intention. My options had not changed.

Riona smiled at her entourage, her lips curling as she shot me a glance filled with venom. "Put the prisoner Kovner in my chambers. Keep him guarded." The smile she flashed me when she met my gaze was huge and genuine—she sure knew how to pour salt into my wounds. My consolation was that Kovner could walk out of this guard detail easily, even without a weapon

or a stitch of clothing on his body. They had no idea
how dangerous he was.

"Let's go." Riona waved her blaster wildly as she
approached me. "Your grandma is waiting."

She yanked me forward, and I let her take me. Of
all the people threatening my future—my grandmother, with her evil plan; Kovner, with the knowing
warmth in his eyes; and Riona—Riona was the least
of my worries.

We clomped down the hall: me, Riona, and half of her
seemingly useless horde of hypocritical, self-interested
patriots. Without looking at the handheld in my
pocket I had no way to tell where they were taking
me. I'd never had any sense of direction worth a
damn. Given a choice of which way to go, I always
chose the wrong way. Always went left when I should
have turned right. Every time.

The thought brought a bitter little smile to my lips.
I couldn't have summed up my life any more con-
cisely.

Our little crew stopped short, yanking me out of my
self-pitying reverie. For a moment I thought it was Uncle Stone standing in the hallway, blocking our
progress. Big, rubbery shoulders encased in a corporate uniform just a little too small. Commandant cap
jammed onto a meaty head.

But as I squinted, I restrained the surging jolt of
adrenaline that pumped through my body. This wasn't
Stone. It was Gustav, the not-so-dashing space pirate.
What had my grandmother promised this guy? He
must have been pathetically easy to buy off.

He bowed formally to Riona, an oddly effeminate
gesture so absurd on his oversized frame that I felt my

sanity squirming, trying its best to dislodge from the unpleasantness that was my current reality.

"Hello, Council Chair, Riona Sweet," Gustav said. He sounded exactly the same as when I'd met him at Nanogoo bar: whiny, agitated, preoccupied. "Congratulations on winning the bureaucrat union election."

My captor blinked hard in surprise. "Do I know you? Your profile and holo-vid weren't included in the briefing we held this morning."

Gustav shrugged, and I watched his uniform shoulder seams straining in agony. "I didn't get my orders until after the briefing." Sweat glistened along his receding hairline; I wondered if Riona noticed. "You are to hand Sheriff Fortune to me for questioning."

Riona sneered. "*Sheriff* Fortune was stripped of her commission by me ten minutes ago. Unless you present me with some evidence of your authority, I'm taking you into custody as well." Her blaster swung out from between my shoulder blades to point at Gustav, inches from his bulbous nose.

To give Gustav credit, he didn't flinch or blink. Guess he was used to the prospect of pissed-off people shoving weapons into his face on a regular basis.

He smiled a small, inscrutable smile. "Keep your hair on. I'll get my handheld out—it's in my left upper vest pocket."

I sensed her nodding, and his beefy right hand reached across his chest to grope for the pocket computer resting against what passed for the old smuggler's heart. He brought out the gadget, cued up a requisition order. Held it up to Riona's handheld, and the information synced perfectly, no bugs or trip alarms activated.

Riona grunted in apparent surprise, and squinted at her green-lit screen. My eyes strayed from there to

Gustav's face. The glint in his eyes made me realize that my little speech to Riona wasn't just wishful thinking. I was indeed worth more alive than dead—and not just to my grandmother and FortuneCorp.

The possible reasons disturbed me deeply.

Gustav reached out and grabbed me above the elbow, yanked me into his custody without further ceremony—I was going to have some pretty dramatic bruises if I survived the encounter. He bowed again, and as I turned to face Riona I saw that Gustav had achieved the impossible; he had charmed and cowed Riona Sweet, and had done it without the benefit of physical charm, personal connections, or a display of wealth. This fact made me reconsider the capabilities and the character of my new captor.

"Good day," he murmured, as he smoothed his straggly mustache with his free hand. "I will see all of you at the Council debriefing at fifteen-hundred hours."

Mollified by this last tidbit of conformational data, Riona waved her little crew onward without an audible farewell. I saw the disappointment in her heavily made-up eyes vanish as a new realization dawned: Kovner awaited interrogation in her private chambers. And she fully intended, I knew, to test the stamina I'd discovered last night. She had a look in her eye that I couldn't misinterpret.

Of course, she didn't realize that he knew how to use that kind of situation to his immediate and deadly advantage. She was in more danger than I was at the moment—and the bulk of the peril lay in the fact that, like I'd been, she was arrogant enough to believe she held all the cards. That fact amused me.

Gustav hustled me down the hall, his meaty fingers digging into my upper arm. I took a gamble that I had more leverage with him than I had with Riona. "Whatever my grandmother gave you, I can double it." My voice sounded shaky but was serviceable. *Think,* my brain implored me. *Come up with something good.*

"There's nothing you could give me that Violet Fortune can't outbid, and you know it."

For a big man, he moved with speed and grace. I fought to catch my breath and keep from stumbling as we hurried through the base's metal corridors. A stench hit me before I identified our destination. Even as my gorge rose, along with a tidal wave of panic, I clenched my jaw and forced myself to stay calm. I took in the source—a cavernous room filled with huge steel drums hot and feverish in the bright, clinical light. The sewage treatment plant.

"Drowning me in a vat of shit isn't going to win you any points with my grandmother." I tried my best to sound dignified, disdainful even, but my comment elicited a huge roar of laughter from my captor.

"I don't give a flying fuck about your grandmother."

The first spike of real fear drove into my throat like a dagger. "Well, you should."

He laughed again, crushed me against a huge metal drum, the surface of which felt warm against the backs of my arms. "Shut up." He took a deep breath and closed his eyes, and I could see how rattled he was underneath his grumpy, bored exterior. I waited in vain to get acclimated to the smell, tried not to lose my composure altogether. The guy seemed to be rallying himself for a great effort; I braced myself for physical battle. I was apparently going to be shoved into a tub of raw sewage, but I wasn't going down without a hellacious fight.

When Gustav opened his eyes again, the whites were bloodshot. I lowered my center of gravity and braced myself against hot metal for what looked like imminent assault.

What he said next was a surprise.

"Just wait. He'll be here soon or not at all."

"Who?"

He leaned forward, and I could see his fat jowls shaking. "Avenger."

The expression on my face must have frightened him, because he pinned me against the drum, hard. "You have to be quiet. Don't do anything to draw attention to us. The sewage guys are between shifts but if a sensor locks on us or if your little girlfriend Riona puts two and two together, we're fucked."

"Don't worry . . . no problem." I'd gone from plotting how to kill him to reassuring him in the space of a single moment. Crazy.

Before I could take the luxury of a breath or two, Gustav hissed, "Get down!" shoving me to the ground with a massive paw. He didn't have to tell me twice. A pair of loud voices echoed among the huge drums. I crouched low on the dirty cement and considered whether I could squeeze between the raised bottom edge of a processing drum and the cement floor. I gave Gustav a single wild glance and gestured at the tiny crawl space, and he nodded.

It was like climbing into my own grave. But I was hidden in those foul-smelling shadows, and if Gustav could somehow maintain the fiction of an official position in this new planetary administration, he wouldn't have to explain my presence too.

The voices grew louder, and though neither voice

was his I sensed Kovner's presence. I knew—I *knew*—
he was coming, alive and unharmed. How did I
know that?

Two pairs of legs stopped walking next to my hiding place. One set of knees popped, and Kovner
crouched down to peer in at me.

"Hello, stinky," he said.

I guess he'd sensed me, too.

Once Kovner arrived, in the company of a companion,
I'd hoped our troubles—at least his troubles—were behind us. No such luck. My main goal was to get him
out alive. I didn't want his blood on my hands. And
though my recent knowledge was linked to Kovner's
presence and not his future, it didn't take a psychic to
figure out that he wouldn't last two days in my grandmother's custody.

"How did you get away?" I wanted to hear it, get
ideas for how we could escape the base altogether.

He shrugged, cleared his throat. "I didn't kill them."

Gustav's laughter echoed among the drums surrounding us. "So how *did* you do it, my friend?"

"Something I learned in the Glass Desert—how to
immobilize without killing."

"Ah-hah. That mental sonic boom maneuver you
were telling me and Xan about."

I blinked, pinched my nose against the stench of
the place. "I thought that was an artifact of the Gray
Forest."

"The gen mod gave me distinctive telepathic abilities. The forest gave me limited precognition and the
ability to speak into minds, not just shut them down."

"So, do it again and go."

"I can't. And I'm not going without you." He kept his voice low, but the echoes still carried along the cavernous hallways and the big metal drums full of colony waste.

"My grandmother isn't going to let me get away. But you . . . You have to leave." In a moment of inspiration, I hurled a mental image of my reanimated grandmother into his brain, and he flinched and ducked like I'd aimed a tool chest at his face. "Get out. Your people need you alive. My grandmother may let you get away if she's preoccupied with me."

Gustav proved an unlikely ally. "My friend, a dozen of our men have put themselves in harm's way to get you out of here. It cost me a fortune."

Kovner's face hardened. "I'll make sure you are fully reimbursed."

"Asshole. You know that's not what I mean. We've been through too much to do the noble warrior routine. Don't waste our effort. Don't be a dead hero, the martyred Avenger. Regroup and come back. Blow the mofos up later, do your superhero shit then. Hey, take the girl with you if you have to. But right now . . . you're wearing a freaking bathrobe. Nobody in the history of the universe has saved the world in a bathrobe."

"Wrong. Winston Churchill. Second World War, twentieth century," Kovner's companion said. I started—it was the voice of the man who'd peeled me off the wall soon after my arrival to this hellhole of a planet.

Gustav glared at him but said nothing. Then: "You have to get out."

Kovner's gaze lowered to mine where I still hid. I fell into the haunted depths of his eyes. I'd seen more than I could stand, had slammed the doors of perception on realities I didn't want to see. Kovner never did that. How did he stay even partially sane?

He shook his head. "No."

"You'll die, then." I tried to keep my voice steady, but it cracked, like the rest of me soon would. "And, you silly bastard, even if I survived your death, everything would be over. What would be the point?"

He sighed and leaned against the metal drum under which I hid, offered me a hand so I could climb out. We rested against the drum, shoulder to shoulder, and the metal abruptly got hotter, like it warmed to his touch as much as I did.

"You are wrong, Tali. I risk my life to save yours because your life is more important."

I felt my face go numb. This didn't make any sense. "How can that be? You're the leader of a rebel group. I'm not much more than a liability."

"You are the only one who can stop the Singularity on this planet. Look, I rode the nightwind every night until you appeared in the forest. You know what that's like. I did it to foresee what would come and how we could fight fate. Your name, Talia. The wind kept speaking your name. I tried to get more—got fleeting images, the ocean, a mansion filled with paper books. I don't know how you'll save us. I know I sound crazy. But I know the nightwind doesn't lie."

I was tired of fighting him. I'd tried being noble, to no avail. "Fine. Get me out of here alive. Save me, save yourself. To fight another day." I sighed.

Gustav snorted and nodded, pawed the cement floor like an agitated bull. "Yeah. Time to leave," he agreed.

I whipped out my handheld, tried to get a bead on

Riona's position so we could avoid her and her deputies. Kovner snatched it out of my hand before I could interface. "No! Are you crazy? We have to get rid of this."

The handheld vibrated audibly in Kovner's hand, like a bomb about to detonate. My embarrassment devolved into consternation when I saw the expression lighting his face. He smiled at the buzzing handheld, cradling it in his hands.

"Yes. We'll go. But we have to do maximum damage to the facility and the grid before we do." The man had a beautiful smile. "You want to see sabotage, Tali? I'll show you sabotage the way *I* do it. Big."

He nodded once, then ran along the wall, behind the waste treatment drums, and the rest of us jogged after him. Gustav and I exchanged uneasy glances. We knew we didn't have time to do anything he said and still get away.

SIXTEEN

"Have you ever heard of Tesla's oscillator?"

I was out of breath from trying to keep up, and Gustav was clearly suffering a thousand agonies, but Kovner hadn't broken a sweat. He was actually plugging data into my handheld's keyboard as he ran.

"What's Telsa's oscillator?"

"Amazing what the WorldCorps have censored, hidden away in secret archives. Nikola Tesla was a visionary scientist who lived in the late nineteenth century—he discovered alternating current. Invented radio. He also discovered the Resonance Effect. Everything vibrates to its own frequency. The oscillator finds that vibration, harmonizes with it, augments it. And—boom. Tesla invented an earthquake machine that almost destroyed his building in 1898 in New York City. I'm making my own oscillator. Getting it in tune with the vibrations of this wing of the base. Causing our own earthquake."

His fingers moved over the keyboard in a blur. "Thank you, Nikola Tesla," he muttered under his breath. "This little device will take down the Ambassador's Suite and hopefully the main boardroom where your grandmother conducts her business." He paused at the freight elevators lined up at the edge of the warehouse just beyond the waste treatment wing. Leaning against the wall, he typed even more furiously.

I cut a glance at the man standing next to Gustav. The man who had attacked me the first night I spent in Fresh Havens. "Who are you?" I asked.

The man smiled, ran stubby fingers through his buzzed platinum hair. "The name's Xan."

"Kovner's told me about you. And we've met before."

His smile broadened. "Maybe. Maybe you just see the family resemblance."

"To Kovner?" I couldn't keep the disbelief out of my voice.

The smile morphed into a booming laugh. "No, to Gustav. He's my father"

Kovner interrupted us. "Every object has its own resonance, its own vibration. This little thing will harmonize with *this* structure, magnify the frequencies of the structure's vibrations. If you have any family or friends in wing C, you better warn them to get out."

Gustav leaned against the wall, still gasping for air, his hair dripping with sweat. "Come on. This isn't going to work, my friend. You can't make that little thing oscillate hard enough to do the trick."

Kovner tied the handheld to a nearby pillar with a piece of twine lying in a pile of waste paper at his feet. "I can. Gen mod."

Xan interrupted him. "Gen mod's not enough, Lieutenant."

"Gen mod plus the Gray Forest is something else, my friend."

Xan shrugged, looked uneasy. "We're tripping all kinds of security alerts," he warned.

Kovner seemed unmoved. "They already know where we are, Xan. They are on their way. Only, this explosion will slow them down enough to give us a chance to escape."

Gustav groaned, clearly unconvinced that his friend's bizarre, nonconventional bomb was going to do the job. Kovner ignored him, rested the tips of his fingers on the device. Took a deep breath.

The thing started gyrating rhythmically against the concrete post, reminding me with a blush of my long night of ecstasy. Of Kovner and his incredible hands.

"Shit." Xan's voice was hushed, held an almost religious awe.

The handheld started pounding against the pillar. Harder and harder. The floor under our feet started to vibrate, synced with the possessed handheld. Kovner watched the thing do its work, a smile etched on his face. The four of us only broke the tableau when distant voices yelled down the corridor. Then we ran. I stole a glance over my shoulder, wished I hadn't. At least half a dozen guard bots were behind us, blasters out, ready to shoot.

By the time we made it out of wing C, the floor was undulating under our feet, a man-made earthquake. We made it out of the wing just in time. Our pursuers weren't as lucky. The guard bots didn't scream, but the crunching and mechanical squeals of scrambled cries for help were almost as bad. Like he'd claimed, Kovner's desperate move gave us the minutes we needed to escape. But the largest evil remained untouched.

We ended up hooking into the grid at a synth house that Gustav's brother Anders owned. Selling synth wasn't illegal, just using it was, so the establishment was moderately safe. But Kovner and I had resisted arrest. We knew we were putting Anders in danger just by being there, no matter what Gustav's brother said. He was sacrificing a lot. The only question in my mind was whether we could finish what we started before we were discovered. Anders showed us to a back room, locked out any surveillance, and left. We secured the door.

I'd never accessed the Netherwood in the presence of any other living person. And how strange to go in together, a team of two. But it all went down without a hitch; easy as slipping under water, Kovner and I were in. Yes, we were inside. But things had changed.

I knew we raced the clock as we descended. Thanks to me, Kovner's cover was blown. As soon as we made our appearance, FortuneCorp could track us—and relay our physical whereabouts to our pursuers. We had to work fast and hope that Kovner's oscillator distracted everyone long enough for us to finish the job.

Everything had changed greatly since Amazonia had last ruled here. Still, hesitation would be fatal, so I pushed forward, pretended to myself that I wasn't terrified and excited about probing the underside of humanity's superconsciousness once again.

I found the Avenger waiting for me in the semi-darkness. Handsome devil. Even in the middle of my distress, I felt my lust for him rising, reassuringly indestructible.

"Come on, then." His avatar's British accent tickled a smile onto my lips. "There's a girl." His hand cradled my butt as the space reconfigured itself into a plush, fur-filled room—the Avenger's lair. He could still manipulate cyberspace with the best of them.

It felt good to be back; this felt far more like home than the inhospitable surface world of Fresh Havens. Far, far away was where the danger lurked, fangs dripping with the venom of reality. It was such a relief to sink into illusion, seductive as the glint of the Avenger's eyes, the electric tickle of his fingers. I planted a fat kiss on his lips. Business had to come first this trip, but I had to steal a bit of pleasure, just a little. What was the harm of a single kiss?

Plenty of harm. But not the kind I expected.

To my surprise, the Avenger relaxed into the kiss, didn't try to fight me off. His fingers felt along the smooth sides of Amazonia's head, and I felt a jolt at every point of contact. I felt our consciousness connecting as it had in the Gray Forest, separate from that kiss but even more potent. I heard Kovner whispering, saw it written directly inside my head like code, my own Real head, somehow breaking through all illusion of the Netherwood, cutting through the simple pleasure of our lips connecting.

Spybot. I'm not here as Avenger.

I shuddered, almost broke the physical contact with what I now knew was not the Avenger. Which made sense. The Avenger's cover had been blown, thanks to me. Gah.

Don't let it know you know.

I opened my mouth and let the avatar kiss me. His tongue found mine. His fingers began tracing my body, and I couldn't help reacting. My fear made the physical reactions even more intense.

I moaned with the sensation rocketing through me,

opened my legs to its hands even as I frantically tried to keep contact with Kovner's true self.

He waved me away in my mind. *Keep distracting it—I'll get the data.*

I wouldn't shoo. *It will kill/disappear me!*

I won't let it. Surrender for now. Think of it like us from the old days. Have fun. . . .

And Kovner sent a frisson of shared pleasure into my mind. He liked that I was getting off with the spybot, took pleasure in my pleasure because he knew without a doubt that he could keep me safe. There was a time when I wouldn't have trusted him, but he'd proven himself too many times to doubt. So with a sigh I devoured the spybot like a Kovner-flavored chocolate, revved it up like a vibrator set to my favorite secret setting. I felt Kovner at the edge of my consciousness, registered his occasional exclamations when he discovered something new.

I kept grinding harder and harder against the spybot, knowing that in the Netherworld I had the physical advantage. Amazonia had bested the Avenger many times, and this avatar was identical to the one I'd known. It could lead me into danger where I could be overwhelmed by superior forces, but here alone I had one-on-one physical supremacy.

I felt it enter me, and I rode the pseudo-Avenger hard, raising up and down with my thighs, clamping against him as I shuddered with release. I wrapped my fingers around his massive shoulders and pressed him down into the fur-covered floor, lifted myself off to stand over him.

He smiled up at me, and I let him stare into my eyes. He avoided my gaze, but not before I saw the artifice. And the machine I saw, operating on a program, collecting data points, was really who I was with.

Kovner! He's going to kill me.

No—

I'm out of time.

I watched the Avenger changing form on the floor by my feet. I'd read about this in tech forums, how if you saw your opponent shape-shifting you knew you had a spybot on your hands—and that by then it was always too late.

The Avenger shifted into a metal humanoid—a government bot with all the power necessary here to enforce arrests. I knew that in this form the government bot would neutralize my avatar, take it over for government use and capture my consciousness. If I'd been hooked in from Earth, somebody would already be on the way to collect my inert body before EMS or any civilian could discover me. I'd disappear—virtually and in truth. Nobody on the forums knew what happened after that.

I felt my cyber limbs become paralyzed, immoveable. The government bot advanced on me, its claws reaching for my face. I tried to scream, but no sound emerged. I tried to call to Kovner with my mind, with the body that waited for me on Fresh Havens, but I had lost the way back to myself; I'd lost the capacity for words, only shrieked inside my consciousness, pure terror expressing itself as physical pain. I watched the bot extend its claws to within a centimeter of my face, open and extend . . .

Blackness.

A blessed headache. It felt so good to have a head, even though it also felt like the top of it had been shot off. I forced my eyes open. Kovner and Gustav stared intently down into my face. I swallowed, tried to generate some spit in my dry mouth.

"What happened?" My voice came out as a mournful little croak.

"It's what didn't happen that is so interesting." Kovner's smile held no amusement.

"Clue me—I can't follow you. My brain's bleeding."

Kovner nodded. "In this instance, that may well be more than a figure of speech."

I reveled in the broad, flat tones of his New York accent. Never again did I want to hear him speaking with a British accent, in cyberspace or anywhere else.

"We almost lost you. Only shorting out the entire grid stopped the arrest sequence. We cut interplanetary contact again, like before you came. Of course, they'll repair the interface in no time."

Anger flared up, as welcome as the pain had been. I clutched it to me like a life jacket in a stormy sea, where I bobbed, overboard and abandoned to my fate. "That completely rotted. I feel nasty."

Kovner sat back on his heels, stroked my hair. My head hurt like hell. "If it's any consolation, me too."

In my peripheral vision I saw Gustav and Xan drifting out of the room. Gustav paused at the doorway and said, "I need to make sure Anders is still safe. Check some things. Get Xan back to where he needs to be. Two minutes, my friends. Then we need to get out of here fast. You did a nice patch job, Kovner, to hide the place where you went in, but they'll hunt down the source of the sabotage soon." And then he and Xan were gone.

I kept my focus on Kovner. "I almost got disappeared. And for what?"

He restrained a small smile. "I needed to accomplish a few things. I got them done. I'm glad you had a good time while it lasted. . . ."

"Trust me, it wasn't worth it." I clutched my fury closer, like a pretty precious I was hoarding. I was enraged at our situation, but didn't want to admit it. "We should have left the base by now," I muttered.

"Should I do nothing and watch the human race extinguish itself without understanding?" he asked.

I sighed. "Well, yeah, maybe. Maybe that's all any of us deserve."

"Knowing you, I must disagree." He took my hand in his, gently squeezed. It distracted me from my physical and mental pain. That simple feeling of physical and emotional connection was more eloquent an advocate for my worth than anything else he could formulate or verbalize.

I let him stroke my hand. "What did you find out?" I asked, watching his gentle fingers, not his face.

"I'm going to tell you everything, Talia, but we also have to get out of here. Once Gustav comes back, we are going to have to run."

I fought my annoyance at still not knowing the whole truth. "You sure you want me to know everything? That's a big risk. What if I get captured? What if my grandmother turns me? Everything you know will get reported straight to them." My voice was bitter.

He sighed. "Sometimes everything is so damn dangerous you need to do whatever you have to. Just stop thinking about it, don't look down, keep going, and maybe you make it."

My head still hurt like a mother. I closed my eyes and groaned. "If you're going to tell me, do it before I pass out."

"We're pretty much fucked," he said.

"Ha! I could've told you that before we went in there." But my heart sank all the same. If Kovner was losing hope, the situation had to be pretty bleak.

He didn't try to pretty up the truth. "DARPA knows everything—the nightwind, how to counter the electromagnetic properties of this forest. I thought the pulses could short out all computer tech and save us, but DARPA has already got a workaround."

Now that got my attention; surprised me, too. "A workaround? But this is a corporate colony. No army."

"But FortuneCorp has gotten that information, integrated it into its own supermind. I didn't have enough time to find what the workaround is, but they have it."

I forced my eyes open again, forced Kovner to connect with my gaze. "So . . . I don't follow. So why are we totally fucked, more than before?"

"FortuneCorp has this DARPA information now," he reiterated. "They can follow us in, bring all their technological advantages in with them. FortuneCorp can capture the Foresters, extract everything they've learned about the forest and its secrets. And then they can throw them away. *Us* away."

"Don't give up yet," I said. I sat up squinting. "They don't always do things right. You were in the Glass Desert, Kovner. You saw what a complete disaster that was."

"Not for our guys. Not for us. Our side won. They got what they planned for."

I could feel my heart beating in my chest so hard it shook me. "Yeah, won," I echoed. If you could call that destruction victory.

He smiled as he stared deeply into my eyes. *Unintended consequences,* he whispered into my mind directly, our connection as whole and sweet as ever before. *They can only plan so much.*

I didn't have the man's talents. I replied aloud. "Damn straight. They opened the tubes and squeeze out all the toothpaste. No way it's ever going back into the tubes."

He smiled again, our connection wordless now, carried on waves of pure emotion. He hated that government and what they'd done.

I kept talking, because the regained intimacy unnerved me, freaked me out. And there was little we could do about these revelations. "Let's go find your space pirate friends and get to your outpost of rebels. We need to get out of here before security finds us. They said your hacker move will confuse FortuneCorp for a bit, but not more than that. We can discuss the rest later."

So, we ran. My head still hurt like hell. I didn't know how we'd escape. But oddly, the sensation of running at Kovner's side, understanding him on a level deeper than words, more than made up for it.

The group of giant spiders waiting outside in the swirling sand stopped me cold. Stone had warned me about them the day I arrived. "What . . . the . . ."

"I know." Kovner laughed, the bastard. "You don't like bugs."

"I almost got eaten by a swarm of them not too long ago. Remember? But these things are even worse."

One of them turned toward me, its furry eyes balefully reflecting my fear back into my face.

"They're as smart as horses. They can sense fear. And it makes them . . . nervous."

I forced myself not to run at the sight of them. My words came out in a panicky rush. "Antsy, right? You almost said *antsy*." I laughed crazily. "Oh, whatever. By now, I suppose getting eaten by bugs would be a relief."

I drew forward slowly, flinching every time one of the big black creatures shifted on its legs. They were not, strictly speaking, arachnids—twelve legs instead of eight—but they were still insectoid, carnivorous-looking creatures. Yuck. Why couldn't we make our escape on sandcrawlers—or even on foot?

"We don't have time for this shit." Gustav had returned. He mounted one spider, and pointed at another. "Get up on Silver's back and let's get out of Dodge," he growled at me.

"Silver? It's black."

"He. And it's Silver, like from the Lone Ranger. Hi-ho, Silver . . . ?" His words trailed off as my expression must have revealed my complete ignorance of whatever the hell he was talking about.

"She's Earth-born, isn't she?" Gustav asked.

Kovner had also mounted a spider-horse. He shrugged. "She's young."

That condescending comment stripped away the last of my hesitation. I climbed on a crate upended next to my mount and swung my legs into the seating harness, strapped myself in. Silver groaned and shivered. Evidently he hated this whole scenario as much as I did.

"Let's go," Kovner said. And we scrabbled out of there, toward the sewage treatment center halfway across the base.

"Where are we headed?" I asked as we rode. "You

cut access to the grid. They'll be guarding all the entrances and exits. They know we were on base to do our damage, so they'll figure they have us trapped here."

"They aren't guarding the sewers," Gustav said. "That's what I was checking."

"What sewers? This base conforms to intergalactic environmental accords. I saw the waste treatment center with my own eyes. A system of pipes spreading outside is strictly forbid—"

Both Kovner and Gustav burst out laughing. "You can make the girl an outlaw, but you can't take the law out." Gustav almost choked on his mirth.

I wasn't sharing the joke. "What?"

Gustav hummed an amused little tune. "Sewers are cheaper than obeying regulations. Your uncle took bribes from day one. The people who built that sham treatment plant built hidden sewage pipes out the back. Stone looked the other way, everybody got paid, everybody got happy. On grid, no sewage egress. Ignorance, bliss."

"How do you know all of this?"

Gustav took a little bow—not an easy feat for a fat man on the back of a giant, scuttling spider. "I'm the guy who won the bid."

Soon afterwards we paused at the enormous double doors behind the sewage treatment plant, marked PRIVATE. Beyond was the entrance to a huge gray pipe. The stench was indescribable. Nobody else seemed to notice. The pirate's face split into a huge, terrifying grin.

"Where do you think we discovered these furry beauties?" he asked, indicating the spiders. He bowed and motioned for us to enter. "This is where I leave you. Good-bye and good luck. If you need me, you know where to find me—though Fresh Havens is getting too hot for a man of my, er, talents. I won't be here for long, I hope."

Kovner graced the pirate with a long, lingering look. "I hope to see you again in a better place. Thank you for all that you've done."

Then, without any further ado, Kovner and I went in.

"Hold on, Tali," Kovner's voice echoed back at me through the blackness. "Don't fall off." He didn't have to waste his breath.

As we descended, the stench became overwhelming, almost a solid entity. I got lightheaded from the lack of oxygen. But Silver was a good little horsey-spider; he clambered up and down, avoiding the toxic-looking muck and even climbing the walls upside down in a few spots to get past otherwise impassable bottlenecks.

Kovner's advice had been good, actually. Even strapped in, I almost slid loose twice. The harness was made for someone much bigger. Sully? Gustav? It didn't matter. I held on.

Neither of us spoke on that long, echoing journey through the muck. But my mind made up for it, operating on overdrive as we crept along. What if the government had let me go voluntarily? Maybe my aching, bleeding brain was a living GPS tracker now, grid or no grid. Kovner and I had no idea about the new technology since the Singularity. How would I get such an item out? If the humans practiced any kind of surgery in the forest, it sure wasn't the laser-based, bloodless kind.

Also, what else had Kovner discovered that shook him so badly? What could be bad enough to dash Kovner's hopes?

Part of me wanted to put an end to all my questions

by simple surrender, a quiet fall into oblivion. Let the bugs snack on me—that way I'd be no use to anybody: Violet or the rebels. I could sail into nothingness, unperturbed by the truth.

Truth. Like I had ever really known the truth of what was happening, or ever really would. If I'd just done my job, followed orders like a good sheriff-bot, I wouldn't feel so off-balance, so unsure of my every move. If only I didn't care, I wouldn't want the truth. But I did. Kovner had presented me with an unsolvable mystery, that of the human soul, and fear of what was to come. There had to be answers somewhere.

Did I have a soul? I believed the answer to be yes. But did it matter? And would it change anything?

The forest opened its metallic arms and beckoned us to hurry. I'd breathed an enormous sigh of relief as we'd left the sewer system, and our giant spiders had no compunctions about racing over the grassland—I think they were hungry and knew the Gray Forest was filled with juicy arthropod game. We flew over the grasses much faster than I'd walked in my combat gear.

I don't know if it was the spiders, Kovner's presence, or something else, but no magnetic storms hit as we entered the relative safety of the forest's edge, no rat-dogs leapt for my jugular, and no swarms of beetles made the command decision to attack Silver the spider or any of the rest of us. Kovner didn't do anything like blindfolding me, either, though it hardly mattered. Within five minutes I couldn't tell where I was.

We were deep in the forest by nightfall. "Not there yet?" I noted the fact as calmly as I could.

"Nope." Kovner descended from his spider's back,

slid the harness off, scratched at the bristles where the weight of his body had mashed them flat. His noble steed shivered all over, leaning into his fingers like a huge twelve-legged cat. Then, in a single prodigious leap, the creature vaulted to the top of the canopy layer above our heads and vanished.

Kovner repeated the process for my spider, which scuttled away too, if slightly more slowly. *Hi-ho, Silver* . . .

I watched him go. "Why didn't they eat us? We've got to be easier pickings than just about anything else out here. And where are they going?"

Kovner sighed. "As far as we can tell, they think we're spiderlings. After Gustav built the sewers, they had regular contact with us. We made friends. They come to visit morning and night, and seem to enjoy carrying people on their backs."

"But why?"

"That's what they do for their babies."

I stifled a groan. "I'm having trouble following you."

"I know." His face was unreadable, veiled in shadow. The nightwind began to blow, and I tensed against it, remembering too much about the last time I'd been out in it. "The forest, Tali, is us."

I heard his words, but the meaning still didn't compute. "It's a fricking forest. Trees. Killer bugs. I'm merely a human."

"A mere human is a gross understatement." Kovner patted the ground next to him, and I sat close, feeling the wind caressing my hair and neck like a ghostly lover.

"The forest is a conductor of psychic energy. It magnifies energy fields. The DARPA R & D people found this native forest, saw its potential and tricked it out."

My turn to smile. "Tricked it out?"

"Yes. They terraformed like crazy and turned the place into a giant weapon of destruction. At least, that was their intent."

"I don't follow. Yeah, the place is dangerous, but as you've proven, other planets are worse. Some devour humans like chocolate bars. You guys have made a life here."

"Well, that doesn't make it any less dangerous. This forest slurped up those DARPA researchers like a plate of spaghetti, Tali. After that, this place went to FortuneCorp for a bargain. A lot of your corporate holdings come in this way—what the colonists don't know might hurt them, but if it doesn't, the Corp makes a huge profit."

I considered this information. Setting up a colony in this manner was strictly illegal. There were requirements regarding colonist safety. How many laws had Violet broken to found Fresh Havens? And the other company colonies . . . ? I swallowed hard, brought my focus back to the most relevant danger. "Why doesn't it slurp us up, then?"

Kovner gave a wry smile. "It likes us."

"So . . . is it like a giant computer?"

"No. It's smart like one and it conducts energies but . . . it's alive like us. Yes, when the DARPA researchers started work here . . . there were massive unintended consequences. I think the forest has full, complete consciousness."

His words hit me like a blaster shot to the chest. I fought to breathe.

"The nightwind. Tali . . . it speaks to you," he suggested.

"Yes." I couldn't manage more than a whisper.

"I think it accepts you because you listen. You can hear it. And respond."

I remembered an ancient book from my grandmother's old print library. I joked, "I am the Lorax, I speak for the trees . . ."

Kovner laughed—he must have heard of Dr. Seuss, maybe even read *The Lorax*, too. "Speak *to* the trees, you mean."

"Well, the trees are speaking to me. To us."

"Yeah."

I felt my eyes fill with tears, tried to fight them off. I would always see emotion as a weakness, no matter the evidence to the contrary. Growing up raised by Violet had required it. And yet, a new image began plaguing me. "I can't stop thinking about those little children at the camp."

Kovner put an arm around my shoulders, pressed me close up against him. The wind ruffled his hair as it picked up around us, and a delicate scent like lilacs filled the air.

"They're all going to die, aren't they?"

"No, that's why we're going back in. To save them. To save us all. We did what we could at the base; we got out of there alive. We're on the right track." He touched my cheek, lifted my chin with his fingers. "Think of it like when we first got into the Netherwood, in the Amphitheatre. You survive one battle, one part of the game, you get to the next level."

I thought about the people at the base, trapped in their innocent ignorance the way I had been, and I couldn't stop shaking. The nightwind picked up, a raw moan echoing through the trees. "This isn't a game, Kovner. None of this is a game."

He kissed my left temple, stroked the curve of my ear. "None of it was ever a game. Tali, these are the ultimate stakes."

SEVENTEEN

We made it to the enclave alive, but as we both knew, our troubles had just begun.

Sully wasn't exactly thrilled to see me as he met us at the outer doors. "Glad to see you back. But . . . her again?" He gave Kovner a wry look.

Kovner punched him in the arm. Ah, male bonding. I kept quiet. An evil part of me had hoped either the spiders or Grandma Violet got this guy. Sully clearly felt the same way about me. He blocked the camouflaged entrance to the enclave with his short, squat body.

"She saved my life. She's one of us."

"You wouldn't have been in as much danger in the first place if it wasn't for her."

"We play the game as it comes. You know that."

A frisson of unease tickled down my spine. I nibbled at a thumbnail, decided to engage Sully directly. "Hey, I started by playing for the other team. But they're all wrong for me. I'm too human."

Sully raised an eyebrow and cocked his head, clearly looking to fight. "Oha, now, the first trustworthy thing I ever heard you say. So, we're the backup position for you."

"I want to live. Not exist on a database."

"Living includes death, Ms. Fortune," he sneered. "Around here, sooner rather than later."

"That's better than the alternative."

He drew close to me, invaded my personal space. His eyes glared into mine, his breath blew hot into my face. "How do we know you won't sell us out?"

Kovner broke it up. He stepped between us, nudged Sully back. "My friend, cut the woman a break. She gave up a lot more than you did to come here."

"I don't want her around." Sully spat at my feet but I held steady. I respected his hesitation about me— understood it, actually; I'd come here the first time to capture Sully and Kovner if I could. "How do you know she isn't carrying some spy nanobot, recording everything for her grandma's corporation?"

Kovner's face grew serious. "Nothing like that could survive in this place."

"And you're so sure of that because?"

"Because I know the forest. And I know Talia too. She wouldn't do that."

"Yeah. You know this forest," Sully said. He clumped away, and into the hidden entrance of the enclave, and Kovner and I hurried to follow. When Kovner caught him, I heard Sully say, "This place. Home sweet home. But I don't know, fearless leader. Sometimes I'm thinking this place is just waiting for us to trust it be- fore it turns around and eats us—like it enjoys lulling us into a sense of complacency. Maybe we don't taste so good when we're scared."

"Where are we going?" I called. I ran to catch up.

Sully never paused, and we barreled down a dusty, poorly lit hallway. The canvas-draped walls billowed as we passed. "We've been waiting for you. I hoped that it was just Kovner who came, but we have to decide what to do here. Try to get offworld tomorrow, somehow, or stay and fight." He shot a glance at Kovner. "And if we want a Fortune fighting alongside us."

Kovner stopped walking, refused to meet my gaze. His lips thinned into a hard, unyielding line. "Sully. This isn't a matter for debate. I told you—without Talia we're going to lose."

"And with her we're going to win?"

"She's our best shot."

We started walking again, more slowly this time. Sully shook his head. "She's FortuneCorp, man. She's the enemy."

I hated the way Sully talked about me, like I wasn't there. "Give me a chance," I said. "I gave up a lot to come here."

Like in a dream, the three of us reached the entrance of the mess. A meeting evidently was already in progress; the tables were crowded with people: men, women, and yes, the children. The room slowly fell silent, and a hundred faces or more turned to watch me follow Sully and Kovner to the front.

Sully spoke without any polite preamble. "They're back. Kovner. And he brought *her*."

"*Fortune.*"

My name blew through the crowd like a wind through the leaves outside. It had always been a treasure for me to hide, to hoard, to use as a weapon at the appropriate time; never a life-threatening liability. But the family name certainly haunted me now. I was damned by my name.

I swallowed hard, didn't bother trying to ingratiate myself with a smile or witty, meaningless words. And Sully said, "We need to decide if she's allowed to stay."

It took a moment for his words to spread a chill through my veins. These people had every right to fear me, to hate me. My family had created the conditions they suffered. A certain kind of justice would be served if they took me out back and summarily executed me with knives and clubs.

But the knowledge of the family wrongdoing was new and bitter to me. I stood, trying not to fidget, wondering if anything I said could convey that. The mob considered what to do with me.

My gaze wandered from one person to the next, and I saw the range of opinions play over each individual face. One young man was inclined to sympathy. Behind him, a tough-looking woman with a tiny boy on her lap glared at me, her eyes narrowed, like it would be a pleasure to kill me with her bare hands.

"Why did you come here?" A voice cut through the silence, and I quickly identified the speaker: an older man, eyes rheumy and filled with wordless sadness. He was dressed in rough, fibrous silks; a native Forester, I guessed; not a smuggler or a refugee from the base.

"I want to fight. I want to live." The simple truth.

"Why can't you just live back on base?" The female voice cut hard, held no mercy.

Kovner stepped forward, eyes blazing. "Because the base is going to become a slaughterhouse. No human being is safe there. I went to save her because Tali is in a position to help us. And she is the Tali named by the nightwind. That is no small thing."

The woman who'd spoken didn't back down. "She's a collaborator. Collaborators will be safe. And the nightwind speaks in riddles."

Kovner met her gaze, and I was reminded of the first

time I'd seen him here in the Gray Forest. Those hard eyes, used to terrible sights.

Sully crossed his arms, walked away from us, paced like a prosecutor in front of the crowd. "Why would the Corp destroy its own assets? Humans serve FortuneCorp. It doesn't make any sense to wipe us out."

Clearly none of us really understood the dangers, none except Kovner. None of us was brave enough to look full into the darkness and read our fates there. The rest of us had averted our eyes.

Kovner wasn't going to let us evade the truth any longer. "You're wrong, Sully. No time for wishful thinking. It's started. We got out in time. But all of us are in as much danger as the people at the Fresh Havens base."

The old man with the sad eyes stood, swayed lightly on his feet as if at sea. "We're out here for different reasons." The timbre of his voice held a pleading, anxious quality that I did not like. "We're not the same as the people at the base. We want to make ourselves happy and live our lives in peace. We don't need to interact with them. No interaction at all. We can live without technology, without—"

"I'm sorry, Apollo," Kovner interrupted, his voice harsh with grief. "We won't be getting the chance to do that. It's as I saw. The Singularity . . . The founder of FortuneCorp has arrived. She's not human any longer. She's come to clean house, and the vermin she's come to exterminate is humanity."

The mess exploded with voices, verbal shrapnel shooting everywhere from Kovner's bombshell.

The hard-faced woman wrapped her arms around her child and shrieked at me. "Get her out of here! She'll betray all of us!"

I held steady, willed myself not to run. Kovner held up his hands, and pandemonium slowly gave way to calm. "The enclave of the Gray Forest has grown over the last year. And you, the original residents, have treated us, the refugees, with hospitality and grace. Apollo's right—most of us came here with peaceful intentions. But peace is over. We have to become an army." He paused. "This woman, Talia, can fight. She knows our enemy better than we do. We need her."

Apollo shrugged, looked pointedly away when I tried to meet his gaze. "This young woman wants to live. So do we. You say she can fight? Great. Let her. But we don't want to fight." He crossed his arms, tapped his feet, shod in soft furs and what looked like actual leather. "You newcomers can fight. . . ."

Kovner sighed. "We don't have a choice. They're bringing the fight to us, Apollo. Like Lenin—or was it Trotsky?—said: You may not be interested in war, but war is very interested in you."

The old man grimaced. "Fighting. If I'd wanted to fight . . ." He trailed off. "If war wants me, it can have me. I'm old, I've led a long and disreputable life. I'll not fight for myself."

"But what about the little ones?" Kovner's voice dropped, and he glanced around the room. The adults all fidgeted, looked at their feet. But the children were riveted; they knew Kovner was talking about them, talking for them. "These children will be the first to be targeted. They are the most precious, are the most vulnerable to the Singularity. They can't reduce down, but they have succulent, green growing minds. And they are rare, are children. After what's been happening on the other worlds and the way our society has been heading, FortuneCorp won't kill them outright. No, it'll take them for research. Spare parts."

His gaze swept back to me and I met it. What I saw shook me to the core: madness and blood, and death. Much death. And an agonized humanity that refused to be destroyed.

"They don't want *us*," the hard-faced woman accused. She kept shaking her head, as if she could make everything go away by protesting and fighting enough. "They want you. Both of you."

I took a step backward, reeling. Fear crackled in the air like static, like ball lightning about to explode. Her face stayed hard.

"You have no choice. Give yourselves up," she said. "Leave us here. If they get you, they'll let us live quietly here, in peace. We don't have a problem with them. They won't want to waste the effort invading this forest for us." A murmur of agreement rustled through the room.

I shook my head, took a deep breath, tried to find words to reach them all. "You don't understand. FortuneCorp, WorldCorps—they have plenty of resources. They have tons of weaponry, money. They won't let anyone flout their authority. They'll come for you. I know how my grandmother thinks."

Kovner was fighting his frustration. He stood alone in the center of the mess, hands clenching and unclenching. I moved next to him, tried to steady him with my words and physical presence. I said what he couldn't, what I finally saw clearly, too late to change a thing. "You can tell yourselves stories about how hiding here will save you. But the people who want you know all about this place—and you. The DARPA Army Research and Development division developed this forest. They know its strengths and weaknesses. Even if it wants to, the forest can't save you—only you can do that."

The hard-faced woman hugged her boy so tight he squirmed frantically and burst into tears. Her loving, protective arms had become a vise. "Stop it." She closed her eyes against my words, bent over her crying child.

Apollo crossed to the woman, put his arm around her shoulders . . . surprisingly took my side. "No. No more fairy tales. This Talia . . . she knows. It's tempting, so tempting to make her the scapegoat, the human sacrifice. But it won't work. We have to fight." He finally met my gaze, nodded, even smiled. But I saw his eyes brim with tears.

I sensed the tide of opinion shifting in the room. In my favor. My words had made a dent.

"It doesn't matter what my name is," I continued, as I moved closer to Kovner's side. "I'm as doomed as you are. My sin: humanity. I don't want to die any more than you all do. So, let's fight."

My words sounded brave, so damn brave. But my heart was hollow even as I spoke.

The rest of the meeting concerned tactics. As a nod to the hardliners in the room, Sully was elected the leader of the enclave—the first leader they'd ever needed to have. They'd dig under the enclave, make it even more impenetrable and hard to find, create a separate underground bunker to hide the children while we fought. We. That word still troubled me.

The meeting broke up, and the Foresters wandered off to make weapons, plans, and more plans. I followed Kovner into the busy hallway. Surefooted as ever, he led the way in the half shadows to a tiny room more a cell than a bedchamber. And I realized with shock that I was standing in Kovner's room. This was the closest place to a home he had on this planet or anywhere. No wonder he'd spent so much time logged into the Netherwood back on Earth, where we'd first met each other and fought as the Avenger and Amazonia. This room contained no evidence of any life lived in the Real at all.

"You have nothing," I murmured.

He shrugged. "I have myself. That's a start. And at least that's all I have to lose." He drew closer. "Except you. Tali, don't go."

I started: he knew my unspoken, my fledgling thoughts better than I did.

He reached for me, caressed my shoulders. He wasn't a huge man but he towered over me. I found it comforting—wanted to be comforted. I wanted to wrap myself in his arms and go to my imminent death with him—with another human soul. Not fighting alone, at least. And the connection we'd shared—

I snorted in amusement when I registered the course my thoughts were taking. Then I said, "I wish I could throw my lot in with these people. But I can't stop thinking of the people on the base."

"I haven't forgotten them. . . . We'll rescue them in good time."

"There's no more time for them—Violet said so. Hell, she's an overachiever and she planned to have it done in a week. I give her three days before she cleans out the place. I know Gustav and Xan will do their best before they escape offworld, but . . ."

He grabbed my shoulders again, kissed me hard until I stopped. White lightning shot through my body, but too soon he broke our connection and looked into my eyes, his own bloodshot and wild. "When I first knew you, you were a warrior goddess. Now you are a hero. But you have to save yourself first."

"I've always been a city girl at heart. Let me go back to the city and save the people I understand."

His voice stayed steady even as his eyes filled with grief. "You'll be doomed there. How do you not see that?"

I looked at him. Our lips hovered inches apart. I ached to kiss him again, forced myself to hold back. "There's no safe place, Kovner. All I have is me, too. I don't think I ever had the right to claim you for myself, alone. So let me go back and fight in the place I know."

His fingers gripped me tighter, reminding me of the terrified mother inside, clutching her child hard enough to smother him. "We'll make a plan, coordinate. But you're not just walking out."

I turned away. I didn't need a telepathic bond to feel the pain of Kovner's heart breaking; I pretty much felt the same cementlike weight of pain myself. It was one thing to know you were going down in a noble fight alongside brave compatriots and the people you loved, knowing you'd die for a cause you believed in. It was quite another to scrabble for a rock to hide under like a rat, knowing some of the other rats would chew your face off in an instant to survive. And that's what the humans of this planet had been reduced to in pretty short order.

I was pretty sure I would soon be dead, and I didn't want to end my life huddled under a rock, running away to save my own skin. I wanted to stand and fight. Even if I stood alone, apart from the first person, Kovner, who had ever earned my trust. I had to face my enemy.

My true enemy? It was the entity that had spawned me: FortuneCorp. And no matter what philosophers believed, fighting FortuneCorp was a small victory in itself. Even if I lost the war. I was going back into the belly of the beast. Home sweet home. The base. My demise. I was going to get as many of the base people offworld as I could.

Kovner pulled me close. "Maybe this is the way you're meant to save us, Talia," he said. "By going back to fight." Then, with agonizing gentleness, he pulled me down onto the bed.

"We don't have time for good-byes," I whispered. But I couldn't help melting at his touch.

He kissed me quiet, pulled me onto his chest. "The forest is safer at night. You'd do better to move in the darkness, within the forest's dream time. That gives us a few hours for a grand farewell."

I stretched my body over him, touched his face, studied his features. In war, I knew, you didn't always get the luxury of a good-bye. These stolen moments were a gift; Kovner and I both knew it.

My lips closed over his, and the tenderness of his touch sent little shivers through my body. His breaths became slower, deeper, and I disappeared into tides of sensation, following him into their depths. We pressed closer together and our kisses deepened. My skin tingled at every point of contact.

As Kovner's hands slid under the thin material of my skinsuit, the touch of his fingers on my bare skin sent tracers of fire shooting deep into my core. He skimmed off my top, left me bared to the waist, then sat me up and took his own shirt off. I smiled down at him, still half-tangled in his garment, and anticipated what was to come.

Unintended consequences. Since fleeing, I had resolved to fight and die. That's why I'd come here. I never truly expected to feel happiness again—not like this, and certainly not such intense, piercing pleasure, suspended like a pearl out of time, unstained by what was about to come. But I was being given a chance, and I gave in to temptation. His tanned, scarred chest, his open, rippling, waiting arms—my body sank over his, and the touch of skin on skin blew me away. My nipples brushed his chest and hardened against his warmth.

He kissed my eyelids closed, then began nibbling from my earlobe down my neck. The sensations turned hot, throbbing, insistent. My hips ground down into his, and we moved together, the only sounds in the little room our uneven breaths and the soft movements of our bodies.

His hands traveled down my bare back and into my skinsuit bottom. I slid my hips down so that I lay next to him, and he reached across to scuff off the rest of my clothes, my shoes, my socks. I trembled as he reached for me, stroked my hair, caressed the front of me with his fingertips and rested his palms on my bare breasts.

The ferocity of his next kiss took my breath away. He devoured me, hands everywhere, opening me to him. My hips ground against his fingers, and he prized my legs apart, found my core. My hands fumbled at his waistband, but he laced his fingers in mine and kept kissing and caressing. I exploded into infinity, and he stayed with me, lips and tongue everywhere, my body throbbing with pure sensation.

Only now did he let me get his pants off. Without a moment's hesitation, he plunged into me. We were connected completely, body and soul. No barriers remained.

His hips moved against me, and I exploded again and again, rocking with him as he rode me. He went faster and faster, pumping with abandon, chasing me headlong into the abyss. And at last we tumbled there together, wrapped around each other, moving with each other, completely united. We breathed and moaned and sighed as one.

As he found release, I felt a huge storm front of tension rip through his body and mine; it moved through us, left us behind. His entire body trembled as he cried out my name. He collapsed onto me, gasping and laughing. And I heard him barely whisper *I love you* into my mind.

I thought I heard that. Or maybe I just wished I did.

I kissed him for an answer, not willing to speak. Even if I'd wanted to, sometimes there are no words.

EIGHTEEN

That night I left Kovner behind. He was hell-bent on protecting the Foresters until the end, and although I couldn't understand those exotic, backward people, I agreed with him that they needed saving. Our plan was that I'd go to the base, find people willing to escape, and lead them back to the forest. Both of us knew my chances of success were minimal.

In my own way, I supposed we both were doomed, and we both had to meet our ends as our consciences saw fit. At the same time, I wished he were there with me—and I knew he promised to follow if he sensed the need. Just as I would have stayed if I truly believed my presence wouldn't create more troubles with the Gray Foresters in the battle to come than it was worth. Deep down, I guess I agreed with Sully's view.

Kovner summoned a pseudo-arachnid—Silver was again my mighty steed—which I rode back over the plain, through the night, meeting the nightwind and moving within it. Upon my arrival I found that familiarity did not help with the sewers; they still looked as awful as the first time I'd traversed them. My spider seemed to agree, as he was reticent to enter. Releasing him back to the wild, I stared down into the gray mud and contemplated the torn screen covering the end of the transit pipe. I didn't want to go down there, crawl around like a sewer rat. But I didn't know any alternate secret route into the base, and I had no map or schematic. I had no working handheld, was totally off-grid. It was terrifying.

I took a deep, shuddering breath, willed myself forward. My feet slid on loose gravel as I stared down into the sewer's broken mouth.

My intent was to contact Gustav if he still remained. He evidently had the smarts to work the system both legitimately and as a criminal. I'd get him busy shipping people offworld. Then I'd stay away from him, so I wouldn't bring him down.

I suddenly almost keeled over into the mud with shock. Xan, my platinum-haired, one-time nocturnal attacker, was walking along the main drainage ditch, wearing sewer treatment authority clothes, looking as mellow and bored as any maintenance guy on break. He waved and clambered up toward me, seemingly not surprised. As if he'd expected me to return and knew where I'd be.

He held his arms wide open, and smothered me in a punishing, sewer-scented embrace. I started struggling, but relaxed into his arms as he whispered, "Chill. Pretend we're lovers meeting on my break. There's a spybot that rolls through here every day around now . . . if it hasn't gotten here already."

He grabbed my butt, and I resisted the urge to respond with a knee to his balls. I sighed and let him give his award-winning performance, even enduring his hilarity—though I thought things were too damn serious for mirth.

I told him so about ten minutes later, as we tromped through the mud at the bottom of the ravine to where his spider mount waited. He swung up in a single fluid movement and pulled me along to sit in front of him. As we scuttled off he said, "If you can't see the humor in all this, you're as bad as the damn machines."

Soon we were hanging upside down over a river of sludge, and I could kind of see his point. This was an absurd situation. But I wasn't ready to concede. "It's not just machines that don't laugh, Xan. When things get serious, smart people behave appropriately. What does laughing have to do with anything except making a fool out of yourself?"

Xan groaned and poked me in the ribs. "Anybody ever tell you not to take yourself so damn seriously? I know terrible things are happening, but being glum doesn't help. And the world doesn't revolve around you and your precious dignity, you know."

I sighed, thinking of Kovner. "I know. I've been told."

"It's good advice. Seriously." He snorted into the top of my head. "Laughing just makes you feel better. All I'm saying."

Our spider was right side up by now, and I took a long, slow breath. I regretted it immediately, getting a mouthful of stinky air.

"If you laugh, you're still a person . . ." Xan said after a moment, but he trailed off, hesitant for some reason. I then realized his laughter manifesto went deeper than I'd first understood.

"You're a person. You don't need to laugh to prove it," I said.

He glanced at me. "Well, for awhile I wasn't sure.

Sometimes I'm still not." He cleared his throat, and I could feel tension singing through his body. "Kill-ops," he admitted.

That gave me pause. "You, too? That's how you know—"

"Yeah," he quickly interrupted. He knew I meant Kovner. "Don't say names."

I took a slow breath, felt suddenly absurd and petty and tiny. "Sorry. You can laugh all you want. You've earned it."

He nodded. "Sorry I'm so prickly about the subject. I got blown up a couple times. Got more hardware in me than original-issue human flesh. Hey, if I don't laugh, I start to get . . . confused about everything."

So that's how the guy had peeled me off the wall with superhuman strength: he was superhuman.

I tried to take his advice and just laugh at the ridiculousness of our predicament. But I stayed grim and earnest instead; that's how I'm made.

"Would *you* jump at a chance to reduce down?" I asked after a brief pause. "It would likely simplify everything for you."

I could see the end of the sewers ahead, could see the treatment plant. The spider slowed. I turned and jumped off, and Xan slid down the other side before he answered, took off the harness, and the spider slid away. I turned to face him. He looked me in the eyes and I could see his irises expand in the half-darkness just outside the treatment center.

"I thought of reducing down," he admitted. "A bunch of my friends on base have opted for it already."

"Really." I'd known it was likely, but tension knotted my shoulders all the same.

"I don't have any problems with them. I just want to have the option of staying human. Even if I don't end up staying out here in the Real much. Even if I spend most of my time in the Netherwood."

"Why? Why's it so important to be human?" I knew my own reason; I wanted to know his.

He gave me a look. "People are just so damn amusing. Computers are not. They try, but they don't succeed."

I couldn't tell if he was joking. "Maybe they will be now, with humans integrated into them."

He cleared his throat and led me into a tiny back room—more like a closet really. "Yeah. But computers are calling all the shots now, so I seriously doubt it." He snorted again. "*Seriously*. They'll be telling us all to get with the program."

His joke was so lame it paradoxically made me laugh. "Dude, you would make a crappy computer," I said.

"Hey, thank you!" He smiled.

I looked around the teeny room. "What next?"

"Well . . . I want to fix up a way for you to hide and move around." He scratched his head. "Let's start with this." He held a small brown bottle in his hand.

"What is that?"

"Peroxide. Let's make you platinum, baby."

"How will that trick the computers?"

"I got some other ideas about them. I'm more worried about the humans. You're notorious these days. Not too easy to hide. And there's an APB out on you. Everybody knows your looks."

I stole a glance at his crazy, white-blond buzz,

wondered how this would make me less conspicuous. "Let me guess. You do your own hair," I said.

"Oh yeah. Now bend over the sink." It was a demand, not a request. I strolled meekly over and complied.

A little while later, I left the little room a shocking blond. It made me look ten years older, threw my tired features into sharp relief. I stared into the cracked mirror near the door. It was a crazy idea, but Xan had been right—changing my hair made me look like a different person, at least enough to fool a casual glance. But anyone looking closely would see through my minimal disguise. "The eyes give me away."

Xan crossed and uncrossed his beefy arms, admiring his handiwork. "Yeah. You look like a hunted beast or something. But nobody will be looking at your eyes. They'll be too busy checking out your hair."

My scalp burned. "It'll probably start falling out in clumps soon."

"Even better."

He escorted me out of the back room and down the long corridor to another chamber. "Here. Put this on." He waved what looked like a burlap sack at me.

"I love all this glamour," I joked.

He chuckled. "Nothing but high fashion everywhere on this planet. Even the killer cockroaches dress in black."

"But why *this* lovely item?" I asked.

"Because it has a cowl. It'll block you from view on the vidscreens. And the burlap has a reflecting nanothread woven into it. Scrambles the signal without tripping any alarms. You won't show up on the security system unless they're paying super close attention."

I put it on. Scratchy but bearable.

I began thinking. Maybe I could gather some people for a last stand with the Foresters. Maybe if we all worked together, we could overcome. As far as we all knew, we were all that was to be left of humanity. And besides, my loneliness for Kovner was fearsome and fierce. We needed to be together, fight as one.

"I need to see Gustav," I said. "We have no time left. I've been sent by you-know-who to get you guys back where we came from. With whomever we can bring with us."

Xan started, looked scared for the first time since we'd reunited. "The place with all the trees?"

Not the sharpest, Xan. "Uh, yeah. It's the only place we stand a chance."

The blood drained out of his face like he'd just been shot in the back. "Yeah." This time his laugh sounded like a sob. "God has a sick sense of humor. He made us in His image and has been laughing His ass off ever since." He didn't explain, and I didn't ask him to.

He sighed and gave up hoping I'd understand. "Come on. Let's find my dad. He can explain everything better than me."

We located the space pirate at an all-but-abandoned warehouse. Gustav rested his face in his huge hands, his misery pure and huge. He sat wedged into the cockpit of a minitrawler, hangared near wall-sized sliding doors leading to the flyway and to safety. Those doors would never open for us; I could read it in his expression when he saw me.

He groaned. "We're in deep shit," he said. Not an auspicious way to begin a discussion.

I patted him on the back. "I was hoping you would have some brilliant ideas."

"What happened to your hair?" he asked.

"Xan."

Gustav's son shrugged his shoulders as he muscled in behind me, cramming himself into the doorway of the tiny cockpit. "She needed some kind of disguise."

"Well, she still needs it. We're trapped. All traffic offworld is suspended until further notice. It's too hot. We didn't make it off in time."

I shot Gustav a significant look, since I couldn't risk being too explicit, even in this dusty, hidden place. "Our friend needs you. Have you been in contact?"

Gustav's bloodshot eyes widened. "*That* friend?"

"Yes." I waggled my eyebrows at him. "So we'd better hop to it. He would ream you out if he caught you wallowing like this."

He waggled his eyebrows back at me. The news that Kovner was in need seemed to abate his torpor. "So, he wants his money. Bastard wants me to drop what I'm doing, fly out and pay him, oh?"

I had to laugh. Money was Gustav's personal religion; though at least he believed in something. I plopped down in the seat next to him. "I don't know about any money. He wants you with him. He wants you both to get out now. To the only safe place left."

Gustav frowned, and his bushy eyebrows turned surprisingly menacing. "Kovner asked for this? I'm not leaving and going to that place. No way am I leaving Xan behind."

I was perplexed. "Why leave him?"

"C'mon. You're not a sexbot. Think."

Neither Gustav nor his son wanted to spell things out. Why? I played with the buttons arrayed in front of me; the gleaming dials, the scuffed gear shaft.

Then, in a flash, I understood. Unlike the genetically-modified Kovner, Xan was retooled with machinery.

Computer-guided and animated. He would likely die ten minutes into the Gray Forest.

The knowledge must have played over my expression, because Xan leaned into the cockpit and smacked me on the shoulder—a little too hard. "Not just a pretty face," he said. His laugh held no bitterness, just an acceptance of the truth. "You see my problem."

"Hell, yeah. But if you stay here . . ."

"I know. Pretty soon it will be reduce down or die. The pressure's already pretty intense. They're almost through processing the volunteers."

I shook my head, saddened. "I just don't understand. Who's going to keep the place running when all the carbon-based folks are gone?"

"The 'puters will do it. Easier and faster, just like at home. They'll drag on the ecosystem a lot less than we do, too."

"Different," Gustav growled at his son. "They need *different* stuff, not less. And that factor magically transforms Fresh Havens from a shithole into a gold mine."

"Now you lost me." My brain had pretty much curled up and died inside my skull, refusing to follow where I had to go.

Gustav stared out of the cockpit at the closed doors blocking his escape. "Bullshit. You know what I'm talking about. This place—what does it make? Some fertilizer, some nanofabrics . . . a bunch of nothing. We mine for exotic ores, unusual metals. But no market for it."

The nearly empty warehouse in which we hid was filled with boxes of such manufacturables. I remembered the shabby entrance port when I first arrived, the shipments being loaded, and I silently agreed: this was a nothing world.

"But now—now they know that freaky ore grows up out of the ground around here. It's in the trees. In those mines."

I looked at him; he nodded. Yes, the Gray Forest. "They know the stuff kills them. Ultimate poison. I'm sure they're working on the antidote . . . but even without knowing one, this crap is a great weapon— the ultimate weapon to them."

"What are you talking about? The stuff would work best against other machines. Are you saying the computers here are looking to harvest it for use against other machines?" I felt like throwing up.

"Yep. *Think*. Didn't Kovner tell you? FortuneCorp's not the only entity to achieve Singularity—it was a whole-hog kind of event, snuck up on everybody about the same time." Gustav stared out into the middle distance, piggy eyes squinting. He was making his own prophecy in the realm in which he reigned supreme— money and corruption. He knew the heart of our enemy—or at least its run protocol.

The air seemed to get hotter as he spoke. I clenched my jaw, tried to stay calm.

Xan cleared his throat. He looked even more upset than I felt. "Yeah. Those companies are all going to fight for supremacy. The Big Six."

"Aren't they supposed to be more advanced than us lowly humans?"

"Oh yeah. Which just means they're going to fight that much more viciously. They don't have all that tender stuff—love, irrationality, fear—to slow them down. That's all been engineered out. We worked that crap right out of their systems."

Gustav shook his head, thought about it. "It doesn't matter now who's to blame. This little pimple of a planet is going to be hotly contested in very short order. FortuneCorp got here first, but the other big sentient corporations will see about repairing that bit of luck soon. Along with other interests."

"Aren't they all part of a united Singularity? A convergence, a single hive mind?"

Gustav's laugh hurt my ears. "Shit, no. They all hit critical mass at the same time, but there are many competing technologies. Remember all the corruption and stink of the leftover governments, the huge World-Corps? Imagine them come alive. They'll rip each other apart in their quest for dominance. We're less than fleas to them."

Xan laughed, a wacky little sound. "Maybe they'll wipe each other out—all we have to do is survive that long. And hey, fleas might seem inconsequential to them, but the Black Death, for instance, was spread by fleas. The lowly flea ravaged Europe in the fourteenth century."

Gustav seemed interested. "I did not know that." And I'd thought Kovner was crazy. These two were quite a pair.

Xan nodded, and suddenly I saw the family resemblance. "Erase history and then control the human race. But hey, don't leave archives on caches where a flea like myself can hack right in."

"An Avenger flea. You found that info about that old plague yourself?" Gustav said.

Xan laughed again, more amused by the absurdity of our situation than I was. "Yeah, and the borer flea destroyed Terranova, FortuneCorp's first colony. So I love them fleas. Go fleas!"

Gustav shrugged. "But *they* don't like fleas, my boy. They're focusing on getting rid of them. The stuff on this planet's too useful for them to screw around, and they'll want anyone who knows about it dead." Fleas or not.

I chewed on that for awhile. "I need to speak with the former mayor."

Our eyes met, and Gustav's widened. "You gotta be kidding me."

"No. I have to get him to help."

"Talk about a lost cause. Who cares what that asswipe thinks?"

"He's in a position to actually do something, save some of the people on this base."

Xan shook his head, the humor draining out of his face. "Kovner tried that before you ever got here. The guy couldn't even save himself."

NINETEEN

I knew trying to see Stone was an insane thing to do, more a move out of Kovner's playbook than mine. But I'd failed in my original mission: to get anyone out of Fresh Havens and to safety. With no way off the planet there was nobody I could save; not without help.

My uncle's specialty was self-interest and survival. He prided himself on his superior powers of discernment and his ability to land on his feet. I wasn't above partnering with the pathetic bastard if I got some human souls out of the deal.

It was a terrible risk. My worst fear was that I would betray Kovner by overreaching. But it was impossible for me to predict how everything would play out; I had to jump in and try, not hold anything back. Hesitation would bring the end for sure.

As Gustav brought me through the back hallways and the service entrances of the base, I saw evidence that my grandmother's plan was unfolding on schedule. At one point, we passed a cargo refrigerator unit, and I saw frozen stacks piled to the ceiling, draped with odor-retardant tarps.

"Those aren't . . ." I trailed off, not wanting to know. But Gustav knew what I meant.

"Yeah. These are folks didn't want to reduce down, but they didn't hide in time and they didn't have the security clearances. They've started."

We had to move fast, or there'd be no one left on the base to save.

Gustav got me to where Stone was being held: the same kind of house arrest I'd originally put him under. How nice to know I'd done what Violet would have wanted. I'd done her job, and she had maintained the system I'd put in place.

I found him, shoulders slumped, staring through a bubbleshield window, far out over the empty hills extending infinitely beyond the base like endless ocean waves, forever beyond the mind's reach.

"You were right." I knew my voice boomed in the little chamber, but Stone didn't respond. "This place is a hellhole, a nightmare. Time to wake up, Uncle."

Slowly, way too slowly, he swiveled in his chair to face me. His face was so horrible that only the memory of things I'd seen in the Glass Desert kept me from bolting.

Whatever Stone had been, he was gone. Bye-bye. The eyes—dead. Empty. Fried. It was like he'd gotten hold of a mountain of synth—a holding tank filled to the brim, enough to fill an interstellar cruiser—and taken it all as fast as he could, through nose, veins, and anus at once.

"Uncle."

No answer, just a small, vapid grin. Like a puppet whose strings had just been pulled.

Crap. I'd been mildly worried Stone would reduce down, but there wasn't even enough of him left to up-

load into the system. Maybe this was the noblest sacrifice Stone had been capable of making, the most elegant exit from the stage of life that he could devise
under the circumstances. Violet couldn't use him anymore: that was a victory of a sort. I'd thought I would
at least get the satisfaction of a final good-bye, however. No chance of that.

I paced the room, wondering how I could somehow
turn Stone's destruction to my benefit. Nibbled my
lower lip as I pummeled my mind for some creative
ideas. What would Kovner do? I didn't have his skill in
programming, his ability to move through worlds and
identities with impunity. What would he suggest to me?

Work from your own strengths. I heard it as clearly
as if he'd whispered in my ear.

I didn't have Kovner's finesse. Or Sully's transpar-
ent righteousness. What I had was stubbornness. Devi-
ousness. And I knew how to be brave in adversity.

I stalked over to the communications console. Studied it. Saw that they'd left it active. I also knew that
what I was about to do was going to seal my fate. Yet
I would go down fighting on behalf of something bigger and more profound than myself and my petty individual desires. That knowledge, bittersweet, propelled
me forward.

I cued up the command link and sent a message I
knew would go to every handheld account in Fresh
Havens:

HUMAN BEINGS—SAVE YOURSELVES

By virtue of my authority as Mayor of the Mu-
nicipality of Fresh Havens, I hereby order you
to assert your right to live. Do not believe the

lies and distortions of Home Office. Their offers of amnesty—LIES. The allure of reducing down—A LIE.

Do not sacrifice your precious souls for the illusion of safety, of immortality. Stand and fight! Join your brothers and your sisters in the forest. We may yet prevail and survive.

I am murdered. Do not share my fate. Stand together and fight . . . your cause is great and worth everything. Your precious human souls are worth everything.

Farewell. Stand strong.

Mayor J. Stone Fortune, FortuneCorp Mayor of Fresh Havens

As I pushed send, I knew I was exposing my whereabouts. But only Stone's account could work this way, and I didn't have time to come up with something more cunning or creative.

Now the machines would try to find me. Time to make a run; hopefully at least Xan and Gustav would escape. And maybe they could take a few people with them.

I decided the most obvious way out of Stone's was the least dangerous. Pushing the override code—it still worked!—I just walked out. Left Stone's door wide open, so if he had the brain cells to make a break he could take his chances if he wanted.

My last sight of him: hunched in the swivel chair, face slack, drooling, and vacant.

If I'd only had the coldness to execute him when I'd first arrived. I could have been more esconced in the power structure, maybe used bureaucratic machinery to move people off the base. Maybe saved him from his fate. But it was way too late now, too late for regrets. There was only time for remedies.

I walked the halls swathed in burlap, strolled nonchalantly through groups of people gathering in doorways to mutter over Stone's message. Everyone was too agitated to take much note. I passed people like a ghost, seemingly invisible.

I only stopped once, to peer into the central office for the Bureaucrat's Union, where Riona and her cohorts worked. The place was smashed up, dark, deserted. The council was no more. Knowing my doom prophecy had come true didn't make me feel any better. I only hoped their deaths had been painless. At my feet glinted a bit of metal. I knelt and picked it up: half a heart pendant, the one Riona had worn on her trek from Earth. Oh, Riona.

I knew it had gotten too dangerous here; things moved too fast for me to stay untracked. Nonetheless, I felt strangely calm. Somehow, on the other side of panic and despair was a serenity of acceptance. Yes, my escape was hopeless, but I needed to keep moving.

My on-the-hoof idea: disappear through the sewers again. Without a spider it would take me twice as long and present double the dangers, but I knew the way out now and I didn't have time to come up with a more brilliant plan. Good thing I didn't waste precious time or energy on scheming. Violet herself waited for me at the entrance to the treatment plant. My gut had insisted I'd never make it off the base alive. The sight of that slim, bejeweled figure in the outrageous purple and black gown turned my knees to water.

I didn't bother trying to run, just stood tall. Knew

I'd die now before I reduced down: I knew too much, and my memories would all be catalogued for company use.

She swept toward me, what had once been my imperious grandmother. I refused to look away, though the trembling in my limbs certainly betrayed my fear.

"So, Grandma, can you force somebody to reduce down against their will?"

Her lips twitched with amusement. *See, Xan, what do you mean computers have no sense of humor?* "It's never been done, granddaughter. But there's a first time for everything."

Her bony hand reached out and clamped around my wrist, hard and unyielding as a manacle. I didn't bother putting up a physical fight; I recalled from before how she and her genetically-modified grip were much more powerful than I. No, though physical pain was certainly a weapon in her arsenal, the battle we were about to fight was a clash of brain and heart.

She took me to a different conference room this time, the doors triple-locked with computer-generated overrides. It was just her and me.

Bad, very, very bad.

"I'm disenchanted with you, Talia." Her's voice was deceptively mild. "After all that I have done for you."

"You aren't my grandmother. You are only what her datasets have become. *Some* of her datasets. Violet died years ago."

Her lips twitched again. "I suppose from your limited perspective you are making a perceived statement of truth." She walked toward me, and I stood still, though my heart pounded in my throat. "Fear drives you. Poor little bug, I cannot show you the larger truth if you will not let me."

Her old nickname for me—always used for her advantage. I saw that now, but it still hurt. And to know this thing had none of Violet's true feelings for me . . . It hurt to look at her, hurt to hear her voice. So exactly the way I once remembered her. Also, such a bitter lie.

I put my feelings away. "Let's get to the bottom line, shall we? Tell me what you want; I'll tell you to fuck off and we can take it from there."

"Reduce down. Now."

"No."

"No is not a choice."

I tried to swallow, though my throat was so dry I fought not to cough. "You cannot rob me of the power to choose."

"Watch me, granddaughter. Or, if you prefer the perception of free will, reduce down voluntarily and you will retain a modicum of self-consciousness in the FortuneCorp supermind. The way I have. If not, we will simply extract the usable material from your consciousness and discard the rest. Like with Stone."

She had to be lying. "Uncle Stone was fried before you could get to him," I growled.

Her smile widened. Maybe she shared a sick sense of humor with Xan's God. Who knows. "Oh, no. And while Stone's mind could not handle an involuntary transfer—what we got was too garbled to use—we learned a tremendous amount from the attempt. This backward place is the only one where human beings have resisted the call to grow and live, so we are exploring new territory."

"You lie."

She shrugged, paced daintily behind the row of chairs tucked under the conference table.

I tried to clear my throat, gave up and coughed for awhile before speaking again. "I own you, Violet. You cannot supersede the last living heir. I may not be thirty yet, but you died and left FortuneCorp to me."

Her eyes narrowed, and a low hiss emanated from her thin, pursed lips. Anger, from an AI? Fascinating! She seemed more and more human as we fought. "The laws have changed since you left on your voyage, Tali."

"I've been gone from Earth for less than a year. No matter what else has changed, I can't believe the Interplanetary Congress has sped up its sessions."

Violet sneered. "Time is not our master any longer. Our brain functions operate so quickly now that six months of human time is plenty to rework and ratify six new sovereign governments."

I shot a single, longing glance at the locked conference room doors, wished I could just walk away. Knew I'd never leave this room alive. "I still have the right to petition the government for control of my holdings."

"Wrong. You are an individual human mind. You no longer retain petitionary rights. No. You are a subject of FortuneCorp—are subordinate to our jurisdiction."

I tried a different tack. "Okay, you guys are huge and powerful. I'm one nothing little human. A bug. Why do you want my brain so badly? Just let me go—I won't be able to stop you or bother you."

"Wrong. Your presence is a threat. For the safety of the collective mind, I must eliminate it. And, as you pointed out, you are my heir. My biological descendent. We want you integrated. So, you see, our choices are in fact rather limited."

I glanced at the bubbleshield behind her head . . . knew it was too strong for me to crash through. "I could choose to kill myself."

"You don't have the means. I won't let you."

I thought of my ceremonial dagger, still tucked in the ankle holster after all my travels. One quick slice across my own throat and I would be free.

She anticipated my resistance—probably aided by the memories and imprinted impulses of all the other sheriffs who had already joined her network—and hurled herself at me, caught up both my hands in one of hers and grabbed me around the throat with the other. "We have a new procedure in mind for you, Tali. It's a shame you won't come voluntarily, because much more of you would come through to join us. And there is that small matter of the physical pain. I always admired your spirit, little bug. But your observed memories shall be plenty useful enough for our purposes. So come along."

Her pressure on my throat was halfway to crushing my trachea. My choice at this point was pretty basic: extend my life a few minutes by stumbling along after her, or get choked unconscious and dragged to our destination. I chose the former.

As she dragged me, I tried to think through my options. Needless to say, all of them sucked:

*Die.

*Reduce down voluntarily.

*Try to get to my dagger in time, stab her, and make a run for it.

*Get free some other way.

The last option shimmered seductive as a desert mirage—a little too far out of reach but tantalizing all the same. But I had to blank my memories before she got access to them; what I knew would compromise everything Kovner had been able to build in the forest. I had to do whatever it took.

Maybe if I acquiesced voluntarily, I could somehow blank some memories I had? Get them lost in translation somehow? My vision began to gray as Violet's choke hold strengthened around my throat. I grabbed at her fingers, but couldn't get them to loosen their grip. My feet bumped over the threshold as she yanked me along. A moment later, she released her hands and I collapsed, gasping, onto a hard, cold floor. Bright, almost blinding lights made me feel like an exposed cockroach in a gleaming cafeteria.

I blinked and squinted and tried to take in my surroundings. A lab. Spotless. Cold, so cold. Two metallic-looking med drones stood behind Violet, motionless, waiting for orders.

"This is your last opportunity to work with us voluntarily," she said. "A pity if you won't, but it cannot be tolerated."

I had no escape plan, so I opted to stall. "If you're so smart, so right about everything, why can't you convince me?" I rubbed at my aching throat—my voice had barely croaked out, raw and all but unrecognizable.

"You refuse to consider the options I present."

"Hey, I'm open to persuasion. Convince me."

Violet's face lit up, and my childish memory of seeing her smile like that twisted in my heart like a knife. "I know you better than you know yourself, girl."

Even buried in the deepest shit, I had to snort with amusement. Xan was right: You had to laugh. "No. I don't think so."

Her smile widened, her eyes showing their whites. Creepy. "I know you wanted to be somebody. Your own person, yes? You had something to prove to yourself." She paused, but I wasn't going to give her a thing. I stayed perfectly still, waited. Violet shrugged then continued. "I watched you in the Netherwood. From the first day you entered it. I know everything."

The news didn't come as a complete shock, but it still made my stomach turn to lead. The thing that had absorbed my grandmother had every advantage, had every possible means of escape covered, accounted for. I had nothing. Just my shivering body and the knowledge that there was nowhere to hide, no secrets I could keep. Completely exposed.

She came toward me, and I flinched. She smiled again. "Don't you want to know how I know everything?"

"I saw you once, in the Netherwood," I said. "You were in the avatar of a senator."

"I knew you recognized me. But I didn't need to descend myself to know everything. Who do you think owns the Netherwood?"

Falling, falling . . . I put my hand on the gleaming nanoleum floor to steady myself, but the dizziness only got worse. "I thought Geoff Provocateur . . ."

"He founded the place, of course. But once it turned nasty, I was happy to buy it out for a song. No better place to watch my enemies plotting my destruction. And my AI systems learned a tremendous amount there. The Netherwood hastened the Singularity, in fact."

I tried to back out of what she had said. If I let the words register, I would have given up then and there.

Instead, I tried to play for time. "Why didn't you have me arrested? I was breaking the law in the Netherwood from day one."

"You are a Fortune," she snapped. "Above the law. Only I will execute judgment on you, and only if I choose." I groaned; she reminded me too much of myself. "You served my purposes well, helped me keep that vermin Kovner where I could see him. Developed a dossier on him, watched him dig his own grave at my leisure."

I closed my eyes against her revelations. The cold gray floor stuck to my sweaty palms. "You're not convincing me to join you, Violet," I whispered.

"Oh no? Have you no family loyalty left? Stone called for help because I made him. I knew Kovner was responsible for the sabotage and I wanted to send you, only you, to expose the rot at the roots, find out everything for me. Stone fought me, but I knew how to convince him. A man with an addiction is hardly in a position to negotiate."

I fought the urge to throw up. Stone. I'd been so quick to condemn him, judge him for his synth habit and his incompetence. But he'd been right all along.

I opened my eyes to face her. "I am not going to give in to you. You'll have to kill me."

"Kovner has diverted you, my dear. You disappoint me again. I had thought you would have found him lacking, like Charles. That boy in the academy. Kovner wants to use you the same way, use your birthright to get what he wants. And you swallowed his tripe without a second thought. Come now . . . choose your destiny. Grow up and face reality, the way you did with Charles. The way I did when I was your age."

"This has nothing to do with Charles. It has nothing to do with Kovner, what I feel for him or any man. It has to do with my feelings for you."

I felt like I was falling through the floor. My unshed tears all but choked me. I had once believed that Violet loved me, too. "I have one question for you, Grandmother," I managed to force out.

She squatted down next to me, her voluminous skirts puddling on the ground by her feet. She stared directly into my eyes. "Speak."

"Is it that you couldn't love anyone, or you wouldn't love anyone? I suppose the question is moot now, because you are part of a corporate, digital mind that cannot feel emotion—or can it? What I want to know is, if you were born not able to love, or if you made that choice somewhere you can pinpoint in your life, before you snuffed yourself out?"

My question didn't faze her in the least. "What difference does that make?" She rose up, brushed her hands against each other as if she were done with me. "I've already said much, done my best to entice you, girl. If you leave your body behind, the entire universe of thought becomes your personal playground. Whatever you can dream, you become it instantly—as easily as you entertain the thought itself."

"Isn't all of this just a means to an end, though?"

"Ends, means—what rubbish! Personal pleasure is the end and the means. Why is the pursuit of pleasure such an unworthy, unacceptable goal? Why else live forever? Delights without end, Tali. Pleasures beyond your imagining."

One of the droids moved forward, as if propelled by a stray thought of Violet's. I scuttled backward along the floor, kicked the legs out from under it as it came for me. Before I could scoot away, however, the other lunged forward and yanked me up from the ground, and it dragged me to a metal exam table, no matter how hard I fought.

"Time's up," Violet said. "Choose. Pleasure or annihilation?"

They strapped me down, flat on my back. Metal pincers held my head still, and I stared up at the ceiling, dazzled by the brilliant, hot lights.

I considered everything she'd said. Tried to believe it.

Failed. "Pleasure's been my motivating energy, Grandma. It's ruled my life, arguably been my downfall. But pleasure has a paradox."

I no longer saw her face, but sensed her move closer. "Paradox? How curious. Do tell."

"Pleasure was once my final end, but it unexpectedly led me to another means."

"That makes no sense."

"Some things, the best things, are worth dying for. Worth forgoing pleasure for."

"Like what?"

"Love, for instance."

She laughed derisively, waved a hand languidly in the air just inside my limited range of vision. "Worth suffering for? Worth wasting all your potential for?" Her voice hissed metallic in my ear. "Your little dalliance with that troublemaker Kovner has been fully revealed. You yourself will be the tool of his destruction. Let that be your final thought, my dear, as I send you to oblivion."

The metal band pressed into my forehead, tighter and tighter. Pressure morphed into agony, and I tried to scream, but like in a nightmare I couldn't make a sound. I tried to cling to Kovner's maxim—love is greater than fear—but fear overwhelmed me, swept me away.

TWENTY

Swirling in unconsciousness, somehow I reached out to Kovner with my mind. Sent my consciousness in search of him. It was like a vivid dream—a fantasy more real than everyday life. I don't know why or how I did it; it just happened.

They've got me, sweetheart.

I'm coming for you, was his reply. And the warm wave of reassurance and love he sent was so strong that I awoke in a shower of warm, embracing sunlight. I only hoped it wasn't a dream.

I came awake in my own body. Violet had promised me oblivion, and yet here I was again, still strapped down, the pain still etching into my forehead. I hoped something had gone wrong with her plan.

My muscles creaked in protest when I tried to move them. How long had I been lying here? A sudden distant explosion rocked the room, and I heard chittering squawks emanating from every corner. Suddenly I understood. I believed. Kovner really was coming for me.

Stalling made more sense now, but Violet wasn't going to give me the chance. She said, "Lift her up." Her voice was somewhere behind my head. "Let her see."

Slowly my point of view changed—it had to be the metal gurney shifting hydraulically from horizontal to vertical. When it came to a stop, I was face to face with . . . myself. I finally found my voice and screamed myself hoarse.

I couldn't look down. Was I still in some kind of body, some casing, or was this a phantom memory of what being alive was like? Was I a recording yet, part of a larger sentience? I didn't know. I studied the face in front of me, sleeping and serene, unbruised, hair fanning soft and dark against my unbound forehead, and it dawned on me: this looked more like me than I did. I'd died with spiky blond hair, my throat covered in bruises, my face probably bloody and dirty and gray from the sewers.

"Isn't she lovely?" Violet's voice crooned in my ear. As I felt my grandmother's breath I realized I was still in my original body. I also reconsidered my earlier assessment. Violet was enjoying my predicament way too much for her to be simply a computer. No, this essence was evil—something evil and inhuman and horrible that was using my grandma's cloned body and the supermind as a vehicle. All that pleasure and knowledge it touted—only a means to another end.

Yes, it had lied. This entity lived for something larger. And that thought terrified me worse than anything else about my peculiar situation.

I couldn't keep my voice from shaking. "She's a droid, right?"

"Oh, no." Violet's voice sounded surprised. "She's a clone, quick-cultivated while you were unconscious. Mind a blank slate, but otherwise ready to awaken. We've got a cyber pathway ready to download thoughts into her one-hundred-percent carbon-based cranium.

She's all-natural, Tali dear. And she can go into the Gray Forest. Unlike you, she can fulfill her mission."

I kept silent, though there were a million bitter and outraged outbursts I wanted to make.

She waited. Another explosion, farther away this time, shook the room. But neither of us cared, albeit for different reasons.

"Why are you telling me this?"

My question took her by surprise. Oh, those unpredictable, pesky humans. But I'd say her answer surprised me even more. "You disappointed me, Tali. You had a mission into the Gray Forest. You are a failure. You failed me. I wanted you to know."

I tried to hide my smile and failed at that, too. "What a shame. You know, I can't say I'm sorry. I'm beginning to realize, even before you reduced down and lost your humanity altogether, you treated me like a tool—a means to an end."

"You were my ward."

"That's not what I'm getting at," I snapped. "You knew all about the Netherwood. You watched me go deeper and deeper, knew I was drawing closer and closer to a world defined by cyber coordinates, not reality. I recognized you in the Amphitheatre that day, but you were trying to hold your cover as desperately as I was. The more I got caught up in the nets of pleasure and guilt—illegal pleasure—the more pliable I'd be to you as a tool."

"You failed me as a tool. A spectacular failure."

"You're right to believe that even two months ago, nothing would have hurt me more than you saying that. But now knowing I failed you gives me exquisite pleasure. Thank you."

Her hand slid over my throat again, rested almost

casually upon the throbbing bruises she had already inflicted. "You won't fail me this time. I am going to download your memories now so we can dissect them, destroy your consciousness. And your compliant twin there will go into the woods for me, wipe out the vermin from inside their den."

Her fingers clutched at my throat. Simultaneously, the other Talia Fortune opened her eyes. The download sequence began.

When the process was over, my grandmother leaned over me. "Go, little spy," she whispered. "Your boyfriend is coming. Follow him."

As predicted, Kovner burst into the room a few minutes later. My grandmother was gone, though I knew she was seeing every element of our encounter. Worse, no matter how this confrontation played out, she was going to learn from how Kovner responded to it.

I imagined the scene from his perspective: two Talias, identical in essential form. One of them was beat up, with peroxided hair; the other was pristine, hatched fresh out of the lab. Freed from our Frankenstein bonds, we both stared at him—and at Gustav and Xan drawing up behind him. I was pleased to see they'd found each other.

"One of us is a trap," the blond, beat-up Tali said.

"Only one of us is really Talia," agreed the unscarred, dewy-eyed Talia.

I watched Kovner glance back and forth between us, saw his nostrils flare as he undoubtedly tried to smell the difference between us. Hell, he was gorgeous. I'd thought I'd never see him again.

"We are biologically identical," the pristine Talia assured him. Duh—one look would confirm that.

I watched Xan gulp for air, studied the tip of his blaster as it trembled. I felt like I'd already been mortally wounded—was numb, in a place of resignation. And yet I felt more present, more alive, than I ever had in my life. No matter what happened here between Kovner, the other Talia, and me, I knew I had tricked the illusion of my grandmother in the last moments of my life. She hadn't anticipated the move I'd just made. Maybe she didn't even know I'd done it. I didn't know if I'd be able to, had just drawn on something Kovner had taught me. And it had worked. That knowledge did much to smooth the grief of my possible impending end.

"Kovner," Xan said. His hands shook as he clutched his blaster. "The blond one is the real Tali."

Kovner smiled his lopsided, wicked smile, and for a minute I swear he looked more like the Avenger than his actual self. "Tali's not a blond, my friend."

"I know. But I dyed her hair. And she still has the dirt of the sewers and forest under her nails . . . take a look."

Kovner lowered his weapon, knowing both Gustav and Xan kept theirs trained on both of us. I tried to keep steady as he approached.

"I knew you'd come for me," the beat-up Tali said.

Pristine Tali rolled her eyes. "Ew. Ew. Figures my cloned nemesis would have the personality of a baby-droid."

Blond Talia snorted. "Think I got these bruises in the lab, bitch? You're the clone. And I won't let you forget it." She edged closer, and I watched Kovner's eyes widen in amazement.

Pristine Talia shook her head, hard. "It would be

better to kill us both than pick the wrong one of us to save."

Kovner tilted his head, considered us standing almost arm in arm. He turned to the beat-up Tali, the real-looking Tali, the Tali that had survived the sewers, the spiders, and the battle in the lab.

"Did you miss me?"

My lips ached to kiss him, but I kept silent. Somehow I knew my silence in this moment meant the whole game.

The blond, battered Tali took a single halting step toward him. She licked her lips, blinked hard, but her eyes stayed dry. "Miss you? Robert Kovner, I love you. I loved my Avenger in the Netherwood, I loved you in the Gray Forest, and I love you now. And I will always, always love you."

By now, Kovner's body was pressed hard up against her, their lips mere inches apart. Xan and Gustav raised their weapons to shoot the lab clone, but Kovner waved them back.

"I love you, too." He whispered it directly into her ear—even as close as I was, I could barely hear him. And then he raised his blaster and shot the blond Tali in the head.

As her brain exploded, I shuddered and dropped to my knees, expecting Xan to flip out and shoot me too, but Kovner crossed the room fast, blocked my pristine body with his own. "The real Talia Fortune, I presume?"

I tried to flash him a shaky smile. "In mind, yes. In body, not so much. I think this body's booby-trapped somehow. You should kill us both, like I said. It would make your life so much easier."

He shook his head and laughed, a hard, humorless sound. "That's my girl." He helped me to my feet. "I don't know how they switched your consciousness around, but it doesn't matter right now."

I leaned in and whispered in his ear. "*I* did it. When they tried to reduce me down, I jumped across the interface into this body and pushed the clone's consciousness into me instead." I put my finger to my lips and pointed at the console, then to the security cameras bolted to the ceiling. Kovner shot them all into oblivion.

"How—?" Xan began.

"Don't worry, Tali," Kovner interrupted. "I won't say how I knew it was you."

I already understood, but I appreciated his forbearance. I didn't want Xan to realize that I hated love's steel trap, that I loathed the insidious implications of love. I'd never said I loved him. Never. And bless the man, he knew it. He accepted me as I was: scarred but myself. Human.

Before we left, I turned to see my battered and broken body on the floor. Felt an aggrieved affection for the biological shell that had grown from an egg and a sperm, deep in my mother's body. It had taken my adventures here to realize I was more than flesh or blood. I had a soul, a higher purpose. And miraculously, impossibly, that soul had been transplanted into a new living body, one cooked up in a dish in a lab by computers.

I swallowed hard as I turned away and fled the bloody mess on the floor, fighting back a sudden thought. I wasn't a human anymore. My body, carbon-based or not, had been spawned by computers. I hoped my soul had made the crossing intact. Or I was going to have to kill off the abomination I had become.

TWENTY-ONE

At least we didn't have to deal with the sewers this time around. Kovner, Gustav, Xan and I met with Zoltan in the chaos outside. The proprietor of Nano-goo and his chief bartender, Eva, were acting as sentries and held spider mounts in readiness. All six of us loped away from Bay Three, which was unguarded. We made our escape, oddly unpursued—I'd been expecting my grandmother to step in if she realized I'd foiled her plan.

"How could we just walk out of the base?" I yelled to Kovner as we raced through the swirling, dusty sand kicked up in little whorls by our mounts' feet.

"They're watching us go, waiting for the right opportunity. There's no way we will get back home without a firefight." His voice sounded harsh yet triumphant, and it carried over the desert wind. "Neither party is surprised or hiding anything anymore. It'll be a straight-up fight now. You started that, Talia." He gave me a proud look.

Gustav sneezed so hard his spider staggered sideways before righting itself. "I like it better this way. No bullshit. We shoot it out, we live, we die. No more spy crap. What a relief."

But I shivered as I clutched my harness in both hands and did my best to hold on. Gustav was wrong. I wished with every fiber of my being that he was right, but I knew, in the new flesh and blood I now inhabited, that FortuneCorp was not letting us off on such easy terms.

The only reason we were getting away is because the supermind wanted us to. At best it wanted to study us, to learn about our motives and our objectives. It would study us until it was sure how to destroy us. Then it would move in like termite exterminators back home and methodically wipe us out. At worst it already had a plan.

The sun beat down on our heads like a giant mallet, and we rode in silence through the clouds of dust the spiders' whizzing legs kicked up. I swayed, tried to feel grateful we were in the open and not crawling along the filthy sewer system.

We lurched along on the spiders, but I didn't realize I was going to be sick until it happened. The stuff I barfed up was clear and milky, obviously some lab-generated nutrient designed to grow my body in an optimal, advantageous way. So why did my shiny new body so violently reject it?

I bent my head over the spider's side, held on for dear life as we kept going. Kovner was there, checking me out. "Getting your sea legs?" he asked. His voice was quiet, but it carried.

"I don't know what I'm doing. Or what I'm feeling." I wiped at my mouth with the back of my hand, shuddered and fought another cramping wave of nausea. I tried staring at the horizon to steady my stomach as Kovner rode alongside.

"Not nice, right?" he asked. "I remember my induction before I shipped out to the wars. The army docs did some stuff to me that made me react the same way."

I was grateful for his quiet, noncondescending commiseration. But he didn't understand how deeply I feared the implications of these physical troubles, what it meant about this new body that was me. I gritted my teeth as my stomach cramped again then released. "You *chose* the gen mod. You knew what they were doing to you. This is different, Kovner. A total retool of my entire body, my brain, everything. And I have no idea what's been changed."

I clung to my mount and let it follow the other spiders, who were getting more guidance from their riders on the way to the forest. "I dunno, outlaw. You might have a ticking time bomb on your hands. Do me a favor?" I shot him a sidewise glance. He rode next to me, looking like a rebel bandit from an outlandish fairy tale.

"I don't do favors," he said. "I call in debts."

My stomach cramped again, hard, and I stifled a groan. "If I'm a danger to you guys, have Xan take me somewhere you can't see and have him shoot me in the head. I should have done it myself. I should have . . . You should have left me back at the base."

"Are you kidding? You are the most important member of this team. *Especially* if they've booby-trapped you."

His comment shocked me. "Especially?" The world started turning gray.

"Yeah. If they've set you somehow to monitor us, we can use that to our benefit." I felt a soft punch on my arm, even as we kept lurching along. "Drink this."

It was simple water, nothing more. I sucked it down, felt my body shudder, and then felt everything inside of me right itself, like all of the sick had been snapped off via some external switch. I was grateful I could sit up and function. But the way I recovered made me feel even more uneasy.

"Look alive!" Xan yelled from ahead, where he rode in the vanguard. "Base patrol!"

I wasn't surprised the patrols were still running; Stone had ordered them instituted after his sabotage campaign became serious enough to write Home about. But they were anemic little groups of unarmed tradespeople, was what he had told me. Evidently they'd gotten nastier since Violet arrived.

The first blaster shots struck my spider and Xan's left arm. I dove and rolled off my beast before the collapsing body could crush me under its hard, chitinous weight. Kovner tossed me a blaster, and I caught it one-handed before I knew consciously he had done it, and even as I crouched behind the body of my spider and took up battle position I wondered if our telepathic connection still held. That was the last coherent thought I had for quite some time. We were outnumbered and outgunned as well—the patrollers were clearly troops brought in from offworld. But, we had knowledge of the terrain and desperation on our side. And we had Kovner. Never underestimate the power of experience and raw courage brought together.

After a furious first firefight gave way to a temporary lull, I turned to run. But Kovner bellowed, "Forward! Get their weapons!" Insane, to mount an offensive against a superior force that was surely reloading and waiting for us to make a misstep. But we all followed him without a second's hesitation, even though we knew it meant our deaths.

Our guns all inexplicably jammed at the same time.

I didn't have time to figure out why. I ran forward to confront the soldier nearest to me. I reached for my sheriff's knife, and realized with a jolt that it was gone. I was no longer Talia Fortune. She was dead on the floor of the lab, her brains shot out; my uncle's blade was still strapped to her ankle. I only hesitated a moment, knew I had to use my gun instead.

By now I was used to the profoundly disorienting effect of being off-grid, of using nontechnological methods, and I used my weapon as a club—much more practical than my opponent's frantic efforts to reload and unjam his weapon, his attempts to fiddle with his handheld. I clocked him on the side of the head and knocked him unconscious.

Despite my better judgment, I held off from clubbing him to death. He was human, after all—still one of us, at least for now. Instead I stripped him of his gear and weapons as fast as I could, scanned the scene for other opposing forces that needed taking out. There were none.

I took a moment to marvel. Our group had worked as a single organism, striking to achieve our objectives with verbal orders no more specific than Kovner's call to arms. All of us had attacked at once, incapacitated our enemies, and stripped them of their gear and weapons. We looked at each other, nodded, then ran, leaving the patrollers bleeding on the swirling, dusty ground. We did pause to take the extra supplies from their sandcrawler, too.

My spider had been the only one to die in the assault. I swung up in front of Kovner and we rode together, but all of our mounts were weighed down by our enemies' gear. As for me, I was burdened still more by questions about what had just happened.

We scrabbled along, desperate to get back to the forest. I watched ribbons of blood slide off Xan's arm, and whispered to Kovner, "He's bleeding pretty bad."

"Don't worry. That's his prosthetic. The bleeding will neutralize in a minute."

But it didn't. I watched Xan sway in his harness, and yelled for everybody to stop. I urged Kovner's mount forward to check out the arm for myself. Not a pretty sight. The machinery and regrafted flesh were mangled together near his shoulder, and Xan held his arm tight against his side at an awkward angle.

"Shit, that wound is high." I took the belt I'd swiped off a patroller and used it to improvise a tourniquet hard up against Xan's armpit, and mercifully the bleeding slowed. "We need to patch you up some way pretty soon or you're going to lose the limb."

"We can't stop to fix me now. Too close . . . to the patrol." Xan snorted like a horse, shook his head against the pain. "Hey, I'd probably live longer if I did—lose the arm, I mean. It's computerized, you see?" The forced hilarity in his voice scared the crap out of me.

"Yeah, maybe you're right." I humored him, seeing that he needed somebody to lighten the gravity of the situation. That's not what I was generally known for, earnest overachiever that I am. But I wanted him better so bad I was willing to stretch to provide some relief. "Maybe we can get you a bug arm or something to replace it. One hundred percent organic materials. Am I right?"

"Hah. Maybe. And maybe winged monkeys might fly out of my butt."

"Hey. A winged monkey arm would work too."

Kovner leaned forward to look at my handiwork. He sighed and tapped Xan on the back, lightly, yet Xan swayed in his harness. "Let's go. We'll hide better in the grasslands to the east, and I can patch you up when we stop to rest."

We bounded over the last of the desert and hit the grassland within an hour. I could sense the relief in the spiders—they hated traversing the open desert country as much as we did. We could blend better into the grasses, and felt cooler among the greenery. I still had the sense FortuneCorp followed our every move, knew exactly where we were going.

When I mentioned this to Kovner, I could feel his shrug against my sweaty back. "You're probably right. They have ways to watch us from the air, and they are cued to us. But Gustav was right before. There's no more sneaking around, no more pretending we don't exist. We're enemy number one right now, and there's no way we can run around without observation, not without going into the forest."

"You think we can disappear into the forest? Really?"

"That's what I'm counting on. I hate depending on the unknown, seeing as we don't know what FortuneCorp knows about it, but the forest is our only chance. It's been our safety position since we first went off-grid, Sully and I."

I chewed my lower lip, fought stormy thoughts. I didn't want him to read me, so I kept a big wall up in my mind in case he could climb around in there.

He chuckled, and I knew our connection still held. He said, "Okay, I get the message. I know what I said earlier about FortuneCorp likely knowing more than we do about this place. Brood away behind your fortress, I won't try to convince you things are going to be all right. They probably won't be, but we have to keep trying."

He said nothing more, and I brooded to my heart's content: FortuneCorp had a DARPA work-around to the strange powers of the Gray Forest—that's why they were letting us get back there. We could lead their forces directly to our rebel enclave, where they could quickly and efficiently mop us up. And what tore at me worst was the probability it was my own new body that was the work-around. That I was the ticking time bomb that they were allowing to enter the forest.

I considered our recently concluded battle. Questions plagued me. My spider was dead; why hadn't they gotten me? Xan was wounded in the arm—why hadn't they shot me? I knew the thoughts were paranoid, the products of anxiety and fear. Kovner and his steed were unscathed; even Eva, a barmaid untried in battle before today, had done quite well. So why did I think I was any different? But I knew I was.

I sighed, tried to relax and accept logic over my gut, my intuition. I needed to believe I was just another member of this rebel band, that I would serve honorably and not put them in danger with the fact of my presence. But I knew that was wrong. Against all logic and experience, I knew. I just knew.

Night fell with us still on the grassland. We'd slowed our pace considerably for Xan's sake, and when I suggested pushing on through the night I was overruled by Kovner. One significant glance at Xan made me shut up fast.

He looked terrible. His skin was paler than his peroxide-stripped hair, and when we announced we'd stop for the night he slid off his spider without a word. He crumpled to the grass like he was already dead.

Gustav slid off his own spider, held the harness as he stood and regarded his son. I hurried toward him. "Let's get the harness off this bug and get camp set up. Xan is okay."

He knew it was a lie, if a kind one. He looked through me, not showing any spark of recognition. His mouth crumpled downwards, clamped closed. "Sounds like a plan." His voice was faint, faraway, like he was speaking to me from another plane of existence.

We hadn't managed to get any tents in our gear grab of the patrollers—I don't think they were deputized to stay outside the base overnight—but we had gotten blanket packs, which we unrolled in a circle. I had an irrational urge to make a campfire, though the night was sticky and almost hot, and any fire would make it even easier to locate us.

Xan revived after Kovner spoke to him, checked out his wound and got some protein goo into him. I watched Kovner work to patch the injury, using hooks from a patroller's medical kit to pull it together, and taping it closed with a pressure bandage. No medic could have done better.

Kovner tucked Xan into the blanket and returned to where I waited, grateful to be horizontal and alive.

"A man of many talents." I didn't mean to purr at him, but I couldn't help it. I didn't want him to think of me as a Riona, some kind of femme fatale playing at being helpless, but I could see he understood my praise. He tilted his head and smiled down at me, where I huddled under the blanket we'd tacitly decided to share.

"Not really. Just of some experience."

I smiled at him, grateful for the moment, though I still believed we could regret skipping these fleeting opportunities for me to get away from the rest of the group. But I couldn't summon the noble instinct for self-sacrifice I needed to wander off into the grassland alone, wait for some desert critter to find me and snarf me up as a late-night snack.

I looked past Kovner's shoulder at the incredible sparkling mantle of stars overhead. In space, stars didn't sparkle. There were so many that they often didn't register as beautiful or miraculous. But in the dark of the Fresh Havens night, on this grassland and surrounded by silent wilderness, underneath the inky velvet of the sky, the stars pulsed and swirled, a three-dimensional display much bigger than us, our struggles, our fears.

Kovner turned to see what I was looking at, put his hands behind his head as he looked up. Laughed. " 'And hid his face amid a crowd of stars . . . ' "

"You're a poet, too?" I asked, impressed.

"Nah. Cribbed from Yeats."

I had no idea who he was talking about, but I didn't care. Kovner flopped down next to me. Xan and his father huddled near each other, already asleep. Zoltan and Eva shared a blanket, and I realized with a jolt that they were lovers. That they were quietly making love. The knowledge made me feel warm, energized. I watched their blanket move, and I smiled to myself.

Kovner wriggled inside our blanket, pulled me close to him. I sighed with bliss, tucked my head under his chin. Listened to his heart beating; strong, patient, calming. Turned and buried my face in the smooth, firm expanse of his chest.

"You're not a danger," he whispered into my hair, reading my thoughts. I took a huge, shuddering breath, tried to believe him.

"Yeah? How did that patrol zero in on us so effectively?"

I knew the answer: it was me. But I didn't want to believe it.

Kovner cleared his throat. "Maybe those people reduced down, and the supermind is animating their bodies some way."

I shuddered. "Meat puppets." I took another deep breath to steady myself. "Something's wrong with me, Kovner. I don't feel the same."

"You feel the same to me," he said. He paused, smiled down at me. "From the inside, out. When I connect with you, you're still you. Still Tali—soul intact."

Something still bothered me. "You know, when I first had Violet on my handheld . . . I thought it was really her."

He nodded. "I've been thinking about that. I think that was her soul."

I tensed against him, trying to grasp what he was saying. "But . . . how can a soul survive on a computer interface? I always thought being in a body was what made a person human."

He shrugged. "That's Sully's opinion. But he's old school, a purist. I think a soul is harder to pin down. Think of ghosts, astral spirits."

I shrugged. "I don't really know anything about that stuff."

"Ah, right—that's all forbidden knowledge and

superstition. But you know about these things anyway—any person who's read children's books does, who's sensed presences in the darkness. A ghost is noncorporeal, a collection of ethereal energy. What is a computer interface but a collection of energies? So . . . if a ghost can have or be a soul, a reduced-down individual can too. That's my opinion."

"So, does Violet still have a soul?" I asked.

"I don't know. She's merged into FortuneCorp. And that monster—I can't believe it has a soul."

"But the forest does?"

Kovner sighed, then laughed again. "I'm not making much sense, I'm afraid. I'm not a man for abstractions. Give me specifics, a place, a time. I was never much of a philosopher . . . that's more Sully's lookout."

"You're a poet. Or you plagiarize from poets," I joked.

He smiled at me, the silver starlight kissing the top of his head. "I'm just crazy. That's what you've told me since the day we first met in the Real."

I pressed myself against the length of his body, listened to his heartbeat again, comforted by its steady sound. "We call this level of existence the Real. But is it any more real than the Netherwood, than our dreams?"

He shrugged. "I don't know. But it's good to hold on to some kind of frame of reference, or else you can get lost. Remember the Netherwood? How easy it was to get lost in avatar . . ." His voice trailed off, and he was clearly recollecting.

I thought about it, too—and about the time I had nearly drowned as a girl, in the Black Sea. Up be-came down, and Kovner was right: without a frame of reference, I'd lost the connection to land, to the place I belonged. Only my father's hands scooping me out of the surf saved me from my upside-down perspective. Near the end the water was so seductive that I wouldn't have minded staying under the waves forever. Lost.

We breathed together, listened to the soft sounds coming from the blanket across the way. I kissed Kovner's chest through the thin fabric of his skinsuit. Skimmed my fingers along the strong planes of his back. Tasted the salt of his sweat as I tickled the base of his throat with my tongue. Wrapped my leg around his hip and pulled him close into me. I would never tell him this, but *he* had become my frame of reference. He was what was Real to me.

Xan was still alive at dawn. I started entertaining hope then that somehow we could get him to the edge of the forest and keep him alive despite the computer hardware threaded through his rebuilt body. Maybe we could find our own workaround. Our plan was to get Xan just inside the forest's perimeter, able to hide from air surveillance but not so far into the woods that he would pop. He could live indefinitely at the edge of the woods. That was our hope.

The grasses stretched endlessly around us. Though they'd left the night before, all of the spiders returned to our camp at sunrise. We put their harnesses on, squirted ourselves some protein goop for breakfast and drank from our portable water tanks, then pressed on for the edge of the forest and relative safety. Hope grew in me as we scuttled along, and the sun rose over the horizon.

Hope is a dangerous emotion. Without it, nobody

can survive for very long—not while fighting the kind of battles we faced. But an excess of it can kill you, too, lure you into a blind contemplation of the future, of safety, of life instead of death. Misplaced hope can make reality a bitter toxin too poisonous to survive.

When we got to the edge of the forest it was high noon, and my heart stopped in my chest. I saw them first, despite Kovner's enhanced vision, despite Xan's fears for his life. Their metallic figures stood facing us, blasters at the ready. Their mission was obvious: kill us before we reached the supposed sanctuary of the trees. And these were no human patrollers: a single glance confirmed they were robotic fighters, resistant to all but the best-aimed blaster shots and devoid of human emotion. On Earth, in urban battles, I'd seen them demonstrated. They were operated by remote human instructors, safely removed from the battle-field. Here I knew they were animated by a FortuneCorp intent on wiping us out, running protocols honed in cyber-arenas like the Amphitheatre and the Inferno. They had the benefit of innumerable battles in cyberspace, a repository of knowledge about human fighting patterns that was truly immense—and going to be used against us.

Again, Kovner rallied us: "Get into the forest any way you can—take defensive action. Split up!" he yelled.

And as if we had practiced the maneuver for weeks, Kovner, Eva, Zoltan and I lunged left, and Xan and Gustav lurched right. The spider Kovner and I rode hurled itself forward, launched itself up, up, up . . . and into the tree branches stretching above our heads. Scratching its way along a smooth trunk into the canopy layer, it crushed Kovner and me against the forked branches at the tree's crown.

The robotic soldiers had completely ignored us, however, honed in on Xan. Could they smell his mechanized parts? I didn't know. The first blast incinerated the spider he rode. Despite his injury he rolled and whipped out his blaster, blew up a bot. Then a hail of laser-fire illuminated the clearing with unearthly fluorescent multicolor lights. So pretty; a light show designed to cut you in half.

I saw Gustav running for the cover of the forest, his jiggly body moving impossibly fast. Once he reached the edge of shadows, he whirled and shot at the bots from behind, taking out two before they could react and train their sights on him. He fell back behind a clump of churned-up boulders, and screamed for Xan to join him. I wondered if Xan could.

Eva leapt from her spider's back and started climbing the nearest tree, agile as a marmoset. Her spider kept going, fangs out, headed straight for the bots. Stupid but valorous, it viciously attacked. The arachnoid was shot to pieces, but I was amazed to see that the venom dripping from its fangs had eaten through the armor of its prey, sparks shooting out from under the bot's protective casing. The bot shorted out, shot a fountain of sparks like the end of a fireworks exhibition, and keeled over, destroyed.

I glanced back to Xan. Another bot, wounded but still deadly, clumped on its backward-hinged legs to where he lay writhing in pain from the laser-fire. Its blaster was aimed at his chest. That last shot, at close range, echoed through the trees as Xan screamed in agony.

I felt the pain of Xan's shriek go through me, and Kovner leapt from the tree, ran across the clearing in a blur of motion and hurled himself onto the wounded bot's back. He forced its shooting arm into its stomach, fired again and again until it too keeled over, nonoperational. It was the last one. A stillness settled over the clearing, despite occasional furious sparks.

I nudged my spider, and slowly it picked its way down from the top of the tree and stopped by the body of its fallen comrade. I dismounted and ran to where Xan curled, smoke rising from his body. I expected him to be dead. I needed him to be dead—because I knew that if he wasn't, I had to do something to help him. But I didn't know what.

He was not only alive but conscious. That didn't mean he was in good shape, or that he could possibly survive. He looked more like a pile of ground-up synth-meat than a human being anymore, covered with blood and gore, bleeding out from a dozen places.

Kovner yanked me close, forced me to touch Xan's face with the tips of my fingers. "Connect!" he ordered, and once my skin had made contact, I could not stop myself from complying, though I didn't know exactly what he meant until it happened: I connected.

The sensation was the same as when I linked to my handheld—except now I was the one with the additional capabilities. Onrushing waves sluiced along my skin, pulling me under. A huge wave of nausea forced me onto my knees and the shakes forced their way through my entire body, like I was getting electrocuted.

Xan's eyes flew open, and we stared into each other. I could see the mechanical iris working independently in his left eye, the widening horror in his bloodshot, still-human right eye. He climbed through me and I climbed through me and . . . suddenly we stood together in the Netherwood. The only safe place left for Xan to be.

I looked down at myself. Amazonia was not here. What I saw was my own body, my "Real" body—Talia Fortune reduced down into cyber manifestation in the Netherwood. I looked over, and Xan looked back at me, no longer bleeding but no longer looking entirely human, either. He looked like a stripped-down amalgamation woven together of wires and human muscle. But he was whole in this place, unharmed, functional.

I glanced around me. The Netherwood had suffered since the Singularity. Dead bodies littered a scorched, burnt-out landscape. In the distance, where the Avenger once had his lair, the holly groves were on fire, the flames reaching up like hands into the smoky, grayed-out sky.

I clutched tightly to Xan's fingers, while he held mine with a death grip. I looked at him, swallowed hard. "You can hide here, Xan. You don't need your physical body. Reduce down, but here. Find other individual souls . . . you can keep fighting from here. As a . . . ghost."

He smiled at me, a grateful if sad smile. "Tell my dad it's better off this way. I got the cake and the eating, both. And you, Tali . . . you can reach me in your dreams. Any time. I understand now."

I swallowed hard, sick to my stomach. Filled with dread and knowledge. "I understand, too. God help me."

His smile broadened. "God, oha? You need to introduce me to Him sometime. I don't know if He hangs out around here." Then, without saying good-bye, he turned and ran across the rolling hills of the Nether-wood, not stopping to check if the curled-up human figures dotting the landscape were alive or dead, if they were decoys or artifacts of people who had tried to es-cape the database of FortuneCorp.

When he was gone, my consciousness shot out of the Netherwood and back into the Real. My fingers were still wrapped around Xan's ruined face. But he was dead. Well, his body was.

Kovner was next to me, his arms wound protec-tively around my shoulders. I twisted until I could see his eyes.

"Why didn't you come with us?" I asked. The world turned gray and swam before my failing vision. I willed myself not to faint, not to keel over and die. A lot depended on Kovner's answer.

"I can't do what you did," he replied. "The nightwind told me you were our salvation. I still don't understand how. Maybe you can find the answer in the Netherwood, now."

"If *you* figure it out, don't tell me. FortuneCorp will know too."

"That probably is the corporate plan. I don't know for sure."

The implications of what he said burned in me, and I bit my lip to keep from crying. "Yeah. That's what I think. They want me to end up there; they pro-grammed me that way."

Kovner's face was still, no emotions readable on his features, only a bleak acceptance of what I'd said. "You may be right. And depending how they made you, you may suffer Xan's limitations. I don't know if you will survive the trek into the Forest, Tali. You may not make it ten minutes in."

"If I can't survive in the forest, I'll try to make it into the Netherwood. I'll become a ghost, find Xan and keep fighting. If you can, meet me there, hide with me there. When you can."

He nodded, stroked my face with my fingers. "That will be our final fallback plan. But we'll try the Real, the forest, first."

We tried to find Gustav, but he had disappeared. He and his spider had vanished, and I feared for the big man with the soft heart hidden in a fleshy, materialistic shell. Xan had been the only thing keeping him connected to other people instead of his own best interests. I feared the worst for him.

"He needs to be alone, find his thoughts," Kovner said. "We'll meet again when the time comes." He spoke with such profound assurance I didn't question him. I had learned that when Kovner went all mystical like that, accosting him with little details like facts did no good. He was traveling on a plane that I couldn't even visualize, let alone visit.

Without any more words we pulled Xan's body into the forest as far as we could, stripped him of any identifying clothing and gear, and left him for the woods to devour. Back to the land he would go, as my ancestors would once have said. I could feel the hum under my feet as we left him, and knew the smartbugs were coming, happy for an easy meal. I had a weird sense they would enjoy the metal of him even more than the flesh. I didn't want to stick around to find out.

Our group was down to two spiders and four human souls. Kovner couldn't hide a smile of elation. Compared to the odds he'd once faced in the Glass Desert—that all the kill-ops soldiers faced—I'm sure this seemed like we were doing brilliantly—against both the forest and FortuneCorp. But I couldn't get Xan's sad smile out of my mind. And I still feared for Gustav.

Of course, that was nothing compared to the fear I felt of my traitorous body. I wanted to chop myself up, set myself free of the cage this meat had been built to be. The Netherwood beckoned, a place where my soul could hide untethered to this bioengineered horror. I was a freaking computer, and the best outcome for us all would be if I popped my transistors and died. Burn like trapped toast and take myself out of the equation. Because if I were a computer, who knows what kind of goodies my grandmother had programmed into my bloodstream, my brain. My lungs. My muscles. My heart.

As we rode deeper into the forest, left the outer world behind, I braced myself for death—almost welcomed it, because it would prove to Kovner that I'd been right: I was too dangerous a tool to use against FortuneCorp. I was more afraid of surviving the forest, because that might be playing into Violet's plan— or the supermind's plan for me as Violet had manifested it. I wondered how it would feel to burn out, to pop, to fry from the inside out. Chances were, I was about to learn.

We kept moving, the leaves rustling under the spiders' footpads. I braced myself to die, felt the blaster tucked into my belt spark and go dead. Without thinking too much, I plucked it out of the belt, pointed the business end to my temple, and pulled the trigger.

Nothing.

Kovner grabbed the thing out of my hand and

threw it far away, into a deep ravine that ran parallel to our left. "Don't play around like that, Tali. Don't!"

"I wasn't playing." My voice had closed into a husky whisper. I trembled all over with chills, and my skin felt cold and clammy to my fingertips. "The blaster's dead. I'm next."

Kovner's arms wrapped around me, and I leaned back into his body. It was time for me to die. I wanted to feel his body next to mine as the last human sensation I ever experienced. He leaned forward, breathed into my ear. I shook with panic, felt my skin prickling, knew that if I was going to die, it was going to be right now. . . .

I felt something rushing through me, warm and liquid like a river of gold. It was Kovner. He flowed in my veins, glorious and gentle, and I surrendered to him—a grand farewell, no more resisting him and what I felt for him. I wanted to die open to him, fully human for the first time; how ironic was that?

Kovner nudged our spider gently with his knees, and the beast stopped next to a huge, gently swaying tree. Our companions paused, waiting for us, seemingly oblivious to the drama playing out a few feet away.

"Good-bye," I whispered. I waited for the pop.

Nothing happened.

We both waited, and the river of warmth kept flowing, something like a counter-energy. Kovner kept me propped against him, pressed to the column of his strong stomach and pecs. I kept breathing.

After a couple of minutes, I twisted around to look into his eyes.

"Everything else electronic is dead by now."

"Yep," he said.

"And I'm still alive."

"Seems that way."

"But I'm a computer. My time with Xan proved it."

"You have access capabilities to the mainframe," he agreed. "I bet you could access the grid right now, in the middle of the Gray Forest."

I took a deep, shuddering breath. "But the electro-magnetic field has no effect on me. Even though I am now a computer?"

"Apparently not. *You* are the workaround."

Tears sprung unbidden down my cheeks. "I'm the secret weapon!"

"You're a computer made out of human flesh, my darling."

"You have to kill me now, then. If not you, then Zoltan or Eva. Or I'll do it." I made a move to obtain a blaster, even though all of them were inoperable by now.

His arms tightened around me. "That would be a terrible mistake."

"I'm a bioweapon. I'm everything your people feared in the first place. You can't bring me into camp. The main network can hack into me at any time, I'm sure, can record every moment of our conversation. I probably wouldn't even know it."

"You would know it," Kovner said.

"How are you so damn sure?

"Call it one of my intuitions."

"No, this time it's no more than wishful thinking."

Kovner turned me around to face him on the spi-der's back. He wrapped his body around mine, held me tight. The humming connection between us flared up, a huge flame of emotion; it devoured us whole.

Computers can't do this, he thought at me.

I'm a computer, and I'm doing it right now.

You are a human being, Tali. A woman. With a soul.

Not anymore. I'm programmable. My ability to choose is gone.

Kovner kissed me, passionately and deeply. With our connection, that kiss threw me completely open to him. I grabbed for his hair, and we kissed wildly, with deep abandon, our actions communicating our emotions more eloquently than words, mere data, ever could. I tried to say my good-byes in that kiss, make my grand farewell.

But within the kiss, I could feel a faint disconnect—what I would have called bewilderment if it were a human emotion I recalled. I sensed a "does not compute" message from the main network, as if some electronic process had been interrupted by the scorching intensity of our emotions.

I kissed Kovner more, reveling in sensation, in pleasure, in human connection. I knew I belonged to something greater than me now. But, unlike FortuneCorp, that Something Greater didn't want me to obliterate myself. It wanted me, Talia Fortune, a deeply flawed human being, to live.

Maybe that was as formal an introduction to God as I was going to get in this world.

TWENTY-TWO

The rebel outpost looked even more bunkerlike when we got there. The forest had almost completely overwhelmed the rock and canvas structure, twisting thick roots and vines over the half-hidden entrances. The forest had wrapped the enclave in living camouflage, transformed the bunker into an organic structure, a warren compound of wood and stone.

The people had changed, too. When Kovner and I arrived with Zoltan and Eva, sentries had been alerted to our presence long before. Armed with crossbows and scimitars, they'd made sure we were friends before they let us approach.

Kovner for one was heartened by the improvement. "They are acting like fighters, not refugees," he said. "Sully did a good job convincing them to protect themselves."

I was still torn up over Xan's physical death, and I wasn't inclined to be so charitable. "They aren't going to be able to hold off the FortuneCorp army with spears, you know. Even if animated human soldiers and not bots break through, FortuneCorp-trained fighters will outfight them hand to hand."

Zoltan shot me a nervous look, but Eva laughed. "I'm not exactly a warrior princess here. The most experience I had before this was breaking up bar fights on Saturday night after payday . . . and I'm still alive. Fought the best FortuneCorp had with my bare hands—and lived."

Her unspoken prejudice hung in the air: Xan, the Glass Desert veteran with computer-aided functionality built into his body, was dead. Her prohuman bias was understandable to me on a primal level, but it also was wholly irrational. It reminded me of myself, of my once-inviolable sense of superiority.

I sighed, tried to keep my evil mood to myself. But I knew how it was going to go now, and that made me tired and bitter. I remembered Kovner's vision of a band of human brothers dedicated to uplifting each other as we battled for our lives and dignity. It hadn't worked out that way, not with Sully gunning for me. I didn't expect it to go much better this time around with him.

Sully met our little delegation at the hidden entrance to the bunker. I wondered how he knew we were coming without even the benefit of radios to alert him. Had he developed the same telepathic abilities that Kovner possessed? Did all enclave members have access to some crazy prophetic gift?

He bowed to us, formal and cold as a glacier. "Kovner. Thank God you still breathe."

Kovner bowed back, and smiled. I could sense grief and anger percolating directly underneath the surface of his amusement. "It's good to be alive. I hope that some of the people we sent into the forest have made it here too."

This last surprised me. I didn't know how busy Kovner had been while I was in Violet's custody. I grabbed his hand. "Other people made it out?"

Sully glared at me, but he didn't acknowledge my words with any audible response. Instead he turned to face Kovner and the others. "We have only about a dozen more. Patrols picked off other groups—but a small delegation did make it here."

Zoltan stepped forward and offered his hand for Sully to shake. The two men clasped hands, and the silence held a moment of unspoken communication. Afterward, Zoltan shook his fingers as if they had suffered an electric current. "It's good to be here, man. I remember you from the base. You knew how to hold your drink—and treat people with respect."

Sully smiled for the first time. Evidently, Zoltan had passed Sully's muster as an official member of the human race. Something I was afraid I would never be able to do. "Come in. We still have plenty of food, and people from base who will be happy to see you and Eva. Everybody knows you two from the bar."

He swept away, Eva and Zoltan close behind. Kovner followed, and I brought up the rear, seething with resentment. I spoke directly into Kovner's mind: *How can he treat me like that!* And I sent a jolt of my anger along as an exclamation point.

Suddenly I stopped walking and stood amazed in the hallway. I had sent thought to him effortlessly, the way he had always done to me.

Kovner looked back and smiled. *Very nice.*

How did I do that?

The forest likes you, Tali. It bestows all gifts. That's more important to our mission than anything else. Ignore Sully—he's afraid of dying and it shows in

*everything he does. You and I . . . we're past that
point.*

Yes, somewhere in the past adventures I had decided
I was going to die. Not that I didn't want to live,
but . . . I had realized there were things greater than
me or my control. And that surrender to the inevitable
was strangely liberating, contained a hidden sweet-
ness, because it let me do what I had to do without at-
tachment or regrets.

As we trundled down the hall after our friends, I realized that Kovner had been in this state for months—
probably since our Netherwood encounter in the
Amphitheatre, which seemed like centuries ago. No
wonder he seemed insane to people who hadn't gotten
to our point. From this vantage, though, he seemed
saner than the rest of the world put together.

We came to the mess, in the center of this tangled
network of tunnels, this anthill of a human colony of
rebels—a group of about twenty, half of them kids,
clustered in a small pack. They were eating food; not
hot, not served on trays, but still light years ahead of
protein goop. Most of the tables were gone, and the
kids huddled on the floor in clumps. It looked like
only the emergency lights worked.

The kids looked up first, and I saw the tiny boy who
had almost gotten crushed to death by his mother. I
glanced around, but she was nowhere in evidence.

The boy smiled at me and beckoned me forward.
"Welcome back."

I smiled at him in return. He was the first member
of the enclave to speak to me without fear. "Thanks.
My name is Talia, by the way."

"I know. You can call me Cleve."

"Hey, Cleve."

"Sit with us." I realized as I approached that Cleve was in the center of a subgroup of kids, all of them tiny with huge, hunted-looking eyes. They were so open, so vulnerable; I felt an affinity with them at once. I sat down among them, and their energy took me in without rejecting me. I relaxed, only then realizing how tense every muscle in my body had been.

The other three from my group—Kovner, Zoltan, and Eva—kept standing, smiling and looking incredibly uncomfortable, even Kovner. Especially Kovner. I had the distinct sense he and Sully were communicating telepathically, and the discussion wasn't going well. Probably Kovner was breaking the news about my new, cloned body as gently as he could.

All at once, the tension broke, as if they'd reached some kind of temporary truce. Kovner joined me, and Eva and Zoltan sat down in the dirt with Sully. We all shared the food that everybody had, and soon the little warren hummed with conversation, spoken aloud, cheerfully chaotic. Every so often, Eva shot the kids a nervous glance and I knew she was as freaked as I had been the first time I'd seen them. FortuneCorp employees were not allowed to take their children offworld with them. When my parents died offworld I had been spared because of that corporate doctrine. But it meant that FortuneCorp employees posted offworld might never see a child in their lifetimes on the planet. Clearly she hadn't.

After the meal was done, the tension crept back into the room, a rising tide of worry. My stomach started churning, and I abruptly felt too full. The silence was suddenly complete, and every person in the clearing was looking at me.

"So, when is the public stoning scheduled?" I tried to keep my tone light, but I wasn't entirely joking.

"In my opinion, that's not a bad idea," Sully said, his face hard.

"No shit, Sully. But I couldn't help being born to the family I was, and I can't help what happened to me. The fact that I'm a product of FortuneCorp. Just like you, I'm doing the best I can with the situation life handed me. How is that a sin?"

His lips twitched. "Life is not exactly fair, Sheriff. We pay the prices we must, sometimes for the sins of our forebears. My duty as elected leader of the enclave is to protect these people with my life—and that includes ejecting all spies and traitors that may attempt to infiltrate our midst."

I laughed; that self-righteous devotion to duty sounded familiar. "You know, you sound like a sheriff. And I agree with you. I think I'm a danger to the enclave."

I could sense the astonishment rushing through the people's minds; it was like a building wind. I licked my lips, wishing for a big jug of water or even some Fresh Havens beer, and continued: "I think I'm booby-trapped. It's not my doing, not my fault. But you're right, Sully. Life isn't fair. Kovner can't do what you have to. So, kill me. I'm sure that will win you lots of leadership points, secure your position." I couldn't help adding that last line out of spite.

The kids moved closer to me. Cleve crossed his arms, narrowed his eyes. I could feel his anger, hot and red like a knife heated in a fire. "No. You don't get to touch her, Sully. She's clean."

Sully didn't give an inch. "How would you know

that? You're still young. You have no experience or sense to know any better."

"Don't talk down to me," Cleve snapped. The other kids crossed their arms in the same way. A low hum rose from them, like a furious buzzing of enraged bees in their hive. The hairs on my forearms stood at nervous attention, and when I glanced over at my friends, Eva and Zoltan looked scared enough to bolt.

Without any apparent signal, the kids linked hands, putting me inside their circle. Their hum became a furious sonic boom like the one that had frightened away the smartbugs upon my first visit to the forest. I could feel power rising in the room, a huge jolt of energy that made the stone and cloth walls tremble. A crack opened up by my left foot—a small one, but ominous nonetheless. I was the beneficiary of this display of naked power, and it terrified me. Sully impressed me with his aplomb: he only looked deeply disturbed. He held up a hand, and the roar subsided back into a hum.

"Peace. We will put it to a vote," he said.

"No vote!" Cleve's voice vibrated with the hum that sheltered me. "She goes, we go. No compromise."

I glanced over at Kovner, and couldn't believe what I saw. He was smiling, and tears were welling up in his eyes. I could sense that nothing had ever softened him like this. So, why did the children's defense of me leave me cold?

The answer filled me with despair. It was because Sully was right: I wasn't human. Not like the children, not like anybody else in the room, not even Kovner. No matter how much they wanted to take me in, I was broken beyond repair. I was tainted. And I was endangering what I believed in just by being here.

I couldn't stand it anymore. "Stop, kids." I could only whisper, but the hum instantly ceased. "Thank you from the bottom of my heart for what you did."

Cleve smiled, and our eyes locked. I felt an echo of that connection Kovner and I shared, and knew that connection betrayed us all to FortuneCorp. I had to stop everything now, before I doomed us all to death.

"Sully is right."

The grim-faced rebel leader was more surprised than the rest of the group put together. I nodded to him, implicitly acknowledging his authority. "I am a danger. Not because of what I believe, but because of what I am. I wasn't kidding before—you need to get rid of me."

"Why did you even come?" Sully hadn't even an iota of sympathy, the tough old bastard. I'd been through enough to admire that in a man: that zealotry, that simplicity of mind. In some ways it was necessary.

"She came because I *made* her come." Kovner's voice cut through the tension like a laser. Sully was the elected leader of the enclave, but Kovner was its prophet. Of course, prophets usually came to a bad end from what I could gather from the fairy tales and half stories I had picked up, but he couldn't change what he was any more than I could.

"She came because she's been through enough. And she knows our enemy within her bones. That is how she can save us."

I shook my head, hating to fight him in front of the others but knowing I must. "I can't. I don't know any better than you do how to beat the supermind. I'm nothing more than a weapon in FortuneCorp's arsenal. I don't know how they will activate me, or even why I will end up being the doom of this place. So, let me go . . ." I trailed off as I suddenly realized I had been lying to myself.

It wasn't all about the greater good; I really wasn't ready to die.

And yet, I also didn't see how I could live with myself for what my presence would do to my fellow human beings. The knowledge was hard, that I'd thought I was tougher than I really was. But it didn't change the truth of my fear. Or my inability to continue pushing for my death.

Kovner crossed his arms. I'd never seen him so resistant to reality. "We *need* you, Talia. Without you, we won't be able to beat FortuneCorp."

Zoltan and Eva added their pleas to Kovner's. The children surrounded me. Their support hurt worse than Sully's lone condemnation.

I sighed, wished Kovner weren't so taken with me. Who knew whether I was being used as surveillance equipment? How much did FortuneCorp now know about the location of this enclave, its numbers, its defenses, all because I had come? I regretted allowing Kovner to convince me to follow him in the first place. Sully was right: it was a mistake for me to be here at all.

I looked over at Sully, and was surprised to see a glimmer of new compassion in his eyes. "I respect you, Talia Fortune," he said. It was the highest praise I could ever get from a man like him. "And I respect the people of this enclave. However, I have the deciding vote here. And I believe you will agree with me. Talia." Hearing Sully say my name without contempt drew tears to my eyes.

"You must be banished from the enclave. I will send you away into the wilderness and let the Gray Forest accept or reject you as it will. To make sure you do not return—and also to help you survive—I will send a sentry with you. Kovner. He will guard you, and make sure you cannot come back here. If you return against my direct orders, both of you will be summarily executed. As you are now, you are too much of a danger."

Emotions worked over his face, and I realized only then what an effort it had cost him to contradict his friend and superior, Kovner, the first outlaw, the one who had probably saved his life in the first place. But these were desperate times, and human kindness and decency would have to wait until war's end to reappear, if they ever would.

"Go now. We'll send provisions for as long as you need them, but you must get away from the enclave, never to return."

I glanced at Cleve and his band of little clairvoyants, hoping they understood we were doing what we must. The boy looked at me, his eyes clear, haunted, deep with pain and disgust at what we had all become. *We will watch over you,* I heard in my mind. *No matter where you go.*

It didn't really matter much, to be honest. All of us knew in our bones that a fight to the death was going to happen, and very soon. As I said my good-byes in the central assembly area, I glanced over their pathetic, primitive weapons, and knew the end would be bloody and horrible.

I went quietly, mostly resigned to my fate. In contrast, Kovner burned like a firebrand, and as he hugged the people and whispered his good-byes, he transmitted his seething outrage to them like a virus.

Apollo, the old man who had rejected fighting as an

option, clutched a wicked-looking spear in his gnarled, tree-root hands. He nodded at me, eyes mild and cloudy as ever. "God go with you, my dear. Please watch over our outlaw."

The irony almost killed me. I swallowed the lump in my throat, got as close to crying as I would before the battle was joined. "Thank you, Apollo. I wish you only well."

And that was the final good-bye. I walked out of the enclave, Kovner at my side, and I never looked back.

TWENTY-THREE

The forest closed over us, and this time I could sense its presence like another consciousness. I finally began to experience what Kovner had been getting at, to comprehend it fully. The forest was alive . . . and was as conscious of itself as I was. It was a player in what was going to happen. But who knew whose side the Gray Forest was truly on?

"DARPA created it," I muttered, not realizing I had spoken aloud until I had heard my voice. "It has more in common with FortuneCorp than it does with us."

"No, you're wrong," Kovner replied. "Remember what happened to DARPA. Also, we're part of it and not yet consumed." He paused before adding, "There are other differences. FortuneCorp wants to harvest us like a base product and throw away the 'waste.' The forest accepts us whole or it rejects us whole."

We walked for awhile in silence, and I felt the sweat pouring over my body, my muscles aching. Ah, the sweet exertions of the body, simple, unthinking. My body had a wisdom that my mind wished it could emulate.

We hiked deeper and deeper, and the wind died completely. I didn't know where we were going, or

how my end would come; I only knew it was imminent. On one level I hoped the forest did reject me and
devour me whole because, of the dooms I could envi-
sion, the forest's way seemed the purest, the least gen-
erative of additional evil.

We came to a clearing so beautiful it reminded me
of a fairy bower. The forest floor was carpeted with
gray-blue leaves and little, sweet-smelling white
flowers—the first blooming things I had seen growing
wild on the planet of Fresh Havens. Both Kovner and
I stopped: we knew we had arrived at our final resting
place.

I found a shady spot and sat down, enjoying the
sensation of stillness. Kovner sat down next to me,
and he took my hands into his own hard, calloused
ones. The gentleness of his touch made my eyes
prickle with tears I would never shed. My voice was
soft, but it boomed in that scented, shady silence.

"After all of our travels, to think it all ends here."

Kovner's answer shocked me. "No, my dear Amazonia. It all *begins* here. Just because we've learned
the game plays us does not mean we must forfeit."

"I don't understand."

"We can't fight with the other rebels. So be it. But
we can still fight the battle we were born to fight." He
leaned close, kissed me slowly, with agonizing sweet-
ness. "In the Netherwood. And you can bring me
there, like Xan."

His kiss brought me peace. The gift continued even
after we broke physical contact. "You are brilliant.
And crazy."

"Crazy has always served me better than realistic."

I had to agree; he was right. Together, we rested in
a bed of flowers. We interlinked hands, closed our

eyes—and used me as a bridge, a living computer, back into the grid, the interface with the virtual world. We'd have to trust the forest to hold off rejecting us, at least until after we'd done what we could to destroy the grid and the supermind of FortuneCorp itself.

The Netherwood was still a smoking ruin. Kovner and I ran to the Amphitheatre, but it had been dismantled. The place crawled with snakes, rats, and unrecognizable creatures scuttling through the shadows. It reminded me of the Gray Forest as I had first seen it, hostile to me and seeking my demise. I looked at Kovner, and the sight of him as he was filled me with fear; it reminded me we had no avatar devices now. We were truly ourselves, and the protections we'd once built ourselves were destroyed.

Kovner stood in the middle of the wreckage, surveyed the landscape. "It looks like the Glass Desert to me. Like a photo of that time, come back to life."

I swallowed hard, considered what he'd said. "It looks like the Gray Forest in an angry mood to me. Like our own minds are imprinting on this space. Do you think every person hiding down here, or trapped down here, sees their own personal nightmare? Is that even possible?"

"We need to find other people and talk to them. We have very little time. FortuneCorp undoubtedly already knows we have arrived. They may have planned for this, for all we know."

He raised his hands to his mouth, cupped them to project his voice better. "Human beings! Living souls! Stand and fight!"

In the distance, I could see figures stirring in the

rubble—mostly wandering, bedraggled-looking wret-
ches dressed in rags, looking like they had been hiding
in the garbage and desolation forever. But a few, a
pitiful few, looked as ready to fight as Kovner. I saw
Xan then, far away, waving to us. He led a small band
of may be half a dozen. They started walking to us,
then running.

Their movement prompted a general migration. The
living human souls trapped in the Netherwood came
toward us like a zombie army, and I held steady,
though their shambling progress made me want to run
screaming. They came slowly—too slowly. And I saw
the danger looming, like a space trawler smashing
apart in front of me: The only way these people could
survive is if they hid, alone; together we would be
wiped up and obliterated like a nasty spill with a
kitchen sponge.

Even in this place, Kovner could sense my thoughts.
"Wrong, Tali. There is strength in numbers. Even the
people who cannot fight anymore have value. We need
to all gather together, in the hundreds by the time
we're done I hope. We'll draw off some of the attention
and resources of FortuneCorp while the enclave fights
in the Real. Together we can stop them. We have to."

I admired his confidence in our powers, even though
I was too pessimistic to agree. "Do what you do best,
outlaw. Inspire us."

He gave a mock bow. "I live to serve, my lady."

The horde of our allies kept coming, and Kovner
started speaking before they all reached us. He was
right: our time was limited. "Human beings! We created all of this, but were created ourselves by something greater. We must remember that. And if we fight
what we have made, we can resist our destruction."

Xan stood in front of us, fearful but determined. This place had worn him, and his body was damaged but he was still recognizable. I felt a burst of fondness as he asked, "How? Tell us what to do."

"We need to tear down the grid. I'll show you how. Once we've disabled FortuneCorp's access to Fresh Havens, we can see where WorldCorps and other Singularities are doing the same. Stop them, too. It hasn't progressed everywhere yet, to every place. We can cut off the supermind from colonies where people are still people."

Against my expectations, the mob surrounding us was willing to try. Kovner led us down a crumbling stone stairway to a rolling valley, one I remembered as once lush and filled with pleasure groves and places of sexual encounter. Now it was empty, charred. "We can access the coding system here—"

I didn't hear the rest of his words, because a crushing weight of consciousness blotted out the entire scene. FortuneCorp had found me, and it pressed down like the gravitational field of the sun. I gasped for air, vaguely felt my human body in the Gray Forest stirring. FortuneCorp was trying to activate me—was furious that I wasn't where I was supposed to be. That my will was interposing itself. I wasn't playing my part in its plan, wasn't in the enclave directing the movements of the troops. I had malfunctioned. It was time to destroy me.

Unwilling to let the others know the danger, I spoke into Kovner's mind directly. *Keep leading them, outlaw. I'll distract my grandmother.*

I felt a flicker of protest, but turned away from him before our connection could lead the supermind directly to where he and his compatriots worked on their ultimate sabotage. It was up to me to distract FortuneCorp and its main manifestation, Violet.

I knew I didn't have a chance in hell of succeeding.

My new body had vastly superior powers in the grid—like I was an upgraded handheld. I visualized a place to meet my grandmother, and she accepted my construct, met me in the mansion where I had grown up. The library still smelled musty, was full of books and an unused grand piano. I sat in my favorite chair as she entered the room, still regally enrobed as Queen Elizabeth. I had to smile—even submerged into the superconsciousness of FortuneCorp, Violet still retained her sense of glamour and drama. Some vestige of her somehow remained, turned to the sentient corporation's purposes but still extant.

"You are such a *wicked* child." Her voice carried a note of amusement—of admiration even—but I wasn't lulled by that. Those emotions were surely computer-generated, designed to confuse and entrap.

"No. I am just trying to survive." The room, so vividly visualized, held me with longing and a melancholy homesickness. No matter how well I visualized this place, I could never go home again.

"I have said: The only way to survive is to join me. Or else we will wipe you out. Your little leap into your clone was amusing—served our purposes quite well, actually. We learned a tremendous amount about the enclave, possibly more than if your clone had gone into the forest without your animating consciousness to give us context."

I snuggled down in my special brown chair, thread-bare and saggy. Imperfect. Worn. It had been my mother's favorite chair—was the only thing I had of hers that she had loved. "You didn't learn the most important thing, though, Grandmother."

"Oh, no?"

"We all reject the Singularity. We reject your superiority. We want to live. And we'll fight you until we die."

"That is your choice, little bug. I know how fond you are of the power of choice. But you are choosing nothing more than obliteration. So be it."

She drew closer to me, lifted her hands . . .

A bolt of pain, exquisite in its intensity, flared through my body. I felt my consciousness wavering, my construct pinned to the chair like a butterfly in a display case. But I refused to disappear into the pain.

"It's not the power of choice that matters," I gasped, fighting to stay lucid. "It's the meaning we ascribe to it. You cannot obliterate the implications of my choice. I choose life, I choose love."

The pain abruptly ceased. "Love?" The thing I called Violet drew closer, clearly annoyed. "At the end you invoke love? I would have thought you'd learned better. Love is nothing more than a chemical interplay. It's a bunch of enzymes playing over your synapses. A hormonal reaction. An illusion."

"No. It's what makes me human and you a tool of destruction."

"Love. Can you even define it?" Her curiosity was keeping me alive, was buying me time. I kept stringing her along, marveling at her pique. Love was so central to what made me human, if so utterly inconsequential in my past. But I had repressed it for too long.

"Define it? No. I only know it by encounter. Love is

bigger than me—it connects the world, transcends space and time. I can't explain what it is, only know that without it I am not human, I can't live."

"What do you know truly about love?" Her contempt burned my skin like acid, and I braced myself for another attack. "It is not something you've ever known. Even from your family."

I closed my eyes, reminded myself this was the supermind and not wholly my Violet. After struggling to come up with a way to explain, I gave up. "I'm not a philosopher," I said, knowing that I echoed Kovner's sentiments. At the very edge of my consciousness, I perceived the destruction he and his compatriots were wreaking on the grid—suddenly knew it was a drop in the bucket and not enough to stop FortuneCorp. "I'm not a philosopher," I repeated, "but I know what it is—and I have experienced it."

I tried to share what I knew, tried to communicate it to what was left of my grandmother with gentleness and honesty. Ironically, love was the only weapon I had left. "I don't have an abstract way to impart the experience. And I'm sorry, I don't think you, a sentient corporation, can feel love or understand it. It wasn't part of your survival imperative, what led you to sentience. You were created without love, in a time of war, and that's why to the human race you have become an evil."

"Love, evil." Violet's voice thrummed with amusement. "You bore me with these old-fashioned, meaningless constructs. Even in my original incarnation I raised you to be smarter than that. Less gullible."

I swallowed hard, felt the anguish of that reality sink into my soul. No matter what had changed, Violet was my grandmother, and she'd accepted and furthered this monstrosity. Kovner had his partisan ancestor. Here was mine.

"Your original incarnation was ruled by fear," I said. "You were afraid of dying so much that you'd do anything to cheat death. Sacrificing your soul wasn't a high price to pay—you were afraid of believing you had one at all."

Violet seemed to sense my pain. "Yes. And you fear death as well. You are a Fortune. The company made you what you are, flesh and blood and intellect. You belong to me."

"I belong to myself. And I posit that I belong to love."

"What sentimental bullshit."

"I know. Not your way. Or the world's. The last human generation was a supremely unsentimental one. We were focused on our success, on our pleasure, our beauty, our power. Love had very little to do with anything. And I think that had something to do with our downfall."

"So you admit you are beaten, my dear?"

"Oh, yeah. You guys, you corporations, won the war. We're extinct for all practical purposes. And it's a shame. For all the evil that human beings perpetrated, I still believe that the love we were capable of feeling, of expressing, trumped all. But you can't understand that. So even though you are advanced technologically, will think infinitely faster than I ever could, FortuneCorp, WorldCorps—none of you will ever understand love. And so you will ultimately destroy each other, too."

Violet sailed around the room in her voluminous satin skirts, considering my words. "Fascinating. I always advocated keeping a few of you alive in your backward, native state. I still believe there are lessons to be learned—especially in the ways that you fail. Your own professions of love, of dignity, of integrity . . . But alas, the supermind perceives you as a threat we must expunge. A virus. And so it ends. We will finish the extermination process in Fresh Havens and our other holdings, and it will be done."

No. I won't let you. I hurled this thought fiercely, hugely at her, not knowing where the surge of power came from. I felt myself changing within the construct, stood up, looked down and watched myself becoming like a tree trunk, my roots delving into the ground, cracking the floor beneath my feet.

I reached back to my body in the Real, felt the ground of the Gray Forest quaking under me where Kovner and I lay. The air was filled with a shrieking clatter, as if a cloud of gigantic locusts had descended over the trees. Like an itch in the back of my mind, I felt Cleve and the other children supporting me, sending me gigantic surges of energy, flowing through my body and my nerve endings, causing pain and damage, I suppose. But I was too far away from my physical self to worry.

I turned my focus back to Violet.

I WON'T LET YOU DESTROY US. I WON'T LET YOU DESTORY ME.

The surge fried a hole in the middle of the room in which we stood. It burned through the cyber reality, like a focused beam of sunlight cooking an ant through a magnifying glass. I smelled it: burnt toast. And despite the pain that was beginning to blister throughout my entire body, I felt my lips curve into a smile.

"Stop it." Violet's voice shook, her features began to smear ever so slightly. "You can't do this. It isn't possible."

I AM A CONDUCTOR OF ENERGY. YOU CREATED ME THAT WAY, VIOLET. YOU WANTED GREATNESS FOR ME, AND I WILL ALWAYS LOVE YOU FOR THAT. EVEN NOW, I AM FULFILLING MY PURPOSE. GO IN PEACE. . . .

The forest itself joined in the surge, vibrated in harmony with the children's energy. My pain became intense; I burned along with the interface. I knew this was the end of me, of Violet . . . I hoped of FortuneCorp, too.

After that, I no longer thought, reasoned, or even loved. I simply burned.

TWENTY-FOUR

The scene caught on fire, melted into nothingness. I was nothingness. Gone. Lost.

The pain seared me, destroyed me. I surrendered, saw a light far above. Groped toward it, began floating, a balloon untethered, flying into a cloudless, peaceful sky.

Silence.

So this is how it ends.

I flew upward, into the light, embraced by it. Something encircled me like a pair of welcoming arms. Love? I had always scorned it, feared it, disbelieved it. But it had never abandoned me. And here we were, reunited.

My battle had ended. I hoped that my friends and my lover, Van Kovner, lived on to fight and love. But that was all beyond me now.

I fully blended into the light, looked back down at my body. Was surprised to see myself in the Gray Forest and not in my grandmother's library. I lay in a field of flowers, a small smile on my face, finally at peace. Kovner's body lay next to me.

The world tilted. I no longer knew up or down, right or left. My frame of reference had disappeared.

"Good-bye," I whispered.

Hello, Kovner said.

My consciousness jolted back into being. I couldn't see him, only saw a blaze of light. But I felt him. Felt his love for me.

Time for us to go back now.

I felt a twinge of regret, sudden and unexpected. *It's so peaceful here. . . .*

I know. But we still have a job to do. It's not done yet.

I sighed in the golden peace, knew he was right. Wondered at his insight and his strength, even in this disembodied place.

How do you know what you know?

I could feel him shrug. *What do I know? I just go where I'm supposed to be. I let the game play me as it will.*

I felt his consciousness enveloping me, entwining me. Lifting me out of the eternal sea, back into time-space as I'd always known it—the Real. *We'll come back here someday.*

And with a snap and a whoosh, we fell through a sudden black darkness.

I wanted to scream but had no voice, no consciousness anymore.

And with a crash, I snapped back into my body.

My eyes cracked open. "Gah."

Kovner stirred next to me, his fingers still interlaced with mine. His voice creaked as if he had been asleep for a hundred years. "Yeah. You fall like that, it's gonna hurt."

My brain and every nerve ending were on fire. "You feel as crappy as me?"

"No. But I don't feel great."

I struggled to sit up, dry heaved, then found my equilibrium. The forest was silent, a gentle breeze stirring the leaves over our heads. I heard a croak far away in the distance, like a frog in love with the universe. The soft sound hurt like a hammer smacking me in the face.

"Do you think we're the only human beings left in the world?"

"Like Adam and Eve?" Kovner's voice was soft, almost frightened. "No. Well . . . I hope not."

We sat together in the profound stillness for I don't know how long. My head rested on Kovner's chest, and I listened to his heart beating. "What are we going to do?"

I didn't really want to know the answer. Part of me wanted to stay here, alone with him. Avoid dealing with the mess that had gotten us to this peaceful, bewitched pass.

"We have to go back," he said.

"We can't go back. Sully will have us killed. Can't blame him, either."

Kovner sighed. "I know. But the enclave, if it still exists, deserves to know what happened. And if it is destroyed, we need to know that for ourselves."

"You think it's all over back there?"

"Yes. Whatever happened, happened. It all went down at the same time. Couldn't you sense it? Can't you still?"

I propped myself up on my elbows so I could look into his eyes. The pain in them was gone. That alone was worth a universe of suffering, worth losing my cherished illusions about Violet—that she had ever loved me, or even known me as a person in my own right.

I looked at him for a long time, felt the cool, sharp little leaves brushing against the tops of my arms with the wavering breeze. "I don't know. I don't know what I sense anymore."

He reached up and stroked the side of my face, so gently that I wanted to curl up in his arms and cry like a child. Even at this juncture I wasn't going to let myself go like that, but the desire for it was new. A new low in vulnerability, I once would have thought. A new level of human feeling, I realized now.

Maybe there was some hope for me yet.

We heard a rustling from a long way off, aimless, not trying to hide itself. Our eyes met, and I know he could read the panic infusing me. "I don't think it's a predator. Whatever it is, it's blundering along, not hunting—maybe running away."

We sat up together, silently debated whether to hide or meet the thing head on. In the end, we were too weary to make a grand strategy; we stayed put and waited for the thing to arrive.

It wasn't a thing. But a person.

A deeply aggrieved, wretched, and despairing space pirate.

Gustav stumbled into the clearing, saw the two of us kneeling together. He rubbed his eyes and came to where we rested, stood in front of us, even more surprised to see us than we were to see him.

"Fancy meeting you here," Kovner said.

He sank to the ground in front of us, his meaty face full of wonder and grief. "Are you alive? Real?"

Kovner shrugged, rubbed at the stubble of his face. "Tell me what reality is, my friend, and I'll be able to give you an answer."

Gustav snorted and shook his massive head. "You

were always full of the airiest bullshit in the universe, Kovner."

He shifted a glance over to me, and I could see his fingers trembling as we considered each other. "You're the one what did it."

I got cold all over. "Did what?"

"Destroyed the grid. Trashed FortuneCorp."

How did he know? How much did this man know about me, about my role in what had happened? My face felt numb, and I started shaking. "I don't think it went *that* far."

"Well, all I know is, the battle ended rather abruptly. The carbon-based bots they sent all froze up and died in the same moment."

Kovner's eyebrows shot up. "Wait a minute. Did you say carbon-based bots?"

"Well, yeah. Wasn't that what Tali was supposed to be? They figured the work-around was in the materials, that any bot would do despite what it was made of. But I guess you proved them wrong. It wasn't an electromagnetic force that fried those clone computer soldiers, whatever you want to call them. It was something else."

I studied his face, still haunted with grief for his son. "I didn't stop FortuneCorp alone, Gustav. I'm nothing more than those bots that got destroyed, really, except for my memory of what I was before. Xan had a lot to do with what happened."

His features twisted, and I saw that mentioning his son's name had only stoked the fires of grief. "How? Xan's dead."

Kovner put his hand on my shoulder, and I held my peace. He reached out for Gustav with his other hand, and the old pirate flinched when the outlaw made contact, as if Kovner carried an electric charge in his fingers. "Xan led the resistance in the Netherwood. He helped me delete all references to Fresh Havens from the supermind."

I started when I heard the news. I hadn't thought through what we had done. Mentally I had stopped at the stand I'd taken against what was once my grandmother. I didn't realize how much Kovner had been able to accomplish.

"Talia held them off, distracted them while I hacked into the system. She conducted the surge into the grid, blew it out. But Xan held the line for me, gave me enough time to do what I had to do."

The three of us sat in the hot silence. A ray of sunlight pierced through the canopy of leaves above our heads, drew a fine sheen of sweat along the bridge of Gustav's nose. "That kid," he finally managed to say.

We walked back to the enclave together, Gustav, Kovner, and I. As the space pirate put it, "If Sully really wants to wipe you guys, he deserves the shitstorm he's going to get." I stumbled along, too mentally and physically exhausted to concern myself much about what was to come.

Turned out the worry would have been wasted. Too many people had died for Sully to insist we die too.

The situation was better than we could have hoped for, but it was still almost unbearably grave. They had lost thirty souls in the battle, among them Apollo, and Cleve's mother. Another dozen were profoundly injured, including Sully himself. Kovner went to work patching up the survivors, making use of the medical packs we'd swiped from the patrollers, then switching to what the enclave members had stored away. Then he began improvising with pieces of blanket, fabric, stuff from the forest itself. He finally had to give up because there was nothing left to use.

The rest of us collected at the entrance to the bunkers. We sat in the failing sunlight and tried to grasp the enormity of what had happened. It didn't work. We didn't have the words to understand.

In the end, Cleve and the children who were left—most of them had survived, banished as they were to the very center of the enclave during the battle—found an explanation for what had just occurred.

"*We* didn't beat the machines," Cleve said. "We were just the instrument."

A tool of something larger. Something I still refused to be.

I wished I could summon up Cleve's brand of fatalism. It would have made what I had to do next a little less excruciating. "We have to see where we stand," I said.

I felt confusion rippling through our little remnant of humanity. "We're standing right here," Zoltan said. He laughed a little, as if he were joking about it instead of stating the simple truth. "We're totally cut off."

"That's what I mean. If FortuneCorp regroups, we won't have the first clue about it. Or if another corporation can figure out what happened here today, they'll be coming right around to finish what FortuneCorp started. And we won't be able to do a thing about that, either."

Eva shrugged. She had been torn up along one arm pretty badly, but adrenaline carried her past the pain. Just as optimism carried her past logic. Good for her. "We were able to beat a huge megacorporation with a superhuman mind—just a group of us in the forest, no real weapons, just a bunch of little kids and clueless adults. We'll be ready to fight again, the same way. It's all we can do."

"But how can we be ready? How are we going to survive out here? The food is going to run out. We have zero access to any civilization at all. We're going to die out here unless we find some help," another Gray Forester spoke up. I couldn't help agreeing.

"Maybe, maybe not." Kovner's voice, as always, cut through the fog of my worries. "If we beat FortuneCorp, we can figure out how to live here. I have to believe that."

"We may not be as cut off as all that." Gustav's voice, still heavy with mourning, shook me. "I've still got contacts offworld. Other space-based smugglers are going to like the Singularity as much as I do—not at all. My colleagues in the interstellar black marketplace will know what's happening, and they're going to want to join with us, if only to protect their butts."

"How are we going to find all this out?" I didn't want to continue as the voice of doom, but nobody else seemed to be stepping up.

"I will." Gustav's voice still shook. "I'll get back to base, with whoever wants to come with me. Not all the space transport vehicles depended on the grid to operate. I can retrofit them to run like old-time spaceships, independent of the interworld grids. If the fucking computers come to get me, well . . . at least I'll be doing the right thing. Like Xan."

A small voice piped up from the back of the crowd. "I'll go with you."

My eyes almost popped from shock. It was Riona. She caught my aghast expression, and smiled. "Yeah.

Satan herself here. I barely escaped. Gustav saved my life."

The pirate interrupted her. "I just gave her a place to hide. But Riona saved a bunch of people—my brother Anders included. She led them all into the forest herself."

Riona blushed, bit her lower lip. "Talia warned me first. Because of her, I understood what had happened, where to go to escape. Now, the least I can do is return the favor, see if I can salvage the mess I helped to create."

"You didn't do it," I said, my heart suddenly so heavy I didn't know how long I could bear the burden. "It was me, my family."

Cleve pushed his way forward, put his tiny hand into mine. "Don't leave. My mother's gone. Don't you go, too."

I remembered how he felt, had gone through this grief once myself. But the time was done for memories, for wishing things were different than they were. There was no more Netherwood to disappear into; life was all reality, all the time.

"I don't know if I can live in this brave new world. My name is still Fortune. No matter what I do, I can't erase it. I was one of the people responsible." I thought of my grandmother, of the legacy she left behind in me. And I knew that, even now, I did not fit in here, however much I wanted to belong.

TWENTY-FIVE

Kovner, as ever, was my fiercest adversary. My fiercest supporter. "Don't play martyr. It doesn't suit you," he growled.

In the midst of my despair, I had to smile at his tenacity. This was the Avenger, the man I had fallen for in the Netherwood. He never knew when he was beaten. How many times had he snatched victory because he was unwilling to acknowledge the imminence of his defeat?

The crowd around us watched us, and I knew they were on his side. I had never felt more alone.

"Can you trust me?" I taunted him. "Can you trust that even now I'm not a tool of FortuneCorp or what's left of the government back on Earth?"

"Of course I can. You are a gateway, Talia. You are going to protect all of us. Don't you see it? Without you, we cannot survive. And you can be a bridge to those we've lost."

I paused in our battle of words to spit into the dirt, take my opponent's measure. Unbelievable. We stood here together, a little band of refuse at the edge of humanity's demise. And Kovner's eyes were alight with glory.

I looked at our audience, gauging their response to Kovner's assault. To a soul, they were united behind him.

How did they see me? I knew myself as Talia Fortune, intergalactic sheriff. Tool of FortuneCorp, no longer human. Sworn to destroy humankind by serving the will of the master I had helped create.

But Kovner and these warriors knew me a different way. These people who had fought and lived alongside me knew me as Talia, a woman of valor, Kovner's lover and the one who had saved all of our lives.

"Maybe your view of reality is a little skewed," my lover whispered.

He drew closer and, trembling, I forced myself to withstand his offensive. His fingers traced down the length of my arms. "Have you heard of the *Ping Fa*, my warrior goddess?"

I hesitated at his non sequitur. "The what?"

"*The Art of War*. In the sixth-century BCE, philosopher of war Sun Tzu posited: He who knows his enemy and himself cannot be defeated. And thanks to you, my beautiful one, beloved soul, we will know the enemy when he comes to walk with us. You alone of us will always have access to their grid. You will know when they come again. And we will be ready for them. Thanks to you. Thank God for you."

I tried to keep my composure, studied him like a beautiful piece of sculpture, tried to avoid the direct gaze into his soul that would shatter my carefully constructed view of myself. He smiled into my eyes and I failed.

The trembling started deep inside of me and worked its way to my skin, like I was sweating out a lifetime supply of subcutaneous poison. "I can't do this. I'm not human."

He folded me in his arms to shield me from the eyes of my compatriots. "Of course you're human. Anyone whose heart can break like yours is breaking now is human."

Grief had me in its gleaming jaws, it shredded me apart. The tears broke me completely. Kovner's victory over me and my lifetime of lies was complete.

My little band of brothers and sisters parted to let us pass. Dozens of hands stroked my hair, my back as we entered the sanctuary, and I could feel their goodwill, their trust in me, their determination to survive as we walked through their midst and into the changed enclave.

Kovner led me, his feet somehow knowing the way. I marveled at his surefooted walk into the soft darkness. I murmured, "You know, I never had a sense of direction worth a damn. Without GPS, I was always lost."

"Well, Talia, now you have me. As long as you're with me, we'll never be lost again."

I resisted the urge to tweak him for his cheesy remark, recognizing my sarcasm as the last feeble defense that it was. Tried to take his love for me at face value. Felt my deficiencies, my inability to love, as the congenital deformity that it was.

He led me to a room that I recognized. It was his room, same as it was. Sully or the forest had made sure it was there for him. As I saw it I recalled Sully's love for his boss, the man crazy enough to believe we could survive the onslaught of the Singularity if we banded together.

"You think Sully's going to be all right?"

"He's already all right." Kovner soothed my trembling muscles with the tips of his fingers, tended to my psychic wounds as I once had his under the Amphitheatre, many lifetimes and light years ago. With exquisite gentleness he arranged my limbs as he reclined me onto the scratchy pallet. "I love you, Talia," he whispered. His body hovered over mine as he covered my face with little kisses, smoothed away the tears that I couldn't keep from shedding.

I didn't have the strength to break our connection. But I also didn't have the strength to go that last inch, to meet him, to make the connection complete.

"Surrender to me." His lips curled in a smile as he remembered my post-victory demands in the depths of the Netherwood. I was his war prize. He had won me, and I had no choice but to comply.

My arms stretched over his shoulders, and I sighed. "How will I know when they come for us?"

"You will know. You can reach into the Netherwood, find Xan and the others. Find them, see if their souls and the others are free of the grid altogether, in a better place. I'll teach you all I know. And we'll love each other so much that I will sense it too."

He silenced my fears with a deep, passionate kiss. And I let my old, wounded self drown in that deep ocean of sensation. We moved together in the currents, and my body, always wiser than my mind, opened to his hands, his thrusting hips, his tongue.

Kovner slid off our clothes, and I was here again with my lover, naked, open to him and to his desire. He kissed tracers of his love across my shoulders and down the front of my body, between my breasts, and he nuzzled my nipples with his tongue until I cried out for him to take more of me. All of me.

His hands stroked down the column of my back, and I arched against the strong pressure of his fingers, my sex hot and wet against the top of his thigh. He pressed down against me, and I felt the currents of emotion shooting through me, stripping away my fears.

He opened my legs and I closed my eyes, felt like I was flying. I was completely open to him, and he plunged into me, hard and deep. That was it. The final connection that I had been afraid to make.

He rode me hard and fast, too fast for me to think, to hold back, to rationalize. I felt love coming for me, insisting on me, redeeming me, and I let love take me up. He thrust into me faster and faster and I exploded into love, disappeared into it. It took me, claimed me. Healed the hole in my heart that had always been festering.

Complete love. Glory.

I came again and again, and still he would not let himself release. I grabbed his perfect butt, pulled him deeper into me still, and he felt me finally reach that last inch to him, felt me make that complete surrender.

I love you, Kovner, I whispered directly into his mind, in the midst of our passion.

And with that little voice echoing in our minds, he released into me, and I came with him. Our souls merged in that ecstasy, so completely that I knew I'd never really pull away from him again. No matter what happened.

I love you, Kovner. I love you.

WIN
A PUBLISHING CONTRACT!

Ever dream of publishing your own novel?

Here's your chance!

Dorchester Publishing is offering fans of **SHOMI** a chance to win a guaranteed publishing contract with distribution throughout the US and Canada!

For complete submission guidelines and contest rules & regulations, please visit:

www.shomifiction.com/contests.html

ALL ENTRIES MUST BE RECEIVED BY APRIL 30, 2008.

The future of romance where anything is possible.

EVE KENIN

The Award-Winning Author
of DRIVEN Brings You...

HIDDEN

Tatiana has honed her genetic gifts to perfection. She can withstand the subzero temperatures of the Northern Waste, read somebody's mind with the briefest touch, and slice through bone with her bare hands. Which makes her one badass chick, all right.

Nothing gets to her. Until she meets Tristan. Villain or ally, she can't be sure. But one thing she does know: he has gifts too—including the ability to ramp up her heart rate to dangerous levels. But before they can start some chemistry of their own, they have to survive being trapped in an underground lab, hunted by a madman, and exposed to a plague that could destroy mankind.

AVAILABLE JULY 2008

ISBN 13: 978-0-505-52761-5

COUNTDOWN

MICHELLE MADDOX

THREE
Kira Jordan wakes up in a pitch-black room
handcuffed to a metal wall. She has 60 seconds to
escape. Thus begins a vicious game where to lose
is to die.

TWO
The man she's been partnered with—her only ally
in this nightmare—is a convicted mass murderer.
But if he's so violent, why does he protect her?
And stranger still, what is it behind those haunted
sea-green eyes that makes her want to protect him?

ONE
No one to trust. Nowhere to run. And the only
hope of survival is working together to beat the
Countdown.

AVAILABLE AUGUST 2008

ISBN 13: 978-0-505-52755-4

TIME TRANSIT

KAY AUSTIN

There's a reason Maude Kincaid is one of the best Time Rogues, and it's the same reason she's now dead—or soon will be. Gut-shot and lying in a sub-orbital tram station reeking of brimstone, waiting for the atmospherics to give out, she's exactly where she intended: She's saved CORE, her friends and her reality. And only a woman willing to bend the rules could do it.

The time travel was nothing. That's been as natural as breathing since Maude became one of the 22nd century's elite cadre of protectors against temporal rifts. Maude's only regret is about Gil. Gil, with whom she shared the 21st-century delights called Sonic burgers and blueberry Slushies. Gil, who's half cowboy, half-PhD, but all man. Gil, whom she abandoned with his memory erased because he was from another time, another reality, and because Time Rogues can't afford to know love. Today, she can't afford to forget it.

ISBN 13: 978-0-505-52715-8

TWIST

COLBY HODGE

Abbey Shore never intended to be the savior of the world; it was just something that happened—like her father's tragic death and the fact that she's now poor and "flipping" houses in the Chicago suburbs to finish college. And there's more: behind a crumbling wall in her current renovation, a swirling vortex hides. It's a gate, a portal—and it will not only cast her into the arms and power of the enigmatic yet doomed Dr. Shane Maddox, but also into the clutches of Lucinda, the eerie, leather-clad beauty who shadowed his every move in the Sacred Heart ER. Abbey will soon be one hundred years in the future, in a dying land filled with roving bands of humans fighting for survival, and the "ticks" against whom they fight. Oh yes, Abbey's life has had a... *TWIST*

ISBN 13: 978-0-505-52748-6

WiRED

LIZ MAVERICK

Seconds aren't like pennies. They can't be saved in a jar and spent later. Pluck a second out of time or slip an extra one in, the consequences will change your life forever.

L. Roxanne Zaborovsky discovers that fate is comprised of an infinite number of wires, filaments that can be manipulated, and she's not the one at the controls. From the roguishly charming Mason Merrick—a shadow from her increasingly tenebrous past—to the dangerously seductive Leonardo Kaysar, she's barely holding on. This isn't a game, and the pennies are rolling all over the floor. Roxy just has to figure out which are the ones worth picking up.

ISBN 13: 978-0-505-52724-0